THE ORC'S RAGE

LYONNE RILEY

Cover art by Skadior Art

Editing by Emily Michel

INTRODUCTION

THIS IS A DARK ROMANCE.

The heroine is kidnapped and kept captive against her will, and the hero is a murderous orc without redemption. *The Orc's Rage* is a high-conflict story with elements that may be triggering to many readers. **Check the full list of content warnings on the author's website.**

Cedar is not just a peasant, but a peasant's servant, sold by her parents in exchange for a cow. When orcs arrive in her village, she is not heartbroken to see them murder her vicious master. But when she's caught fleeing, the leader of the orcs, a foul and scarred beast, takes her as his own.

Lord Kargorr's only mission is to destroy humankind. Since the ice melted and the *grrosek* returned to this plane, he is intent on reclaiming his kin's land. Taking a human concubine is the beginning of his plan to sow an army of half-orcs—but he doesn't expect how much this one human would challenge him. Soon, she might become more than just a concubine.

But will Cedar ever truly submit, even when she's carrying his orcling? Or will Lord Kargorr be the one to bow down when he realizes who she truly is to him?

1

CEDAR

"Cedar!"

The shrill voice grated on her, like metal scraping over metal. Cedar glanced down at the piglet in her hands, which was still sleeping. She'd been sitting with the mother, a pig she called Bread Pudding, since the sow gave birth.

Nobody else knew the names she gave the animals; it was a private thing she shared with just herself and the creatures she cared for.

"I'm in here," Cedar called back, returning the piglet to the pile all huddled around their mother's engorged nipples.

Lissa appeared in the barn doorway, a shadowy figure blotting out the light. Cedar didn't have to see her face to know that she was scowling mightily. The woman was always scowling, ready to unleash her festering anger.

"Where have you been?" Lissa snarled as she stalked into the barn. "I've been looking all over for you."

"Why?" Cedar asked, dusting the straw off her knees as she stood up.

"There's no bread, no vegetables, and no meat, either. What are we going to eat for supper?" The gnarled woman pointed at the piglets. "Maybe we should butcher one of those for tonight."

Cedar put herself between Lissa and the pigs. "They're much too young," she told the old woman in her coolest, calmest tone. If she raised her voice, Lissa would read it as insubordination, and then she'd bring out the switch. "Just let them grow up some and we can have a nice suckling pig. Right now there's barely any meat on them."

Lissa scoffed. "We need something to eat."

"I'll figure it out." Cedar didn't know what she could possibly scrounge together, but she'd come up with something. They had plenty of eggs, and she'd found some wild onions and tubers in the woods yesterday. Maybe the bread was stale, but she could dunk it in egg batter and probably save it.

Lissa shook her head and let out a *hmph*. "We're going to have to butcher one of your precious little piggies soon. Unless you want to starve like your parents almost did."

As a younger girl, Cedar was traded for a single cow. That was all. A daughter for a cow—that's how hungry their family had been. When Lissa had bought her, Cedar knew she would most certainly be a slave for the rest of her life, or until Lissa finally died.

That thought brought her comfort from time to time.

Cedar's hands clenched at her sides as she remembered how her mother had simply turned her back on her daughter when the deal was done, but she stuffed them in the pockets of her skirt so Lissa couldn't see. The old lady didn't miss it, and her eyebrow arched.

"Having a thought?" she asked sweetly, the tone she used

whenever she was itching to pull out the switch. It wasn't so much about punishing Cedar as it was about Lissa's deep-seated need to inflict pain on others, whether human or animal. Everything was Cedar's fault, from now into eternity. When Lissa needed someone to hurt, her servant was there.

"Not at all," Cedar said. "I'll come and get started on dinner."

Off in the distance, she heard a metallic ring. It must be Rodan, their neighbor, working on horseshoes.

Lissa took one last look at Bread Pudding and her new litter. "Don't get attached, Cedar," she said in an imperious tone. "You know better."

Of course Cedar knew. The animals never lasted. When Lissa needed extra copper for whatever new thing she fancied that week, they would be down one more pig, as the cows were long gone. Then another pig, until they had nothing left to eat and no more money with which to buy more.

Then it was on Cedar to figure out how to feed them until Lissa came up with another scheme. She cheated merchants whenever she could, making bad deals and selling snake oil— her supposed "herbal remedies." No one in town liked or trusted her, which meant she had to seize on travelers or peddle her wares in other villages.

Cedar sometimes thought about marrying, perhaps one of the guards who stood on the edge of town to keep watch for orcs. But then he would have to buy her from Lissa, and who would want to take on that cost for a wife of ignoble birth?

It was a hopeless endeavor to think about such things. Sometimes Cedar fantasized about catastrophes that might befall Lissa and bring an end to her reign: an animal attack, perhaps, or an orc raid. Cedar hadn't known the way life was before the ice melted, but when she overheard some older children role-playing as big monsters and battling each other with sticks and stones, her mother sat her down and told her what she knew.

It had begun far north—that's where the first sightings were. A great warm spell came over the land, and crops were dying everywhere. The orcs came out of the melted ice, or so the first reports said. Monsters, each like a man that had swallowed another one, with hulking brows and great tusks protruding from their jaws.

An orc was a beast with clawed hands and a hideous face that tore down everything in its path, spreading like a plague. The orcs rode upon saber-toothed cats that had emerged from the prehistoric ice with them. But they were so relatively few in number—only those that had emerged from their frozen tombs—that humanity was able to hold them back. The orcs kept their locations secret and crept out to seize and take before vanishing again.

They had been spotted in the highlands recently, but never came this far south.

As Cedar stepped out of the barn into the fading afternoon, a man shouted far off down the road. Perhaps an escaped horse had broken through a metal gate, and that was the noise she'd heard.

Thinking she might help catch the horse, Cedar jogged to the path that led away from Lissa's rundown patch of land. Their neighbors were a good way down the lane, with their much bigger plot. And yet, even from here, Cedar could hear old Rodan yelling.

She peered over the bridge that crossed the creek. Another clang rang out, and Cedar paused, torn between going to see what was amiss, in case she could help, and fearing what she might find.

"What's going on out here?" It was Lissa's voice again.

"I don't know." Cedar heard Rodan cry out, and it was an agonized sound.

Footsteps. She thought the ground was moving underneath her as dozens of pounding feet got closer, and prickles covered her skin. From around the side of Rodan's house streamed huge, green bodies covered in pelts and bones.

Orcs.

Beside her, Lissa shrieked, and it startled Cedar enough for her to realize she had to move, or she would die. Because when her mother had called orcs *monsters*, she had understated it.

These were abominations.

With a speed born of pure terror, Cedar ran as fast as she could, away from the sound of Lissa's screams.

KARGORR

His heart was beating fast, so fast, thundering in his ears in that soothing, feverish drum. He relished how it swelled his muscles larger, filling them with his hot blood, until fat veins trailed down his shoulders and hands.

The hands that now held his steel axe aloft. The *grrosek* hadn't forsaken all their old ways, but many of them. It was a good trade though, a stone axe for a steel one. Blood flowed much faster, much thicker, and the humans they came across bent under steel like so many stalks of wheat.

Lord Kargorr loved the sound it made, the blade burying itself into flesh, and he had to admit those puny creatures had invented one good thing in the time the *grrosek* were away.

His horde approached the village from the south, as Kargorr preferred to do. The north was their home, the place they had come from and would always return to, so the humans were never prepared for an attack from the south. The guards had been easy to take down, caught unawares by predators that streamed at them from both

5

sides. But the cries had carried, and other humans came out armed.

Lord Kargorr's number wasn't great, but because this was no fortified outpost—merely a village—it would be enough. He and his warriors cut down every man and woman they came across. Survivors didn't tell stories, didn't spread the word.

He had torn through the farmer himself because his rage had demanded sacrifice. The rage, that heady, delirious thing that drove all orcs at the core of their beings, urged him to stick his sword through the man's belly. A shriek followed, and one of Kargorr's warriors speared a woman like a piece of meat.

It was time to finish this. Kargorr tossed the body down and gestured for his horde to follow. They had left some of their number behind to collect what they could from the villagers' homes and storage sheds. What they took from this village would feed the *parog* well for many moons.

He turned a corner around the farmhouse, and a terrible screech greeted him. It was a bony old human woman with a face like a badger, standing at the end of the road.

He would silence her.

But then something caught his eye. A fleeing shape—a woman in a tunic and dirty green skirt—was sprinting away from the house, off into the woods. The pale skin of her calf flashed, and Kargorr lowered the axe he was preparing to throw at her backside. She was sturdy, and clearly in possession of her senses if she was running for her life. In addition to the sound of their screams and the taste of their blood, humans also made good prizes. Others from his own *parog* had taken humans as slaves, as concubines, or whatever other service a *grrosek* could imagine for themselves, and those humans performed well once they were broken and cowed.

"Chase her," he snarled to Orgha, his closest warrior. "Bring her back to me alive."

While his right hand raced off after the disappearing waif, Kargorr seized the old woman by the throat. It stopped the sound in her lungs, and she thrashed against him.

"Are you her mother?" he ground out, trying to wrap his mouth around the human language. It was so ugly. He opened his grip enough that she could let out a squeak.

"Who?" she croaked.

He shook her like a rat. "The girl."

"She's—she's a servant!"

He cocked his head. From the direction of the woods came a scream, and when he glanced over his shoulder, he found Orgha dragging the woman in the green skirt out of the trees.

"A servant," he repeated, tasting the unfamiliar word. "You mean a slave?"

"W-w-well, no—"

He'd heard enough. He tightened his hand again, closing in on her windpipe, and she let out a harsh gasp. Orgha returned, dragging the green-skirted woman behind him. When she saw his hands around the old lady's throat, she stopped cold. Her hardened brown eyes traveled from his chest to his throat, and then to his face. Her dark hair was thick and fierce, and his gut clenched as she scowled at him. Her face was filled with hatred, and the ferocity of it licked his insides.

Kargorr leaned toward her, still holding the woman gasping for breath and clawing at his huge hand where it was wrapped around her neck. He brought some of the girl's hair to his nose and sniffed her. She jerked back, trying to put space between them, but Orgha held her fast.

There. That smell. The moment it filled his nostrils,

Kargorr's groin ached. It was a bolt of lightning through him, and he knew then that she was his.

He straightened and lifted the frail old woman into the air between them. Then he snapped her neck.

2

CEDAR

The orc stared right at Cedar as the crunch of bone breaking filled the air between them. Lissa's head fell to one side and hung limply there, then he tossed her body away like it was little more than a used toy.

Cedar was next. Surely this monster with the dark eyes that glowed red around the edges would do something even worse to her, something more painful and brutal. She could almost taste the blood on her tongue.

That was when Cedar spotted the other orcs headed toward the barn.

"No!" she called out, thinking of Bread Pudding and the new piglets. Cedar tried to pull away from her captor, the one who had chased her into the woods, but his grip was like iron. "Don't kill them! They're just babies."

The orcs ignored her. But this one towering over her, with the scar that ran from his temple on one side of his face to his jaw on the other, where his tusk had clearly stopped a massive blow... he turned to them and shouted something in his deep, growling language. They halted.

"What is in there?" the monster asked Cedar, and she was surprised to hear familiar words fall from his lips. His pronunciation was poor and his accent was thick, but she understood him.

"Pigs," she said, trying to still her quivering voice. "Just born. Piglets."

She didn't think it would work, telling them to stop, but he seemed to be considering it. Then he called something else in his tongue, and the other orcs resumed their march into the barn.

That was it. Now it was Cedar's turn to meet her end. But the big orc with the long scar didn't raise his axe to behead her. Instead, the red faded from his eyes until they were pure black again, and he tucked the axe into his waistband before grabbing her by the wrists from the bastard who had caught her. Cedar couldn't help the scream that came out when he hoisted her up over his shoulder like she was a bag of goods.

Then he turned to the others and called out something in his own tongue. Cedar watched as Bread Pudding was led out of the barn, and two big orcs hefted her up into a cart, followed by her suckling piglets. Cedar tried to free herself as the horses were rounded up and cinched to the cart, but the scarred orc's grip was like iron.

Then he turned and headed back toward town. Cedar kicked and shouted and clawed, but it was like she wasn't even there. He was an unforgiving pile of bricks.

All along the road were bodies, people that Cedar had known for the last four or five years. She realized she'd lost track of how long she'd lived with Lissa.

Lissa, who was now dead.

Most unexpectedly, a thrill surged through her. Cedar was

finally free of that old tyrant. She was *dead*. Perhaps she should have felt some kind of sadness, some kind of regret at seeing Lissa's body broken and limp on the ground, but she didn't. No, but now she was a prisoner of another kind, with a different pair of shackles.

"Where are you taking me?" Cedar asked, grunting as the big orc's shoulder dug into her belly.

"You will find out," was all he said in return.

As they passed down the main road, other orcs began to emerge from the houses loaded up with bags full of goods. They had pillaged for everything they could get their hands on.

Cedar should have mourned these innocent people. They didn't deserve this, after all. But each of them had looked away as Lissa tormented and beat Cedar day after day, right in the main square, and so for a moment, she let the guilt roll off her and decided she would much rather focus on how she was going to escape her new captor. Who knew what he wanted her for? She needed to get away before she could find out.

But this orc was powerful, as tall as a mountain and hard as a rock, and carried her like she was nothing. She feared that she was now in a far worse prison.

More wagons were hitched to horses and loaded up with goods and livestock, which, besides Bread Pudding, had all been butchered and now lay in piles. This was everything the village had.

Just how many orcs were out there, after all? And what had this one chosen her for?

KARGORR

He rather enjoyed the way the human woman's warm little body rubbed against him as she struggled and squirmed. Her energy didn't wane nearly as soon as he had expected. She had a lot of fight in her.

His warriors led horses pulling carts full of goods, both of which they'd taken from the village. When they reached the most difficult part of the climb up into the mountains, though, they'd have to abandon them, because the carts couldn't handle the terrain. Once they released the horses, he would call the rest of the *parog* to come help transport what remained.

It would be two days before they got that far, which made Lord Kargorr ponder whether it was time to move the *parog* to somewhere easier to reach, less walled off from the human lands, if he wanted to achieve his mission.

The pig and its piglets would prove complicated to get home, but the human woman had wanted them, and the *parog* could use the live offspring in the future. A pig roasted over the fire was the perfect thing for a celebration, and he imagined there would be a few of those to come.

Yes, this woman... she was perfect for his purposes. It had become clear to him when he tossed her over his shoulder and she fought back with all her strength. She was resilient, and her body was tough. She would carry many fine orclings for him.

Until now, Kargorr had been much too busy reclaiming land for the *grrosek* to be bothered with siring offspring. It would draw his attention away from what was important: taking back what the humans had stolen in the thousands of years his own people had been trapped in the ice.

But with this raid, with this woman now hanging limp over his shoulder, Kargorr imagined something else. Many of his warriors had taken humans in the past to help sate their needs, to swallow up the dripping remnants of their rage when they returned from the battlefield. They said there was nothing like returning from the fight and sinking your cock into a perfect cunt.

Perhaps Kargorr could have a vessel to sate his own rage, something soft and giving to fuck when his veins ran too hot and his hands were still covered in blood. A place to bury himself, where he could continue his line and have hardy orclings who grew into fine warriors themselves.

Yes, that's what this feeling was telling him. It was time.

And if this human was as delicious as he imagined her to be, then he would find another, and another to bear him half-blooded *grrosek*, who had proven to be excellent fighters and archers. The half-breeds had the gift of far sight, when an orc himself could only see what lay a hundred paces in front of him. They were skilled artisans, too, with a precision to their movements that made them perfect for working with steel. The *grrosek* had succeeded in making rudimentary steel weapons on their own, until the half-breeds emerged and could hone and sharpen them. They could learn human tech-niques, too, but remained loyal to their *parog,* where they had been born.

As the woman finally lost her strength, Lord Kargorr tucked her under his arm instead. She was light, probably too light. He would have to feed her good meat with lots of melting fat to return her to a state where her womb would be ready. He would keep her in his tent, nested deep in his bed of furs, until she was plump and heavy with his horde.

The woman awoke when they began to climb into the hills. Once more she fought, biting and clawing, but to his thick, dense body she was barely more than a kitten. She left a few long scratches on him, but he would teach her later that such behavior was unacceptable.

The sun was heavy on the horizon when they stopped to

pitch camp, but he did not let her go even then. She was quick, and he couldn't have her running. Once the fire was started and the fresh meat cooked, Kargorr forced her down into his lap. She struggled mightily, which had the gratifying effect of the woman rubbing herself all over his groin.

Still, it wasn't time yet. She needed ripening.

He offered her food, but the woman stubbornly turned her head away and bit her lips to keep them closed. With her dark eyes set as hard as her mouth, he warned her, "I will make you eat if you do not listen."

Still she didn't answer, glaring at him with everything she had, so he shoved the meat into her mouth. She fought him, but he was far stronger, and soon the food was between her teeth and halfway down her throat. She choked and struggled until at last she gave in to her hunger. Then she snatched the next piece away from his hands and set about tearing it apart, chewing it with a look in her eye that made sure he knew she didn't like being told what to do.

Soon the fire died down, and his warriors made their way to their own beds. Kargorr picked her up and carried her to his traveling furs, and when she realized where they were headed, she dug her nails into his hands and bit deep in his arm.

"No!" she shouted, earning smirks from the other orcs. "You can't!"

But Kargorr's skin was tough as leather and his hands were calloused from his practice with an axe, and all her ferocity did was irritate him as he tugged her under the furs and pulled her tight against his body. Still, she didn't stop her wriggling.

Finally, tired from a long day of traveling, Kargorr snapped at her. "Stop. I will not fuck you. Tonight is for resting. Tomorrow will be a long day."

"For you, maybe," she snarled back. "I won't rest until I'm free of you."

He grinned at the ferocity in her voice, in the clench of her jaw. She would make a fine concubine and mother to his orclings.

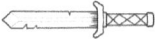

CEDAR

Even after he fell asleep, the big creature did not release his iron grip on her. He had forced food down Cedar's throat in front of the fire while the other warriors, males and females alike, devoured their meals. Some even had loud sex, right there among them. Cedar tried to close her ears to it, because she knew she needed the sleep if she was going to figure out a way past this monster, but still their cries and moans filled her head.

Her plan was to wait until the massive orc had finally loosened his hold on her in his sleep, and then she would seize the opportunity to pull free. She listened to the slow, steady beat of his huge heart against her ear, feeling each of his breaths against her cheek. He was dirty and reeked of sweat, but she imagined so did she. His body had a musky, heavy scent to it, and she could feel his power in that smell—almost taste it.

Cedar did not expect to fall into a deep slumber herself, pressed tight against the orc's bare chest, his breaths hypnotizing her. She dreamed the road leading to Lissa's house ran red with blood, and an orc rose out of it, covered in it, reaching toward her with it dripping from his hands. He had a scar running from one side of his face to the other, ending in a deep groove in his tusk.

But when he grabbed her, he held her close, as if trying to comfort her inside the nightmare he had created.

When Cedar awoke, it was daylight and she was strangely cold. When she opened her eyes, she found herself alone under the thick pelt. Instantly, she was wide awake. She remained prone, pretending to sleep as she studied the other orcs. They were occupied with loading goods and packing up camp, all their backs turned to her.

Here was her chance. Rather than getting to her feet and running, though, she slowly climbed out of the bed, pretending to roll it up when a female orc with a shaved head, except for a massive braid, glanced over at her. Then Cedar walked slowly, without urgency—though she wanted nothing more than to sprint away at full speed—through the camp, past wagons being loaded and a pair of orcs arguing. She couldn't outrun any of these huge monsters, she knew, so she had to capitalize on their distraction.

No one spared her a look as she crept by. The cool wind bit at her exposed legs as she started down the hillside, throwing her thick skirt up into the air. She took one long stride, then another, ready to whisk herself away and find some human town, somewhere else, somewhere she could start over, maybe—when something massive and hot grabbed her wrist.

"Going somewhere?" a voice snarled.

Cedar was brutally yanked backwards, the air thrown from her lungs when she met an unforgiving surface. Slamming into the orc's chest was like colliding with a rock.

"No," Cedar coughed out. Who knew how he would punish her for trying to run? So she thought fast, and then said, "I just needed to pee."

She couldn't see his face as he stood behind her, holding her captive, but she hoped he was considering her lie. The orc didn't move or speak, and his hand tightened even further around her wrists.

"Then finish," he growled, his head leaned down surprisingly close to hers. His hot breath warmed her cold skin. "I will watch you."

Cedar didn't know if she had heard him right. "Watch me?"

The big orc released her arm and, when she turned to him, one of his tusks was raised high on his cheek in a smirk. He urged her forward, clearly unwilling to repeat himself.

She had no choice. Cedar did, luckily, have a little water inside her from not having gone all night, so when she peeled down her undergarments, she had something to give. The orc studied her closely, his arms crossed, and for a long time it wouldn't flow under his watchful gaze. His eyes were dark and stony, but eventually, her bladder released. The orc didn't even twitch as it poured out of her onto the grassy ground, but her own body was white-hot with humiliation.

When she was finished, Cedar moved to pull up her clothes again, but the orc barked a command: "No." He stomped toward her and reflexively she stumbled back, tripping over her undergarments. He crouched down and tore them off of her. "None of these."

"But I'll freeze!" Cedar knew where they were headed. High above these hills sat the snowy peaks of the mountains the orcs called home, and if she had nothing to wear under her skirt...

"You will not. Neither will you leave again without my permission."

He grabbed her around the waist again and hauled her up over his shoulder. Her hip was already bruised purple from the day before.

"Please," she moaned. "Don't carry me again."

"I will today," he answered. "As punishment for trying to escape. Next time, I will have you bound and then dragged along the ground. Remember you are mine now. You will never, ever leave."

Finally, Cedar wondered if he was right, if she would truly be trapped as his bedwarmer, his slave, from now into eternity.

From one master to another. At least Lissa hadn't had a cock. At least Lissa hadn't carried her for days on end like a bag full of vegetables. At least Lissa had given her a cot on the floor from time to time.

Tears bit at the back of her eyes, but Cedar stiffened her lip. She wouldn't give this beast the gratification.

3

KARGORR

After hours of fighting and clawing, the human woman at last went silent. She hung there limply from his shoulder like a dead animal he was hauling home. The quiet, he had to admit, disturbed him. Had she drained of fight so quickly? Perhaps she was not the right vessel for his orclings after all.

Or, perhaps, she was plotting her escape, an urge he hoped he had eliminated after her first attempt. When she made no further movement, remaining quiet, he rewarded her for calming down by carrying her across his chest, which was surely more comfortable. Yet she still didn't speak, nor did she look in his eyes even when they paused midday to eat. This time, though, she took the food from him without objection and ate it sitting on the ground beside him.

At least Kargorr wouldn't have to force food down her throat again.

If she was to make a good concubine, if she was to survive, he would need to at least attempt to bond with her. Should she only see him as another cruel master, she might try to slit her own throat the moment she was near enough to a knife.

"What is your name?" he asked as they climbed higher into the tree-covered mountains.

The human didn't respond at first, and he checked that she hadn't fallen asleep. She was staring into the distance.

"Woman?" he asked again, shaking her in his arms. Her eyelids finally blinked, and she raised her gaze up to his.

"Why do you care?"

"I need something to call you. I will not be shouting 'woman' when I need you."

She sighed and wrapped her arms around herself, and he saw that her skin was covered in raised bumps, and her lips had paled.

"Cedar," she said at length, still looking anywhere besides his face.

"Of the tree?"

She just nodded.

"Cedar." He rolled it over his tongue, considering. She did not ask for his name in return, but he gave it to her anyway. "I am Lord Kargorr."

One of her eyes twitched. "Lord?"

He nodded. "I oversee this *parog*. That is roughly how it translates to your tongue."

Cedar gave the faintest nod to indicate that she had heard him but had no further thoughts. She was closing in on herself, shutting down, and he wondered if his instincts about her had been wrong. A limp female wouldn't do him much good. Though her cunt would serve its purpose, he would gain little pleasure from it aside from sating his urges.

"Are you cold?" he asked at length. She bit her lip, as if deciding what she ought to say. "If you are, you must tell me."

"You stole my clothes," she said, so quietly he almost

couldn't hear her. "You ripped them off of me, and now you ask if I'm cold?"

There was a venom in the words, a deep seething that restored his confidence. Hatred was better than nothing.

"I do," he said agreeably.

"Yes, I am cold." When she once more looked into his face, it was with a measured, deep ferocity.

Kargorr paused and crossed to one of the carts, calling for the warrior who pulled it to stop. He found one of his traveling furs and draped it across her, tucking it under her body with his arms. Then they resumed walking, though Cedar said nothing in response.

She had a shell around herself—but with time, a shell could be cracked to find the soft meat within.

As they neared the final climb to the *parog*, the procession stopped to abandon the carts and horses and carry what they could. A few warriors would remain to stand guard until Lord Kargorr could come back with others, and then everyone would pull their weight by hauling back the spoils.

"We will take the pigs first," he told them. His new concubine was clearly attached to them, and perhaps knowing they were safe and nearby would put some life back in her. He didn't need her affection, but he needed her to live, to carry a will to survive if she was to bear his orclings. It could be difficult and painful for human women, and she would serve him no purpose if she died in childbirth.

Besides, he needed his first concubine to show strength to the *parog* if he was to inspire their confidence in his new venture. He had to demonstrate that he had the instinct to make a good choice.

Cedar's eyes followed the piglets as they were carried up the slopes, and Kargorr followed along behind them so they remained within her sights. Even under the traveling fur she shivered, and he hoped he had not made a mistake by bringing such a weak creature home with him.

CEDAR

It seemed they had arrived at their destination. The orcs were leaving the goods behind, but carrying what they could, and Cedar wondered if the rest would go to waste, if everything the orcs killed for would be for nothing.

Why the big orc bothered to give her his name, she didn't know. He was the same as the rest of them, only larger and meaner. She would have no use for his name once she figured out how to escape.

She had been watching carefully, searching for an opening. Cedar didn't know when her moment would come, but she would be prepared should the opportunity present itself. Perhaps if Lord Kargorr saw her as weak and obedient, he would lower his guard and provide her a moment where she could take advantage of how he underestimated her. If she could make him believe that she had given up any hope, he might give her an opening himself.

But as they trekked higher up the snowy slopes, and the tops of distant tents came into view, that plan lost its shine. The orcs who had partaken in the raid on her village were only a fraction of Lord Kargorr's force, if the massive camp was any indication. Pathways paved with clay crisscrossed between huge tents that were held up by one or two staked wooden poles. Smoke curled into the sky from many smoke holes.

As they descended into a sheltered valley, the camp spread out before her, full of bustling activity. A cheer rose from those orcs who spotted them, and it spread as more and more of the big green monsters emerged from their tents. Lord Kargorr roared something to them in Orcish, and it was shouted back to him by a hundred voices. She resisted the urge to shrink back into his arms at the magnitude of the sound.

Surely once it was known that Cedar belonged to him, these other orcs would not let her simply pass by when she tried her escape. Already there were eyes on her as Lord Kargorr carried her against his chest into the densely packed camp; there were so many eyes, and all of their faces looked hard and unyielding. It was a city of monsters.

She was surrounded.

But among them she had spotted another human, and perhaps that meant there were more. If she could pretend to be one of them, to be another anonymous body, a path could still open to her.

Cedar turned her head into Kargorr's body to shield herself from their stares, and a low rumble shook his chest that could have been a laugh.

"They will not hurt you," he said, voice low so only she could hear.

He stopped at the center of the camp, and orcs appeared from everywhere, shouting and cheering. Lord Kargorr announced something, and then Cedar was moving, being lifted into the air like a trophy. She tried to cover herself as he roared again, and once more they answered.

She was a spoil of victory, nothing more.

When Kargorr was finished with his greeting, he carried her off toward one of the tents that was bigger than the others, a huge pole holding up the center. Against her will, Cedar's entire body tensed. This was surely his home, with his bed inside it, and the coppery fear she'd been keeping at bay crawled back up her throat and into her mouth. This was the moment she'd been dreading since he first caught her.

Kargorr threw back the flap and carried her inside, and she was assaulted by the smell. Everything here was his, that much was clear. The scent of him filled the air, even as another orc came in to light the fire positioned under the open tip of the roof. But Lord Kargorr ignored their visitor and focused on her as he padded to the back of the tent. She couldn't see what was there, but when he dropped her, she let out a scream. Instead of hitting hard ground, she landed in a soft, velvety pile of furs.

"Rest," he said. "There will be a celebration tonight, and I expect you to participate." He enunciated this last word so there would be no misunderstanding of the purpose she was meant to serve. She was a prize to be shown off, a symbol of their success. Who knows what he had planned for her after that, but she had a good idea.

Cedar nodded, holding her words tight inside. The less he knew her, the less she gave him, the easier it would be to eventually deceive him.

Then he left, and when the fire was lit, so did the smaller male orc who'd attended to it. She was alone.

This should be her moment to begin hatching her plan. She knew what sleeping in this bed meant, what Lord Kargorr intended to do with her. Orcs had cocks just as much as human men did, and they used them much the same way. But the furs were so soft, so warm and welcoming, and filled with the smell of him—an odor that was somehow both offensive and reassuring, that insisted he was a beast capable of great and terrible things. Cedar turned her face into it, knowing no one was watching her, and wormed her way under the layers until she was covered. It had all been too much, and there was nothing left in her to give.

As she faded away, Cedar thought of Lissa's head hanging limp off her shoulders and tried to shove down the warm gratification she felt. She had never slept in a place so soft. She had been lucky the few times when Lissa let her sleep in a bed.

Soon, Cedar fell unconscious, wrapped up tight in the furs that smelled of her captor.

4

KARGORR

I t gratified him more than he wanted to admit when he stepped back into his tent after organizing the retrieval and found the human curled up tight in his blankets, the furs drawn to her chin, her eyes closed and soft breaths falling from her lips. This was a good sign. When he left for his next raid, he didn't want to worry about her finding her way out of the camp. Even with guards to keep her put, she was a crafty one.

No, if she felt safer here in his bed, that would suit his purposes well.

He shook her awake with one gentle hand, and her eyelids fluttered open. She looked around with confusion before her gaze landed on him, and then she retreated into the blankets, her mouth in a stiff line. It was tempting to climb into the bed next to her and find out what was underneath that dirty green skirt, but he had other responsibilities, other pleasures to enjoy.

"Get up," he commanded, pulling aside the top blanket that covered her. "You're coming with me."

She hunched further down and tried to snatch the fur back, but he kept it out of her reach. He grabbed her by the arm, and she let out a cry as he yanked her out of the bed.

"Stop," she hissed, shoving his arm away. "I'm coming." She climbed out of the furs, never once looking at him, and straightened her skirt. Her stubbornness put a shine in her eyes that he liked. Now that she was out of the bed, though, she was shivering again.

"Weak humans." Kargorr slung a fur across her shoulders. "I will have new clothing made. After I claim you."

Cedar simply nodded in assent, tipping her chin up obstinately but saying nothing. He pulled her along, and she followed without digging her heels in, which was good. Kargorr didn't want to show off his unwilling new bedwarmer. He needed to display power tonight after being gone for so many days; he couldn't have any of his horde considering relocation to another *parog*. No, tonight was a feast, a celebration, and a claiming.

When he led her out of the tent, Kargorr flagged down the first orc who crossed his path. "Get the human some new clothes," he said, gesturing at Cedar's small body draped in a fur.

The orc woman did not hide her disgust. "We will have to make some," she said with displeasure.

"Then make some," Kargorr snarled, leaning close to her. She seemed to realize at that moment how she'd overstepped, and she hastily bent her knees in respect, thumping her chest.

"O-Of course." She turned and fled. He had no doubt she would do what he asked.

The interaction had caught Cedar's attention, and Kargorr thought she ought to learn his language soon. Only a handful of *grrosek* knew the human tongue, and she would need a way to communicate when he was away.

His lip twitched. It didn't appeal to him much at all, leaving her here alone so soon.

Orgha approached. "It's ready, *kazek*."

Kargorr nodded once, and the warrior departed.

"Cedar," he said, testing her name. "It is a celebration tonight. Look merry. Be festive."

The little human gawked at him. "You killed everyone in my village. And you want me to be... merry?"

"If you aren't, I will be forced to take action and lash you at the head of the table." He leaned down toward her, pausing so his mouth nearly brushed the shell of her ear. "I require your obedience. They will see your obedience, or else they will want to see retribution."

It seemed Cedar understood this, because she nodded once in agreement, and turned away from him with furrowed brows.

"You will do as I say?" he asked, to make sure she was fully aware of the stakes. He didn't want to have to discipline her, not so soon, but he would if it was needed to tame her.

"Yes," she said. But he could tell she was planning something, and he simply hoped he would not have to punish her in front of the entire *parog*. He would do it, without question. Strength was loyalty, and disobedience was weakness. But her skin was fragile, and he did not want to lash the mother of his future orclings before he even had a chance to plant them.

It would only turn her against him.

CEDAR

All eyes were on Cedar as Lord Kargorr led her out into the wide circle at the center of the camp, where a big bonfire was already lit, spitting sparks and smoke. The underbellies of the clouds were painted purple and orange, and Cedar pulled the fur around her shoulders closer as the orcs watched her pass. All hope for going unnoticed was gone.

Most of the orcs were grimacing, and Cedar wondered if Kargorr had made a mistake by bringing her here with him rather than simply killing her. Orcs hated humans. Of course Cedar would be seen as an invader here, as an enemy. She had been dragged into a den full of wolves.

Tables were assembled around the fire: big, dark wooden ones with trunks for legs, which made sense when she saw a few orcs already sitting down. She would look like a child next to any of them. While a low drumming began, Kargorr led her to the largest table at the far end, where there was only one tall, wide chair waiting behind it.

"Where am I to sit?" Cedar asked, eyebrow quirked at the single chair.

But Kargorr only laughed at her question as he sat down. Grabbing her firmly by the hips, he hefted her up into his lap. She scrambled to get away, but he held her fast and leaned over her shoulder.

"Have you already forgotten what we discussed?" he growled quietly. "You will do as I say, and do it with a smile on your face, or you will force my hand."

Cedar straightened. He had mentioned lashing, and she didn't care for the sound of that. She tried to make herself comfortable, her rear end positioned right on the big orc's groin. Underneath there she could feel him, the thick animal that lay between his legs. She knew what it looked like on a human—she couldn't fathom it on an orc. When she squirmed again, trying not to touch it, he grabbed her around the waist with one arm to still her.

"You will not like what happens if you do that," he said, and there was an edge to his tone she hadn't heard before. "Now cease. It's beginning."

Cedar's gaze was drawn up as the other orcs made their way to the tables, filling them up one by one. The orcs of Lord Kargorr's *parog* came in all shapes and sizes, some darker green and some lighter green, like leaves on different trees. They all had the same jutting jaws and great big tusks, though those that looked female had longer and more slender ones. Cedar wondered why Kargorr had stolen her when there were plenty of his own kind for him to choose from.

The drumming slowed. Kargorr hit his fist on the table, shaking it and the big wooden mug that sat on it. Silence fell over the assembled orcs.

He began to speak in Orcish, in a booming voice that carried all the way through the camp. Occasionally the other orcs cheered, and Cedar could only assume he was recounting the battle, how he had slain her neighbor and stolen everything the village had.

Then Kargorr slid his hands underneath her, lifting her up as if she were no more than a goblet of wine. The world swayed as he held her over his head, but Cedar tried not to struggle in case she were dropped. A few of the orcs thumped their tables, and others muttered in disapproval. But Kargorr roared something, threatening and powerful, and let his voice linger in the air. He was asserting himself, leaving no room for dissent from his people.

They did not murmur further.

Cedar was glad to have the ground underneath her once more as he brought her back down to his lap. Another mug was brought to the table, smaller this time, and a male orc bent at the knees before pouring a thick, brown liquid into it. He was smaller than the others, slender, and his face was more finely featured. The drink was some kind of beer, Cedar supposed, or perhaps wine. Kargorr pulled it toward her.

"Drink," he said. She only considered resisting for a moment when she remembered about lashing, and how he had forced her to eat on their journey, and decided that if she wanted to save her hide, she'd do what he asked.

Cedar couldn't escape if she was whipped. No, the more compliant she behaved, the more likely the orc was to give her an opening.

So she took the mug and tossed back the beverage inside it. It was just as syrupy as it looked, and tasted of pine and fruit, and it burned as it poured down her throat. She coughed, and a few orcs among the *parog* chuckled to themselves. But Kargorr nodded with the barest amount of pleasure.

It wasn't until the food came out that Cedar realized what an empty pit her stomach was. There was fresh beef, probably from one of the cows they had butchered before leaving the village and then tossed into a cart. Roots had been roasted and were served alongside bread, and Cedar ate it without having to be asked. The more nutrition she had, she told herself, the more prepared she would be for her escape.

As the *parog* drank more, they grew restless and rowdy. Orcs got up to dance around the fire, and after a mug full of the heady brown liquid, Cedar became entranced with watching them. Their bodies, as big and bulky as they were, swayed and weaved together in front of the bonfire in a sensual dance. Among those swirling around the flames, some were alone and some paired off. As time wore on and more of the alcohol was consumed, the orcs began shedding clothes or simply unlacing their breeches before touching one another. A male orc picked up a female and even slid his cock inside her as they danced.

Cedar's thoughts were milky and warm as she watched

them, enthralled with the sight of him moving in and out of her in time with the drums. She'd once fucked a village boy, and another time, a butcher in exchange for a cut of beef to help feed her family. Both times she had felt so dry, so uncomfortable—not like this orc who was slick and wet, and the orc woman who cried out in pleasure with every thrust.

"Do you like it?" Lord Kargorr asked, his voice much closer than she expected. "Watching them?"

Yes, she thought immediately. But she couldn't possibly be enjoying this, even as her eyes zeroed in on the place the two dancers were connected, as the male orc lifted his partner into the air so her legs wrapped around his waist, and he continued to fuck her as they moved around the fire. He was huge down there, she thought. Bigger than any human cock she'd ever seen, with an odd pair of bulges at the base.

"No," Cedar said, turning away and pushing down the bubbling, giddy feeling in her abdomen. "It's barbaric."

Kargorr repeated the word. "Barbaric?" He considered it. "Ah, like an animal." Then he chuckled, and his head was so close to hers that his tusk brushed her hair. "I suppose we are like animals. We are closer to nature, to our animal instincts. We do not run and hide from them. And you envy that, don't you?"

Of course she didn't. Cedar couldn't possibly admire how loose and free they were, how no one batted an eyelash at them performing such an intimate act in public. Yet her thighs twitched.

Lord Kargorr wrapped an arm around her waist. He pulled her in toward him, so her back was flush with his chest, and breathed in some of her hair the way he had done when she first saw him.

"You don't need to admit it now," Kargorr said, his unfamiliar accent drawing his words out and crumbling them up like pebbles. "But I can still feel you, little deer, moving with the beat."

She turned her eyes away from the bonfire and scowled into her mug.

"I think it's time," Lord Kargorr said at length. Placing her down on the ground next to him, he stood up and shouted something out at the crowd. He reached around her, seizing her breast in his hand, and dragged his fingers down the length of her body. Answering hoots rose into the air. Cedar twisted away at his probing hand, but he held her fast.

"What did I tell you?" he growled in her ear, and she stopped moving.

After I claim you, he had said, and Cedar shivered as he took her wrist in his hand and led her away from the fire.

There was no more time left.

5

CEDAR

Her breathing quickened as the orc lord led her through the camp, toward his tent.

"Please," she said, trying to pull her wrist out of his grasp. "Please don't do this."

He ignored her, and his grip was much too strong for her to get away. Before they reached the tent, he caught sight of the orc who had chased her—*Orgha*, she thought his name was—and waved him over.

"Prepare a bath," he said in her tongue, as if this was for her benefit. "I must wash off before I take her to my bed."

Cedar's whole body shivered. She thought of the orcs dancing around the fire, the thick cock sliding in and out, and nothing she felt made sense. It was as much terror as thrill, and the damn alcohol was muddying her mind, blurring everything into a single new sensation that made her thighs clench and her heart race.

When they reached his tent, Cedar knew putting up a fight would get her nowhere. Lord Kargorr was three times her size and built like a bear, and nothing she did would change how this all ended. So she came along inside as he pushed open the flap, hardening herself, shoring up all the sturdiness she'd built in the years she'd starved and worked under Lissa.

Inside the tent the fire was already burning. Kargorr tugged her to the bed where she'd slept earlier and pushed her down onto it, and she wanted to retreat inside the furs and hide, even though this was going to be her torture chamber, too. Then he left her there, walking to a rack on his wall.

She waited on the bed as first, he took off his necklace, a leather strap covered in teeth, and then lifted off a cloak made of bones and hung it up. Next came his thick leather jerkin with fur around the edges, and he took his time removing each hook. Two orcs entered with a heavy copper tub, and a third brought a bucket of hot water. More buckets came, filling the tub as Kargorr removed everything that kept his body hidden.

Underneath there were scars, yes—but one stood out against the rest, thick and white, crossing from his shoulder all the way to his hip. Even his muscles had changed in those places, where some blade had torn him asunder. Kargorr turned around, and one tusk rose up when he found her staring.

But he didn't gloat. He didn't need to. She was admiring him in the way she might admire something beautiful because it was flawed, a tree because of the lightning that had struck it in half. He had experienced deep pain when this happened, and she wondered what that was like.

"I obtained this at the same time," he said, gesturing at the scar across his face, "as this." He was staring back at her now as his hands dropped to the laces of his hip guards, then his breeches. Finally Cedar had the sense to look away, pretending she was observing the orcs who came and went with even more hot water. Soon the tub was full, warm steam rising from the top, and she couldn't avoid looking at him any longer.

It was as big as she had feared, if not more. Between corded, green thighs hung a creature Cedar almost didn't recognize. His cock was darker than the rest of him, the skin wrinkled as it lay dormant. Even then, she thought, it was too much. Too big. Too everything. At the base, Cedar noticed the thick bulges, two undulations that made it even more deeply unfamiliar to her.

When Lord Kargorr saw her staring, it twitched. But he didn't seem to care one way or another as he climbed into the bathtub. It was only when she remained there on the bed, frozen, that he spoke to her.

"Get in." It wasn't a command, but merely two words ground out in his strange accent. He didn't need to issue commands to get what he wanted. In fact, he hadn't raised his voice to her once—not yet, anyway.

Cedar stood in front of the tub, working through her mind what this required of her. She would have to get in there, naked, with him, unless she wanted to soak through all of her clothes. He watched as she turned around and pulled up her shirt, along with the stays that kept her breasts in place. The cold night air struck her bare skin, even this near to the fire, and made her shiver all over.

"Hurry up and perhaps you can get warm," Kargorr called to her, tapping the tub. Cedar tossed her shirt to the side and hooked a thumb into the band of her skirt, which she pulled down next. After that, nothing was left.

She turned around, covering herself, and headed toward the tub.

"Hiding is pointless," Kargorr said, his eyes not leaving her face. "I will see it all, many times over."

Many times over. A shuddering breath whooshed out of her lungs. He was right. There was no point. But still Cedar kept her arms crossed across her chest, simply on principle, as she climbed into the tub. She found his legs parted in such a way that she could sit between them, and she fit there as if she was meant to. The water was warm, so warm, and Cedar couldn't help a gasp of pleasure as it rose higher with her added presence, all the way to her chest. She saw how filthy she was now as the dirt came off her skin. He was even filthier, with arms darker than the rest of him, still caked with blood from the raid. His cock, thankfully, was hidden down below where she could avoid looking at it.

For now.

From the floor, Kargorr picked up a basket and set it on the edge of the tub. It held rags and soap, and when she gave it a curious look, he held out his arms.

"Wash me, little deer."

Was that all? Cedar could wash him. If this delayed the inevitable, she would wash him well and thoroughly, all night long.

She snatched up the rag and soap and set to getting him wet, then beginning with his hands, soaped him. His fingers were thick and wide, with black nails that became sharp at the tips. She washed underneath them first, then up his palms and wrists, one hand at a time. Everything about him was strange, eerie, foreign. The water ran brown with dried blood as she reached his forearm, forcing her to lean further and further forward.

Cedar worked hard never to look at his face, never to acknowledge that she was in the water with him, completely naked with nothing to hide her. She treated it like a job, doing her best to scrub and scrub his green skin until his arms were shining and clean and the water no longer was.

"There's more," Kargorr said, and at last, she glanced up at him. His eyes were sharp, heated, and his huge lower jaw was clenched tight. He ran his hands down his chest and back up to his throat again, showing her exactly where he wanted her.

She crawled toward him in the water, forced to wedge herself between his thick thighs to reach that far up his big body. Something moved against her leg, but she did everything in her power not to look down at it, to pretend it wasn't there, as impossible as that was. No, his hidden cock occupied a whole corner of her mind as she reached up and dragged the rag down his chest, smearing dust, rinsing it off, and swirling the water around until he gleamed. The higher she reached, the farther she had to lean forward, until something soft but sturdy pressed at her belly.

Cedar's breath hitched and her hand slowed, her focus now on that object making itself known. But Kargorr didn't speak. No, a low chuckle vibrated his chest, and he reached out to cup her hip, dragging one hand up her side. When she finally regained her composure, she steeled herself not to think of the hand or the cock and only of accomplishing her task. She scrubbed harder, but his fingers kneading the skin down her side grew harder to ignore as they brushed over the swell of her breast, and then down under the sweep of her ass. His cock swelled thicker and harder under the water, the head reaching the surface and rubbing her with every circle of the rag on his chest. Each long stroke of his hand left a blaze of heat behind, a heat that radiated across her, spreading to all her fingers and toes.

And then Cedar had nothing left to clean. She shrank back to the other end of the tub, more afraid of herself than she was of him, regretting how she'd leaned into his touch. She wanted more, even more, and that couldn't be right.

"Now," Kargorr said, breaking the heavy silence in the tent, "I want you to clean yourself."

He leaned back in the tub, hanging his arms off the sides, and watched without regard for the heavy cock floating in the water in front of him. Any other time Cedar would've been happy to get clean after days of hard traveling —especially traveling while slung over someone's shoulder for miles and miles on end—but with those hot, dark eyes digging into her skin, she felt paralyzed. Slowly she reached for the rag and the soap again and scrubbed her shoulders, then her arms, dunking them each under the water. She brushed her armpits, and when she lifted her hand into the air to reach better, Kargorr brought one of his own hands down to his crotch. He seized his cock in his rough palm, and she paused where she was, her eyes drawn to his fingers where he wrapped them around himself, squeezing and stroking.

"Keep going," he said, his voice lower, huskier.

She nodded quickly and resumed scrubbing, moving from one armpit to the other, trying not to watch as his hand gripped his cock harder. It stirred something ugly and deep inside her, an empty pit that was slowly filling with heat. His brows lowered further as she reached her breasts with the rag, and here she paused, uneasy at how much she longed just to brush it over her nipple.

Kargorr's eyes bored into her, dismantling her, daring her to deny herself. So she swept the rag over the hanging globe of her breast, and her breathing sped up.

"Ah," hummed Lord Kargorr as he leaned back further in the tub, his hips sliding closer to hers. "Does that feel good?"

"No," she said instinctively, and his mouth curled in a smirk as if he didn't believe her for a moment.

"You're not clean yet." He grunted as he continued to pump his hand along that thick beast between his thighs.

Cedar nodded and swept the rag down her body, then up over her nipples to her throat and neck. His gaze was intense, sharply focused on her and only her, as she drew it down to her belly and circled it.

Then, abruptly, Kargorr released himself, his cock dropping from his hand.

"Get out," he told her, a harshness to his voice. Those dark eyes of his were focused with a painful precision on her and that feeling returned, the terror mixed with thrill. Surely he would want to use that cock now. With her nipples still peaked and warmth coiling in her belly, Cedar had a traitorous thought. What if she wanted it? That big, scarred body that had seen so much—what would it feel like? Would that massive thing between his legs even fit inside her?

She thought of the orc woman crying out in pleasure, of the wet cock moving in and out of her. Cedar trembled, whether in fear or anticipation, she didn't know.

At last, she obeyed, climbing out of the tub. She shivered the moment she left the warm water. Lord Kargorr stepped out after her, his cock jutting straight out in front of him like a spear. He grabbed her arm and pulled her toward the bed, and Cedar stumbled along behind him with a yelp. Rather than pushing her onto it, he snatched up one of the furs and wrapped it around her body.

"Dry off."

Kargorr stood by the fire while she whisked the fur over her skin, his eyes never leaving her. They burned into her, searing the skin off her bones, revealing to him her bare skeleton. She turned away and pulled the fur tighter around herself.

"It won't do you any good," Kargorr said as he padded toward her, reminding her very much of a wolf that had once attacked her pigs. He slowed before reaching her. "You can set it aside, or I can tear it off of you."

Those were the choices. So she slid the fur off her shoulders, and he took it from her, hanging it on a rack by the fire. Then he closed the distance between them, taking her chin in his hand.

"Lie down," he told her, a husky edge to his voice. "Now."

6

KARGORR

The human woman had tried to hide it, but her body felt the pull, too. She'd stared at him as she'd caressed her own breasts, and now her face heated with arousal, red blotches covering her skin.

This would make it much, much simpler for him. He wasn't likely to plant an orcling in her tonight—but he would bind her to him and stake his claim so no other orcs got any foolish ideas. A prize was a prize, after all, which sometimes earned a fight over who would take it home. But this one was his, and tonight Lord Kargorr needed to make sure all of them knew it. Challenges within a *parog*'s ranks were a sign of weakness, a symbol of poor health that could only be blamed on its *kazek*. Kargorr didn't want to invite one by leaving her unclaimed and unprotected.

Thankfully Cedar did as he told her, lying back on the bed in all her nakedness. She tried to cover herself with her arms again, but that wouldn't last long. She was so small, so helpless in front of him, and his cock leapt at the sight of her pinkish, fragile skin. His hands hungered to touch her, to taste that skin under his fingers.

He had taken bedmates in the past, but that had been years ago, before he became lord of his own *parog*. Bringing someone into his tent now was an assertion that he was claiming a prize and intending to sow orclings.

And indeed, after so long kept tucked away, his cock was slobbering. Every time he had vented his rage through his enemies or his sparring partners instead of a warm cunt or a tight asshole, his hunger had grown, and now it was bottomless.

When Kargorr advanced on her, Cedar scrambled higher up the bed, tightening her arms around her chest. He tugged her wrist away.

"I've already seen you," he told her, planting one knee on the furs. Her hand fell away from her chest willingly this time, because he was right. He set her wrist down and did the same for her other arm, so she was splayed out before him, but free to move. Though her body hummed in a tune that felt so familiar and yet exotic, he would take his time with her. Desserts were best enjoyed slowly, a few small bites at a time, to fully understand their flavor.

His fingertips dragged up her arm to her throat, his sharp nails only dancing on the surface of her skin. There he trailed downward again, to one of the teardrop-shaped globes that rested to either side of her sternum. They were round with a loose heft, topped by broad areolas and taut, tiny nipples. He traced one, cupping the nipple with his nail, and Cedar twitched against him. Her eyes were round and rapt, and there was no sign yet that she intended to fight him.

Perhaps she was more intelligent than he typically gave humans credit for. Still, there was a shimmer of stubbornness in there, a hidden gem of insolence, that made him pause.

He would have to cure her of that.

When at last he slipped his finger over one hardened nipple, her lips parted. Repeating it made her eyelids flutter. They were fine breasts, he thought, taking one full in each of his hands. Her hips trembled, and that rosy flush was spreading across her skin as he teased and tormented them. He imagined how they would look even larger when she was full of his orcling and nodded in approval. She had been a good choice.

Heavy breaths fell from her lips as he finally released her and trailed his fingers down her belly, thinking it was much too scant. She needed more roundness to her, flesh on her hip bones and the soft place where she would carry his offspring.

Kargorr prized himself on his self-control, even when the rage took him. But just the sight of her, the games his imagination played with her, were chipping away at it. No, he couldn't have that, not yet. If he took her hard now, she would be much more of a risk later.

He needed her hungering for him. Thirsting for him. Wet and open for him.

Her chest was rising and falling higher and higher, and so he ventured further downward, over the indent of her belly. He would make sure she had extra at meals from now on.

Not once did her wide eyes stray from him, as if challenging him to look away himself. Kargorr slid his hand down her side, over the swell of her hip, brushing her skin with a hint of his claws. Her body pressed into his hand, and her expression seemed as if this was not deliberate. His cock jerked, but he stilled it with a thought and continued his exploration down to the thatch of curly hair at the base of her hips.

Cedar tensed under him, and he shored up his patience to run his hands down her thighs and back again, urging her legs apart.

"Show it to me," he said, his voice coming out more of a growl than he intended.

Her throat bobbed, and in response, her legs opened to him. Inside he was more than pleased to find her small pink cunt shining in the firelight, the petals of it already wide and open to him, swollen up and waiting. He slid the pad of his finger down, over the edges of it, to the place where her heat radiated out. Now that she was exposed to him, Kargorr could smell the tang of her need, the musky flavor of her want, and it nearly blew down his remaining willpower. But he sampled her slowly, ignoring the steady drip of his seed as his cock imagined where it would go.

"So wet," he said. When he pulled his hand away, some of her thick nectar came with it, and he rubbed it between his fingers. Cedar said nothing, but her eyes darted between his hand and his face. To emphasize his point, he licked his forefinger, drawing his claw over his tongue.

He would need to deal with those.

Kargorr sat up and reached for the knife that lay on a table by the bed, close at hand should he need it in the night. Cedar sucked in a breath, like she was waiting for him to use it on her —but he held it up to one of his nails and slid it across, slicing the claw off at the base. Then he smoothed it out, using his tusk as a file, until he knew he wouldn't cut open his delicate new concubine. Repeating the process on his next finger, he flexed them, then replaced the knife on the table.

Cedar hadn't moved, and he rewarded her by teasing her nipples again, worrying them until they were stiff.

"Very good," he murmured, cradling each breast as he imagined how it would leak milk someday.

He crouched over her, his shadow encompassing her as his hand slid down her belly to her cunt, and it throbbed under his hand with the beat of her heart. He dipped one dulled finger between the soft lips there, diving down until he reached where the folds parted for her small slit. He dragged the liquid he found there upward, spreading it around to better tease her. The wetter she was, the better she would feel, though his patience to sink his cock into her was wearing thin.

Her body answered with a tremble. Again he ran his fingers over her tiny bud, and again her hips twitched, her breaths coming faster. Kargorr's blood was warming, heating up inside his veins as it flowed ever faster toward his groin. Cedar's eyes had drifted upward to the roof of the tent as her eyelids sank lower. He found her small channel and dipped inside it, pleased to find her leaking there. Cedar's eyes widened, and a halting breath fell from her lips. His finger easily slid inside her, patiently thrusting in and out as he made a map of her. Fucking was the same as any other battlefield—there were strategies to win and tells that told him how to adjust his plans. When her gasps came harder, he was winning, and it was time to home in on his prize.

His second finger met much more resistance as it pushed inside her, but when she squirmed, he gripped her hips and squeezed his hand deeper in, twisting and reaching to spread her for him. A strained moan fell from her lips, like she had been trying to hold on to it until it clawed its way free. Now he could fully explore her, staying shallow as she opened for him, then sliding in deeper. He dragged his fingers along her inner wall, and her hips jolted up to meet his hand.

There. He pumped quicker, and Cedar's small hands gripped the fur underneath her. Another moan, and now his hand was slick up to the palm with her. He widened the gap between his fingers, expanding her edges, ripening her for him.

"Ah!" She twisted against his hand.

"I would much rather you be ready for me," he said, making her pause. Her body stilled, and he resumed slicking in and out of that tiny cunt, stopping from time to time to pet her sensitive nub. He imagined himself inside that tiny hole, sliding into her, soaking her up, watching her spread lips leaking as he—

Then it cracked. Kargorr's need was too great for his self-control to hold it back, and he withdrew from her, reaching for his cock with his wet hand. He pulled her down the furs toward him by the thigh, trapping Cedar's legs around his hips.

"Are you—" Her words were cut off as he brought the head of his cock to the small slit he'd gotten slick and swollen with his attentions. He took a few halting breaths so he didn't jam himself inside her, and looked up into her round face, her cheeks blazing red.

"I hope you're ready, little deer," he said. "You're mine now."

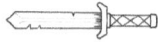

CEDAR

She had to admit that the orc was something to look at without his clothing on. His body was huge, like two men had been combined to create him, all of their muscles joined to make bigger ones. Each of his pectorals was swollen thick, and the breadth of his shoulders reminded her of an ox. His abdominals contracted with each of his harsh breaths, and she had to admire the sharp line of muscle that wound from his hip to his groin, where...

Cedar choked at the sight of his heavy, green cock with the darker head protruding from the skin. Above her, the torch-light flickered off his black eyes, as if they were two pools of poisoned water. She was still slick from his hands, which, much to her pleasure and indignation, had felt wonderful—and she grew even slicker as that thick tool of his pressed into her belly.

This shouldn't have made her throat flare with desire. This shouldn't have turned her insides to liquid, thinking about how he might feel. He was an enemy, a destroyer. She had cleaned the blood of her fellow villagers off his bare skin.

The scar across his face pinched as Kargorr fisted his cock in his hand and dragged it down, through the hair at the mound of her pelvis, over her pearl. She shook, her hips involuntarily snapping up at the sensation of it, and his lip peeled back in a ferocious smile, bringing his tusks up his cheeks. He did it again, rubbing that soft mushroom head over her clit, until she was gasping and twitching under him. Then he slid down through her folds, to the place he'd put his fingers inside her and splayed them open.

Cedar knew what he'd been doing by stretching her, and still, she didn't think there was any way that enormous, green cock would fit inside her without tearing her apart. She crushed her eyes closed.

She understood that her best chance of ever escaping would be to earn Kargorr's trust, to convince him she wouldn't leave, so his guard would be down when she finally saw her opportunity. And that would have to start here.

Besides, a much darker part of her thought, when had a man ever tried to prepare her? To pleasure her? Certainly not the wealthier man in the village where she'd grown up, who she'd slept with hoping he would marry her, but he simply laughed in her face. He'd been rough with her, seeing only to his own pleasure.

But this monster had already brought her close to the edge, and deep down, she wanted more. She wanted *all* of it.

"Open for me, little deer," Lord Kargorr said in his deep, rumbling voice. The way the head of his cock slipped down to the cavern between her legs, the way it naturally started to slide through, as wet as she was—it was as if he was meant to be there.

Cedar gasped as that head pressed in further, and of its own volition, her body began to part for it. Kargorr growled in satisfaction as he kept his grip cinched tight around the root of his cock, his other clawed hand keeping her thighs spread open for him. Deeper he went, urging her to give. Once his head was inside her, she met the thick shaft.

It was too big, too much. *He* was too much. She bit her lip and reeled her hips back on instinct, trying to escape that force plowing its way into her. Kargorr sucked in a harsh breath as he dug his claws into the flesh of her thigh.

"Stay still," he said in a clipped voice, and some feeling she couldn't distinguish, something between fear and excitement, rippled down her spine. This time, he spit on his hand, the saliva dripping from his lips, and slicked it all over his cock.

Once more, he guided it into her, and now slippery, it drove further in, until he met a passage too tight to let him through. Cedar begged her body to allow it, and as he rocked against her, his head barely lodged in her, the lip of it dragged over some sensitive place inside her she'd never felt before. Pleasure ricocheted from that one spot, all across her body, and above her Kargorr groaned.

"Yes, little deer. Feel me." He gripped her hip tight in his other hand as he pushed as far in as he could, then slid out, then back in again in a truly torturous motion that soon had Cedar whining, her hips jerking with each quarter-thrust as she tried to keep her voice trapped inside her mouth. How she wanted more, she was shocked to find. Her walls clenched around him, desperate to be filled. How she wanted it all.

As much as she dreaded giving him the gratification, she couldn't help moaning when he finally bestowed her more. He grinned down at her, a demon-like smile, as he sank further in, and further again on his next stroke, each time withdrawing so she was forced to whimper again. Her body was stretched to its limit, maybe even beyond, and Cedar cursed at how delicious he felt, and at how her own pussy was betraying her by swallowing him up this greedily.

"Now you'll take everything," he murmured to her, lowering himself to one arm so his thick chest and huge, heavy body weighed her down. He thrust in again, deeper this time, spreading even more of her. "You're going to take all of me."

There couldn't possibly be any of him left to take, she thought. Surely he had packed her as full as she could be already. Until he grabbed her cheek in his hand, his sharp claws nicking her skin, and looked into her eyes.

Inside that darkness, she saw nothing. It was empty, bottomless. There was no familiar shred of humanity in those eyes, no sign that he might have mercy on her, that he might be kind to her, that he might *free* her.

No, they were pits, where someone could fall in and get lost forever, with no escape.

And then he plunged in. Cedar cried out as Lord Kargorr fully sheathed himself in her, his cock buried so far inside her small channel that she felt it nudge her other organs, felt it press against her belly. When she clenched, there was no give at all around that thick object inside her.

When he reeled back again, and that huge, fat cockhead of his dragged over her sensitive inner flesh, a sharp spasm of pleasure burst behind her eyes. Cedar found herself clutching him tight, her fingers buried in his arms, holding on for her life as he buried his cock in her again.

And again.

And again.

With each stroke he moved faster, until Cedar's breasts were bouncing with every thrust of that enormous creature inside her, and cries were falling from her lips like snow in the depths of winter. They tumbled out of her so fast she couldn't stop them, and that eerie smile on his thick lips, on his jutting jaw, grew wider.

"See?" he asked as he fucked her, his mouth only inches from hers. "This is how it will feel every time I put an orcling in you, little deer. Every time you welcome me home."

For a moment, Cedar thought he might kiss her. He was so close, and she thought perhaps, if he did, she could feel something for this monster on top of her. If he pressed his lips to hers, if he bestowed upon her that shred of intimacy, perhaps she could see herself underneath him gladly.

But he didn't.

7

KARGORR

He had fucked orc women before. They welcomed him into their tents when he needed it and spread their legs for him with ardor. He had taken them as brutally as he wanted, and they devoured it, rocking underneath him and shouting his name.

But no cunt had ever felt as good as this one, as that of this small human woman. Her big breasts swung with every one of his movements, and the sight of them underneath him made his groin ache. With every strike of his cock inside her, she mewled and moaned, her body squeezing him so tight he thought that only by some kind of magic had he even fit there.

Her small, angular face was appealing, in its own way, and Lord Kargorr liked the look of it with her mouth open, her ripe lips spread. For a sick moment, he even thought of pressing his mouth to hers, of claiming that part of her, too.

Such things were reserved. They were kept tight until the time that an orc found his *yapira*, and then they were given like a gift.

This human was not his *yapira*. She was a tool, a vessel, the beginning of something and not the end of it. He would fill her, and when his seed had taken root in her, he would find another concubine just like her and seed her, too. His cock swelled as he thought of the empire he could build of skilled half-breed warriors that would overtake even more of the human lands, reclaiming the *grrosek*'s ancestral home.

It all began here, with her. *Cedar*. He didn't mean to think of her name as he sank deep into her hot, slathered cunt, but he did, and then he couldn't shake it out of his mind again. *Cedar*. Like the tree, he thought, clutching her closer, grabbing her around the ass so he could change his angle. This drove her wild, her hands reaching for anything they could find to grab onto, and he was gratified by this discovery.

A battlefield like any other.

Cedar. Her cries rose in pitch, and the sweet walls of her cunt began fluttering around him. His control was a testament to his training—usually. But the sight of her, the sound of her, the *sensation* of her around his cock, squeezing him as tight as any perfectly tailored glove, threatened to break that control.

He thrust faster, pumped harder, his balls slapping her flesh as he drove into her over and over. A chase began between Kargorr and the little human's whimpers of pleasure. The more she cried out, the more she clenched around him, the better the chance his seed would take. Perhaps he hadn't meant to fill her with an orcling tonight, but now that he was here, the swollen, pinkish lips of her cunt splayed around his cock, he couldn't think of anything else.

"Now, little deer," he commanded her, and her big eyes flew open. "Now you're mine. Forever and always, you'll be mine. No one else will partake of you again, except for me." He jammed his cock deep in her, relishing the soft pulse of her cunt as she neared her crescendo. "Say it, human."

Instantly she whimpered, "No."

Kargorr stilled, and she writhed against him, her hips seeking his.

"Yes," he growled, leaning his head down close to hers again, but not in the promise of a kiss. This was of a bite. "Say it."

Her body stilled, and panting, she gritted her teeth.

"No."

So instead, he fucked her. Kargorr reeled his hips back and slammed into her, and the squelch was his reward. He pinpointed just where he could best torture her, and took her, used her, again and again. Cedar's cries had become whines as he denied her finish, slowing down just before it carried her under.

"No," Cedar moaned, because he didn't even have to ask the question again.

But she would give in to him, sooner or later. He would crush all of her walls and turn them into gravel, until she was bare and helpless before him.

Her cunt clamped down tight, and her screams abruptly stopped. Eyes huge, she tensed in a wordless, soundless scream. *Yes, Cedar*, he thought, clenching his teeth as her soft edges became hard, as she dragged him in deep and then kept him there, as he plundered her through it. He could feel her around him, from his cock into his belly, up to the base of his throat, where his own groan sprouted. He couldn't help the sound as she demanded his seed and so he gave it up to her, jamming himself fully into her before the dam broke.

She cried out again, and he realized then her legs had wrapped tight around his hips, her body desperate to have him even as her mouth denied him. He could use that, he thought, to shape her into what he wanted. All beings were pliable with the right motivation.

When at last Kargorr erupted inside her, he fisted his hand in her hair and tugged her head up toward him. She shook and shivered all over, her lovely sheath doing the same around him. He pumped once more, twice more, fucking his seed into her, drawing out her aftershocks until her legs fell limp. He remained inside her, simply relishing the warmth of her, the sight of her submitted to him.

Now he had her body. All he needed was her mind, and then she would be his.

CEDAR

She lay like that, panting underneath the orc's huge body, as he continued sliding in and out of her on a wet river of his own spend. Her pussy was too sensitive, much too sensitive, but he didn't seem to care as he earned another whimper from her. His cock only seemed to soften for a moment, after he first expelled himself in her, before it was hard again, swollen and too big for her wrung channel. Kargorr grunted as he pushed into her again, forcing her taut muscle to give to him.

"Again, little deer," he told her. "Say it."

"No," she said, and this time she spat. She would never be his. He could take her this way, but she was her own. The droplet landed on his cheek, very near his nose, and he laughed at her.

Laughed.

But Kargorr didn't stop his languid strokes, his seed audibly spurting out of her as he filled her and displaced it. It rushed down her ass, and she couldn't help a whimper because her skin felt torn. Still, she accepted him, bringing him into her body again and again as her pussy slowly released. Soon it was thirsting for him once more, and Cedar couldn't help but give over to it.

And so the orc fucked her again at a brutal pace, driving

Cedar to wildness, until she was thrashing and calling out to the stars as she gripped Kargorr tight against her. She was incensed that he could do this to her, that he could turn her body into a puppet tied to his hands—and to his infernal *cock*.

When he was finally finished with her, and he'd extorted another monstrous climax from her fragile body, he released her. She wanted to wriggle away, to separate from him and show that he hadn't claimed her yet, but Cedar's muscles wouldn't move.

Kargorr lowered himself until he was nearly crushing her, and she could feel his breath on her face. Again she wondered if he would kiss her. The need to feel his lips on hers didn't make sense to her, didn't sit right. But the way he had taken her, ruthlessly pursuing her pleasure, had stirred something else: a hope. For what?

Cedar didn't know. She didn't want anything from this beast, who had tried and failed to make her cow to him even as he conquered her. He was a brute, to be mollified and then outsmarted.

He never stopped simply looking at her, his cock at last softening inside her. She tried to look back into those empty eyes, but eventually, she turned her head.

With a dark chuckle, Kargorr withdrew himself from her, and she bit her lip as a whimper came out.

The orc looked displeased.

He crouched down over her, forcing her legs apart, and she squeaked as she tried to pull away. But he held her fast as he gathered up his seed in his fingers and, with surprising gentleness, pushed it back into her. He examined her, and Cedar wondered what he was looking for, what other strange torment he had in store.

Abruptly, and still completely naked, he got up off the bed and stalked out of the tent.

KARGORR

It wouldn't do to have her break on him. Now that he'd felt what it was to be inside her, oh, he would have her again. Until the next raid, he thought, he would use her until her cunt was the same shape as his cock.

He stopped the first orc he saw, an older male with a load of firewood over one shoulder.

"Get me some *kuja*," he said, and the orc nodded and darted away. He stood there, breathing in the frigid night air, hoping he might get some sense about him again.

Cedar had taken more than just his cock inside her. For a moment, Kargorr had forgotten everything. It was all a haze beyond the sound of her, the sight of her, the *feeling* of her.

He couldn't let her become a distraction from his goal. His *parog* would be the strongest, with the most territory retaken from the humans. He would have even more prizes, and then...

An orc woman was breathing hard as she approached him with a small clay jar.

"*Kuja*," she said, sliding it into his hands. Kargorr nodded his appreciation, and she turned and left as quick as she came.

Inside the tent, Cedar had found her way under the top layer of furs. Kargorr took the edge and pulled it aside, revealing her to the air. With a yelp, she tried to get it back, but he was already pinning her to the bed.

"I can't," she moaned, and yet her body instantly responded to his, her back arching into his hands.

"Quiet." He lashed her thighs down and spread them apart. Then he took the jar and popped the cork so he could get at the salve inside.

Cedar stifled a gasp as he brought the cold paste to her red slit. He smeared it around, and she was very still as he finished and re-corked the jar.

"It will heal," he told her firmly.

"Oh," was all she said. Kargorr grunted, hoping she would be well again by morning. Now that he had tasted her, he would stop at nothing to put an orcling inside her.

He pulled up the fur, covering both of them with it. Kargorr hadn't realized how much he longed for a bedwarmer until now, until there was a small body in his blankets that smelled entirely of him. He curled his arm under her and brought her in so he could sniff at her hair, and she fought him, pushing him by the chest. She wanted to let him know she was still angry, but he could sense how she faltered inside.

"No struggling now," he told her, with a firm hand around her. He was surprised when she obeyed. So he had drained some of the fight out of her along with her slick juices when she came. "Sleep."

Cedar kept her arms pinned between them, as if putting up one last barrier. But when she fell into sleep, she came in close, seeking him out and winding her arms around his waist.

Good. He drew her against his big body, giving her what her unconscious self sought.

They had crossed the first twist in the path on the road to making her his.

8

CEDAR

She'd never been so warm and comfortable in all her life. It felt like sleeping next to a lightly flickering fire, draped in the softest blankets possible. She'd never slept like this, not in her time sharing the floor with her siblings as a child, not on the bare cot that Lissa occasionally let her use when she wasn't in the barn.

And something under her head was rising and falling in a slow, steady rhythm. Breathing, she realized.

Cedar opened her eyes to find herself pressed firmly against a huge, scarred, green chest. The skin was mottled all over, and she recognized it immediately.

Her breath came faster as she tried to decide what to do. Remaining here, against Kargorr's side, was against her better instincts. But the furs had formed so perfectly around them, and he was so, *so* warm in this awful, frigid place, that she didn't want to move.

Still, this was a golden opportunity, one that might not

pass by her again. He was fully asleep, and maybe she could slip away while he was unconscious.

"I can hear you thinking, little deer," came his rumbling voice, and Cedar flinched, her eyes darting up to his face. Kargorr's big arm, which was still slung over her waist, tightened to stop her retreat. "Your breathing changed."

Is that all it took to wake him up? Cedar had hoped, seeing him fast asleep this morning, that she might be able to steal away in the middle of the night after tiring out his body. But that didn't seem to be an option if he slept so lightly as to pick up changes in her breathing.

His hand stole down her side and over the swell of her ass, then underneath it to the pathway between her thighs. She was horrified when his fingers encountered wetness, as if simply breathing him in, feeling him so close, had done this to her.

Cedar should have moved away, insisted that they get out of bed and demanded food, but instead she let him thoughtfully, languidly drag the pad of his finger through her warm lower lips. It only made her wetter, the way he remained otherwise still, just testing her out and occasionally brushing over her clit. Each time made her involuntarily convulse, but he kept to his unhurried circuit.

Then he slid his finger inside her. Her hips snapped against his hand, so he rewarded her by pushing it in deeper.

"I think she wants my cock again," Lord Kargorr said with a twinge of amusement. Cedar clenched her fists, holding in any sound as he pumped that single finger in and out, curling it to stroke her as it went. But was he wrong?

She hated herself for it.

His hand gently withdrew, then coursed down her thigh to pull it up, over his hip, spreading her wide. Cedar couldn't bear to look at him as he swirled the head of his cock through her fluids, coating himself, brushing over her small button again and again until she was aching to have him.

But she couldn't hold in the sound she made when he slid into her, somehow fitting easily while also demanding she open wide, that she stretch to her limits. He glided right into his seat, deep inside her, and let out a satisfied exhale.

Cedar was surprised to find nothing more than a twinge where she'd been rubbed raw the night before. Whatever that *kuja* was, it seemed to have worked magic, because every glide of that thick orc cock in and out of her broke her down, piece by piece, shred by shred, until she was moaning, her pussy begging for more. It was a traitor.

"Is that so?" Kargorr said, a smirk on his big, square face. He flipped her over, needing barely one hand to move her, so she was flat on her belly, her nose in the furs, and she let out a cry of surprise as he spread her legs apart and pulled her hips up into the air. Cedar was even more helpless in this position as he buried one clawed hand in the soft flesh of her ass, then plunged himself into her.

He could have set a blistering pace. He could have fucked her like he fucked her last night, but instead, for a reason she couldn't fathom, Kargorr didn't. He took his time, dragging his cock up and down along the sensitive underside of her channel, settling deep in her and then merely rocking back and forth. Somehow this was worse, the way he lazily used her, letting her pleasure build and build one small stone at a time. She needed more, but he wouldn't give it to her, denying all of her mewls and whines.

When she crumbled, it took her by surprise. Kargorr barely reacted as she cried out and twitched around him, her knees shivering as she tried to fall to the bed. But he kept her anchored, hoisting the weight of her with his hand as he continued his methodical subjugation of her body. She hated that he could do this, *hated* that she had never felt pleasure like this before, and that she had given herself over to it.

It wasn't until he had pushed her over the edge again,

claws leaving marks on her, that he finally spent himself. He barely reacted save for the impossible swell of his cock inside her, those thick protrusions at the base butting up against her entrance.

"Not for you," he rasped as he finished emptying himself. "Never for you."

She didn't know what that meant, but it reminded her simply that she was nothing to him, only a body to be used until it wasn't needed any longer.

Kargorr lay down at her back, breathing heavily, still buried inside her. When he withdrew, he said nothing, though his hands were shaking. Then he stood up and walked naked from the tent.

Cedar had never been one to cry. Crying made you look weak, and it blinded you to what needed to be done. So she buried all of her hurt, all of her hopelessness, and tucked it away in a place no one could see, not even herself.

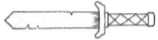

KARGORR

He had considered it, for the briefest moment—sinking all the way into her, really and truly claiming her. His *sarga* had wanted it. They had wanted it so badly that it almost overwhelmed him. The way Cedar turned into liquid, how she moaned and her cunt spasmed around him, had begged him to push completely inside her, to bury his *sarga* in her along with the rest of him. Then, when they swelled, when he poured all his seed into her, they would lodge there.

It was a sacred act for an orc to use his *sarga*. It would label her as his *yapira*, his forever bedwarmer, and this ratty human offal was not that.

Irritated at himself for even having the thought, he left

Cedar in the tent and walked out into the fresh air, hoping to clear his head. He stood there for some time, looking up into the clouded sky that spoke of snow to come. They needed to move into the lowlands soon and continue their expansion southward. That would be the true testament to the strength of his *parog*, if he could take even more human villages and swallow up what remained into his territory.

He heard Orgha approaching before he saw him. Kargorr inclined his head slightly as the shorter orc stopped at his side and tapped his chest in greeting.

"You claimed her, then?" he asked, arching an eyebrow in the direction of the tent. "Everyone heard."

Kargorr got a chuckle out of that. She had tried so hard to not let it show how good his cock had felt inside her, but Cedar was no match for him. Good. It was a positive thing that the entire *parog* now knew. No other *grrosek* would try to encroach on her, unless they wanted a fight with their leader.

It would also, hopefully, make it harder for her to escape when he left on his next raid.

He would post many guards, and she would be under watch even as she went to pee. She had refused his demand for her submission, and it would be impossible to trust her until she did.

Even then, he wondered if her word would mean anything. Taming this one might prove difficult, but tame her he would.

Kargorr answered his right hand with a nod. "She is mine now. She will bear me many fine orclings." As if summoned, one of the *parog*'s other half-breeds walked by, an immense blacksmith's hammer over his shoulder.

But Orgha didn't answer. He was studying Lord Kargorr with one brow arched. "So you have joined the ranks of those taking human concubines."

"It is the best path forward for the *parog*." Seeding many

orclings would also show off his virility. Strength in battle was the only thing the *grrosek* valued more. "I will likely need a bigger tent soon."

Orgha nodded, and though his mouth twitched like he wanted to speak, he chose not to.

Kargorr arched an eyebrow. "What is it? Be forthright."

Orgha cleared his throat. "Still, it should be a temporary solution, lord. Eventually, you will want a *yapira* instead, to rule the *parog* alongside you."

The impudence made him seethe. As if Orhga knew what he needed. As if he understood Kargorr's greater plans.

Lord Kargorr rounded on his right hand, eyes ablaze, and Orgha realized the mistake he had made.

"I do not need anything," Kargorr said, his voice deadly quiet, "but myself. But my *parog*. But my warriors. That is where strength lies, not in one's bed."

"Of course," Orgha said, not meeting his lord's eyes. "You have always ridden alone, and I should not expect that to change."

Kargorr had no use for a *yapira*. He needed to be free of ropes tying him to the ground. He needed to show his blood-thirst and sow many more concubines.

Kargorr gestured for Orgha to leave him, but before he did, his right hand had one last thing to say.

"When will we move south?"

At least Orgha understood his place, understood where he was needed.

"In three days' time," Kargorr said. He needed the hours with his new concubine to properly break her. And then they would move on to the next frontier.

Orgha nodded. "We will begin taking down the posts right away."

The message spread quickly through the *parog*, and soon, even as he stood there, the other *grrosek* began dismantling the camp in earnest. The posts that secured the perimeter were removed one at a time and loaded onto sledges.

He would be needed soon to oversee the move, but in the meantime...

Lord Kargorr found his way to the meal tent and secured a large tray of beef and roots and bread, the spoils of their raid. No one spoke to him, but everyone looked as he took the tray, returning to his own tent where he had left Cedar.

But when he returned, she was gone.

9

CEDAR

She wasn't stupid, just very full of *pee*.

When Lord Kargorr hadn't come back for quite some time, Cedar poked her head out of the tent and glanced from side to side. Maybe this could be her chance, she thought.

But there was some kind of activity going on, and orcs were now everywhere, talking amongst themselves as they began pulling down tents and rolling up the leather. She had tugged on her skirt and kept a fur wrapped around her shoulders as she searched for signs of her captor. He hadn't told her where to go to relieve herself, and now he was gone.

Cedar couldn't hold it for a moment longer, so she ducked behind the tent, searching for somewhere out of sight. A few tents over there were some trees, up against a low hill. She ran to it, peeled up her skirt—legs shivering—and peed in the snow.

Then, off by the tent, she heard a roar. She could have

mistaken it for a bear if she didn't recognize the tenor, the guttural lilt of Lord Kargorr's voice.

She hurriedly finished, then pushed her skirt down and ran out from behind the trees. There, Cedar saw him, that massive beast of an orc, scouring the snow for her. She hoped he wouldn't think she was running. It was too soon.

"I'm over here," she called, and he spun around, glowering at her. "I had to, you know—pee."

His lips were peeled back in a harsh scowl, his tusks dragged down low on his face. That scar looked more brutal than ever with his skin stretched and pinched. When she approached, he didn't speak—instead, he leaned down and sniffed her.

"Hmm." His posture relaxed somewhat, and she hoped he could smell she was telling the truth. "Well, did you?"

Cedar nodded fiercely. She wanted to be out of the cold now, bare legs and all. With a grunt and a nod, Lord Kargorr turned around and led her back to the tent. She exhaled a relieved breath.

"Next time," he snarled to her once they were inside, "use this." He retrieved a closed basket, and when he opened it, she found the inside was lined with some sort of waterproof leather. He placed it outside the entrance to the tent. "Someone will empty it for us."

It was a surprisingly keen invention for people she considered so brutish, but it would certainly prevent Cedar from having to wander off into the snow.

Only a moment later, someone knocked on the post, and Kargorr opened the tent flap. To Cedar's surprise, a human woman stood outside, her head bowed, a neatly folded pile of clothes in her arms. Kargorr grunted in acknowledgement, took the clothes, and let the flap fall closed again.

Cedar watched as he examined the garments, hoping that

she might finally have pants. There was a coat, a tunic, and thankfully... a pair of pants.

"Eat first," Kargorr told her, gesturing at the food that was still steaming.

Cedar didn't have to be told twice. After last night and this morning, she was absolutely ravenous. Kargorr ate bits and pieces off the tray as she devoured her meal. It was delicious, full of fat and flavor and even plenty of salt. She was much too hungry to give much thought to his dark eyes as he watched her.

Finally, when she was finished, Cedar got up and tried on the clothes. He had already seen her, all of her, many times over now, so she merely ignored his gaze as she changed. The leather was remarkably soft under her hands, pliable and smooth, the stitches incredibly even. Cedar herself couldn't sew that well, and she marveled at it before slipping the tunic on over her head.

"I have much to attend to today," Lord Kargorr said, rising at last. "Stay here. There will be two guards on duty." The orc narrowed his eyes at her. "If you try to leave, they'll be the first to tell me."

Briefly Cedar wondered how long he'd be gone, and what she would have to do in the meantime. She thought she might at least have some movement available to her, that perhaps she could have run of the camp. But no, he was planning to keep her prisoner in his tent, for who knew how long.

She almost objected to being left and confined there, but she remembered her plan. *Obedient. Subdued.* That was how she would get free of this place—by playing a part and playing it well.

So Cedar sat down on the bed to show she didn't plan on going anywhere. With a sharp nod of approval, Lord Kargorr turned around and walked out into the snow, leaving her alone.

Alone. She really was alone now, more than she'd ever been living under Lissa.

Still exhausted after the way Kargorr had taken her this morning and last night, and still wearing her soft new clothes, Cedar climbed back into the furs and fell asleep.

KARGORR

He had much to do preparing the *parog* for a move. The mammoths would need to be lured back in, and then all the fences and posts for the tents loaded up onto sledges for them to pull. He had already sent off nine of his warriors to fan out and locate the herd, then bring them back in. He hoped they would return in two days' time, so as not to delay their departure.

But his thoughts would still wind back to what was waiting for him in his tent. Cedar's small, supple body was like the most delicious meal, a food that he longed to get his mouth around again. He ought to get back to her soon, to continue rutting her and securing the bond between them.

He didn't like the idea of seeing her pale pink backside torn open by the lash of a whip, but if she tried to escape while he was away, he would have no choice but to punish her—he'd have to make an example of her, or his *parog* would not respect him. Kargorr would make it in her best interest not to attempt it.

Or was it that his body had simply awoken, and now it wanted to sate years of built-up carnal need? Certainly he felt that just as much. His cock twitched at the thought of the human's sweet cunt, the sight of her underneath him, the way her legs had squeezed so passionately around his hips.

There was an animal inside her, too, and he wondered if he could fashion a key to unlock it.

He barked orders as he patrolled the perimeter of the camp, overseeing the preparation. The *parog* had not moved in two years, and they had grown lazy and started putting down roots. All of those would need to be torn up, and it would be a difficult process when they had accumulated so much.

Kargorr paused when he reached the livestock pens where Cedar's pigs were kept. When he stopped to survey them, the stablemaster emerged from the hut that had been erected nearby.

"We lost one piglet overnight," he said as he approached, then stopped a respectful distance away. "The others are thriving, but I don't know how we'll take them on our journey."

So he understood that this pig was important. Good. Kargorr watched the piglets fumble over themselves to get to their mother. Cedar had been desperate to save them, a sign that she had a softer side, a side that could be appealed to.

"We will bring them," Kargorr said. He surveyed the piglets, and an idea came to him. "They'll have their own sledge if need be."

The caretaker only just held in his surprise. He nodded in understanding. "Of course, Lord Kargorr. I'll make sure they get to their destination safely."

"Good." Kargorr passed the pens, mulling over his idea as he approached the stables. He hadn't seen Liga in some time, and surely his cat would be testy with him if he didn't come bearing gifts. Speaking of bonds he needed to forge and maintain, if he wanted Liga to be pliable enough for their upcoming trip, he should attend to her.

There was no one around as he entered the icehouse, where meat was slung across the ice, venison and beef and even other pigs they'd found and butchered during their raid. He flicked his knife out of his belt and sliced off a good chunk of some prime red meat, and then another piece, thinking of how long it had been since he'd called on his cat.

Bearing both slabs of meat, he left the icehouse and headed out onto the snow-covered plain beyond the camp. He saw the telltale humps of white just beyond the perimeter and held up the raw beef.

"Come, Liga!" he called out, letting the air pick up the scent of the meat. Then he waited.

Out in the snow, one of the lumps moved. It rose up, higher and higher, until it had reached its full height. If he were any human man, Liga could simply snap him up in one or two big mouthfuls. But a cat was much less likely to attempt such a feat against the *grrosek*. There was a grudging respect for one another, as interdependent species often have. The *parog* kept them fed, and the cats carried their riders from place to place.

Liga was female, but one of the biggest in their clan, just like her mother had been. She curled her shoulders as she stretched, showing off her huge, lithe body. When her mouth opened in a yawn, it revealed her massive fangs, which jutted down from her upper jaw long past her bottom one, even with her mouth askew and her pink tongue bared.

After her long stretch, Liga made her languid way toward where Lord Kargorr stood standing, watching him from the side of her eye. Oh, it had been too long, he realized, when she stopped a good twenty feet from him. Her affection would need to be repurchased.

Kargorr tossed the meat toward her, and it landed in the snow. She leaned down, her long, furry neck extending as she sniffed it. She hooked one of her immense claws in it and dragged it toward her, spreading blood across the white fur of her paw. Her ears lowered as she examined it, sniffing again.

Then she pushed it away. Kargorr cursed to himself. First Cedar had refused him, and now Liga. All the females in his life were obstinate, and he had little patience for it. But he would have to lure her in, the way he knew he had to lure Cedar in, if he was to earn her obedience.

"Liga," he murmured, taking a step closer. She raised her head, but didn't growl. That was a good start. He held up the other piece of meat, and her yellow eyes followed, her lip peeling back at the smell. So she wanted it, but she would teach him a lesson in the process.

"I know that you're angry with me." He took another step. "I don't blame you. I've been absent."

As if she could understand him, Liga pinned her ears back, and her hair stood up. But he wasn't deterred. He had tamed her as a kitten, when she was only the size of a dog. He knew she hadn't forgotten him.

"You think I only come to you when I need your help." And she would be right. He took another step, and her hair rose further, but she didn't move to attack or to retreat. "But aren't we friends, too?"

It was different with the mammoths. All the *grrosek* had to do was wave their hands and lash a whip, and the mammoths would go whichever direction they asked. But cats were more complicated creatures, with minds of their own. Kargorr leaned down to pick up the meat she had pushed away.

"Come now, kitten," he told her, and her tail twitched in warning. "Come back to me." He held out the meat and then dangled the second piece next to it. The quick dart of her eyes between them gave her away.

At last, she took a step forward, and he tossed the meat to her. Liga caught it mid-air, and it vanished into her mouth in one massive bite. She padded toward the other piece, but he held it away from her.

"You'll have to follow if you want it," Lord Kargorr told her, and began making his way back toward camp. Begrudgingly, Liga followed behind him, her eyes riveted on the treat.

When they had returned to the livestock pens, Kargorr turned around and offered her the beef. She stopped in front of him, only inches away, where she could take off his face if she so chose. Instead, she lipped the meat from his hand delicately before devouring it.

While she ate, Kargorr stroked her neck, leaving trails of blood along it. Eventually her chill melted, and she leaned into his touch as he scratched behind her ear.

He wondered what sort of meat he could hold in front of Cedar. When she was full with his orcling, he couldn't have her trying anything foolish. He needed to bind her to him, like Liga was.

It was just a matter of how.

10

CEDAR

S he waited. And waited.

Once she was awake, there was little else to do. She had examined the orc's strange armor for some time, discovering the tough leather and steel that had been layered under it to deflect blows. Strings full of teeth and tusks decorated the breastplate, and Cedar was certain that they were taken from his victims.

She wondered how many humans, how many other orcs, even, he had murdered over his life. How old was he, anyway? With as many scars as he had, it was difficult to tell. Not that it seemed to affect his health or stamina either way.

After some indeterminate number of hours had passed, someone came to the door, the shadow of their feet the only sign of them. Cedar watched anxiously, wondering if Lord Kargorr had come back. But then a ceramic bowl was slid under the tent flap, something that smelled incredible.

She went to the door and opened it to see who had left the meal and found a human man retreating.

Another human in the camp. Cedar wondered if he, too, was a captive. He must be some sort of servant if he was bringing her meals.

Had he ever tried to escape?

The food was a simple array of meats and vegetables on top of gruel, but it was delicious, full of flavor and texture. After stuffing herself, Cedar returned to the bed and watched the fire, hypnotized by the flames dancing in the reflections of his blades. An axe, two swords, and a handful of daggers all hung from the wall.

Cedar had only considered sneaking away—but looking at this dagger, another thought occurred to her. Perhaps her path out was different than she imagined. While Lord Kargorr was on top of her, could she fish the dagger out from under the pillow and kill him with it? And as he bled out, she might be able to flee with no one to stop her.

The dagger was small enough that if she wanted, she could probably snatch it and he wouldn't notice. Once the thought had entered her head, she couldn't shake it away. That would be a way out of here, certainly, if all else failed.

She scooted toward it, looking from side to side in case this was the moment the orc decided to return. Then she slid the dagger off its hook and pulled aside the pile of furs that made up the bed. Slipping it underneath, she placed them all back down again. It would now lie directly under her head, for the moment she needed it.

It was as if he could sense her traitorous thoughts, because that was when Lord Kargorr stepped into the tent, letting the door fall closed behind him. He was dressed in surprisingly little given how cold it was beyond the fire that burned in the pit, but orcs must have some natural resistance to it. How she envied that. She was perpetually cold.

He stood there motionless, watching her for far too long.

Then he crossed the space between them in two immense strides until he was standing over her.

"Now." He untied the strings that held on his light fur pants. "Satisfy me with your mouth so I don't ruin your cunt again."

Cedar swallowed hard, thinking of how he fucked her last night, and maybe it would be wise of her to give herself more time to heal. Still, the recollection of it ignited a small flame in her belly, the way he had demanded her release over and over. He had fought for each one, clawed it from her, and she wondered if he'd do it again tonight.

When the pants were loosened, he shoved them down his thighs, and that green cock came out, the one that had already begun to look familiar since yesterday. Would he always be this hungry?

It wasn't fully hard yet, so he wrapped his hand around the root and shoved it in her face.

"Lick it clean." The command was clear. Cedar shouldn't have obeyed him. She wasn't his to dictate, to command, to demand. But as his cock swelled, shedding its wrinkles, even her mouth felt wetter than usual. His gaze was hard, impenetrable.

No, she needed to do what he asked. To show she was becoming pliable for him.

Shifting so she was sitting on the edge of the fur bed, Cedar reached out and took that slowly thickening length in her hand. It jumped, and she gasped as more blood flowed into it. How could she take this monster inside her?

But Cedar had sucked on a cock before, and she had an idea how it was done. She closed her lips around the fat, green mushroom head and brushed her tongue over the thin slit at the tip. Remarkably, he tasted good—salty and musky, a taste that reminded her of a campfire. She drew even more of him into her mouth, gasping at how full his cock filled her, how she had to struggle to keep her teeth away from it.

She sucked in as she withdrew, clenching her hand around the shaft so she could control how much she took. And he allowed it, for a time, her hand working in synchronization with her mouth as she brought him in again, circling his head with her tongue, and then pulling it back out.

But then his hand found the back of her head.

"Deeper," he growled, and shoved her hard against him. His cock burrowed into her throat, and she choked against it. He pulled her head away again by her hair, and Cedar was horrified to find herself growing even warmer between the legs, the heft of his cock in her mouth making her think of the heft of his cock inside her.

Lord Kargorr used her mouth, plunging in until she couldn't take anymore, and then yanking himself out again. She kept a tight hold on the two lumps at the base of him, and at last, she pulled a low moan out of him as she rubbed and stroked them.

The sound pleased her. He usually made no noise, no matter what she did, but this time she had earned it. So she rubbed harder, and with her other hand, stroked the underside of him. His hand gripped tighter in her hair, and his cock filled up even more of her mouth, scraping against her teeth. She wasn't prepared for the hot spurt of seed that rushed over her tongue, down her open throat, and she gagged as he shoved himself even farther in. The tingling between her legs was almost uncomfortable now, and Cedar hated it. She hated that her pussy clenched and unclenched, remembering how he'd slid inside her, and hated how his wet cock slipping out of her mouth made her want that cock elsewhere.

Kargorr's breath was coming faster than before as his hand dropped from her head. She tasted him on her tongue, and the flavor was, to her mortification, divine. A sly smirk pulled up his tusk, and Kargorr leaned down until his puckered, scarred face was only inches away from hers.

"You want it, don't you, little deer?" he asked, pushing her down to the bed. His hand wandered over her new tunic, and deftly, he unlaced it. Next, his fingers found their way to her pants. The fingertips were so thick and calloused, but quick, too, as they stripped her bare. He still wore his shirt as he climbed over her on the bed, caging her in. Her eyes caught on the collar, and this time, Kargorr laughed.

"Is that so?" he asked, and she detested the smug tone of his voice. He stripped the shirt off, and underneath, his body, bisected by the broad scar, stole her breath.

He was a monster, through and through. A creature worse than any beast, a beast as powerful and cruel as any man. Already his cock was thick again as he pulled her thighs apart.

Cedar hated, more than anything, that she wanted that monster to claim her all over again. She hated how her pussy pulsed, open and closing as it hungered for him to be inside her once more. Above her, Kargorr breathed in deeply, and a knowing look came over him. His hand trailed down her belly, his fingers stopping to tangle in the curly hair beneath it before he dove lower.

"So ready for me already." He circled her sex, as if memorizing each petal, dragging her slickness around with him. "Do you want my cock again, little deer?"

She didn't want to open her mouth and risk the words falling out, so she pressed her lips tightly together. Kargorr chuckled as he brushed the pad of his finger over her tiny nub, and her breath quickened. Cedar couldn't hold in a gasp when he dipped it inside of her, like a faun sipping cool water. He swirled it, making her ache for the rest, for more than just his hand could offer her.

"Tell me," he commanded, leaning down closer to her, so close his tusks brushed her face. He buried his finger deeper, then withdrew, and she whimpered as he taunted her clit again. "Say what it is you want, and you'll have it."

Cedar shut her eyes, her legs trembling as he pushed two fingers inside her now, and she easily gave for him. He rubbed along her channel until she couldn't hold in a moan.

Then he attacked, increasing his pace, extending his thumb to rub her at the same time his fingers thrust inside her. Her hips jolted up, and Kargorr huffed a breath against her face.

"Just one word," he murmured to her, his voice strangely soft. Her eyes opened, and she found his bottomless, black gaze looking back at her. She wondered if she was imagining the small spark of light she saw in them, way down in the depths. "That's all it takes. One word."

She knew her mouth was going to betray her before it did, but she didn't try to stop it. "Yes," she said, barely more than a whisper.

The roar that came out of him covered her skin in goose-bumps. Lord Kargorr yanked his hand free of her and gripped his cock. With one arm supporting his weight so he didn't crush her, he lowered his hips until she felt the broad, dripping head pushing inside her.

"There we are," he grunted as he skated along on her wetness, her pussy already waiting to accommodate him. But he didn't give her all of him. No, he only sunk partway in, giving her a taste before pulling out. Again and again he only filled her half full, until she was gripping his arms and rocking her hips toward him, begging for more.

"With your words." He spoke again, and Cedar opened her eyes. "Ask for it."

Why did he suddenly care what she wanted? But she couldn't take this torture anymore. She needed everything. All of it.

"Please," she said, whimpering, and with it, she cut through one of the ropes holding her back.

"Please what?" he asked, giving her just a little more. Cedar tried with her thighs to bring him closer, but Kargorr easily pulled back, depriving her. "Who do you ask for this?"

She cursed under her breath. "Kargorr," she muttered. "Please, Lord Kargorr. I want more."

And so, with a wicked smile, he relented. He buried himself inside her, as fully as he could before those strange lumps threatened to spread her apart. He uttered an Orcish curse and reeled his hips back, still watching her as he plunged in again.

He maintained a battering rhythm, and Cedar found herself clutching him tight around the neck because otherwise, he might just fuck her through the bed. One massive, clawed hand slipped under her ass and lifted her hips, making his way even easier. When the world started to fall apart around her, and bright light shimmered behind her eyes, Kargorr groaned on top of her.

"This cunt," he said under his breath, as if just for himself, "will be the death of me."

And as she clenched and pulsed and all her muscles went tight as taut strings, he gave her everything. Those lumps pressed even harder at her entrance as his seed gushed into her, and Kargorr brought himself to an abrupt stop. He pulled his cock free, even as it spurted more white fluid over her belly, and he sat up, gasping.

Whatever those swells were, Cedar could tell there was some importance to them—some reason he couldn't, or wouldn't, fully take her. And as Kargorr sat there panting, his eyes strangely wide as he stared down at the bed, she wondered what that reason was. He still seemed to be elsewhere as he fetched the water jug, wetted a cloth, and cleaned her up between the legs. Cedar was afraid to move at how intimate, how unguarded, this gesture was. Then he applied the *kuja*, smoothing the calloused pads of his fingers around the edges of her. When he was finished, he rose from the bed and left the tent, without another word.

Something had happened just now, and she wished she understood what it was.

11

KARGORR

When she had said the words aloud, when she had admitted how much she wanted him, his *sarga* had rioted. As he had fallen into her warm depths, they had begged to sink into her, too. How they would please her. How they would ensure she stayed round and full of his orclings forever.

Kargorr shook his head angrily, and once again naked, he stalked to Orgha's tent. Orgha and his *yapira* were inside eating, but Kargorr's right hand jumped to his feet when his very bare leader thundered inside.

"Clothes," Kargorr said, and Orgha quickly complied, giving the larger orc some of his own. "We're working tonight."

Orgha sighed. "I'm bringing my soup," he groused, and his *yapira*, Rathka, gave a sad wave as Kargorr dragged him from his tent.

Kargorr knew he shouldn't be punishing Orgha for his

own discomfort, but he needed to divert his mind, which meant *work*.

They stayed up late into the night, planning which sledges would carry which tents, how many of the mammoths they would need, whether they would have to build new sledges for the additional weight they had accrued during the *parog*'s stay in this area. The sky was lightening when Orgha finally collapsed and gave Kargorr a firm look.

"Are you avoiding your concubine already?" Orgha asked, much too forwardly, but Kargorr let it slide, believing that his exhaustion was getting the better of him.

Lord Kargorr snorted derisively. "I'm merely concerned about moving. There's a lot to be done."

Orgha yawned and rose to his feet. "You've only had the dog for a short time," he said. "It's too soon to get attached. Never would still be too soon, in my opinion."

And with that, he left the tent, and Kargorr thought perhaps he should have his right hand punished for such brazen impertinence.

Finally, realizing he had no excuses left, Lord Kargorr made his way back to his tent. Inside the fire had burned low, so he kicked the ashes and added new logs to bring it back to life. The early hours of the morning were always the coldest, before the sun came up to warm the world again.

He could just make out Cedar's head of brown hair, mussed around the pillow. When he climbed into the bed, he lay on his back, keeping his arms at his sides. Perhaps Orgha was right, and he was getting too attached to her already. It had been merely a few days since he snatched her from her village. He would have another concubine soon, the moment he was able to find one, and then he'd spread his attentions among them.

Cedar let out a small, soft sound, and without opening her eyes, she curled closer toward him. In her sleep, she was drawn to him, the way any baby animal might seek out its mother's warmth. That's all it was, he thought, as he instinctively wrapped around her, bringing her small legs between his, looping his arm around her back.

Still she didn't wake, and Kargorr's *sarga* throbbed inside the breeches he'd borrowed from Orgha.

He had planned to rut her until she was tied to him, too attached to him to leave, but now he wondered if he had made a mistake in thinking that connection would only go one way.

CEDAR

Everyone was packing, preparing for a big move tomorrow. It looked like the orcs were planning to fully uproot.

Still, Lord Kargorr wouldn't let her leave his tent. Her body felt sluggish from not getting exercise, besides that which he gave her in bed. At least he returned frequently, often a few times during the day, seemingly only to fuck her. The other day he had sat up in the furs and insisted she sit astride him, and Cedar was humiliated to find herself eagerly rising and falling on top of him, one of his huge hands curled under her ass to lift her, the other kneading her breast and teasing the nipple. As she got closer to her edge, he leaned forward to suckle on them.

"These will feed my orcling well," he murmured, sinking her down on his cock again.

She couldn't forget that's what she was—a breeding mare to give him children. That was why he took her over and over, often waiting after he had released inside her to hold up her hips and spoon his spend back into her.

This should have frightened her more than it did, but at the same time, she'd never been fed so well in her life. She had chicken and beef, sheep and goat. There was cream and butter and bread, carrots and potatoes, and some other foods that tasted delicious but that she couldn't place in her memory. The morning they were set to leave, Kargorr gave her thick cuts of cooked bacon, and she feared it was Bread Pudding.

"Don't worry." He tore off a piece for himself and slipped it between his lips, chewing thoughtfully. "Your pig does not have this much fat on her."

Cedar was speechless as he left to go do whatever it was that he went off and did.

Later that day, an orc she didn't recognize came inside. Without looking at her, or even greeting her, he began packing all of Lord Kargorr's things. He started on the left side of the room, gathering up whatever lay out on the small table and the lid of his trunk. It was all stuffed into leather bags, and even the table was disassembled while he stayed silent.

He didn't look like the other orcs. He was shorter by half a head and much more slender, without that hulking mass that Lord Kargorr carried with him. This orc's features were finer, with a longer, more pointed nose and a less brutish jaw. His tusks were smaller, too, curling only to the base of his cheeks.

Cedar puzzled over this as he worked. Then the thought occurred to her: he looked almost *human*.

Her stomach tightened. Is that what he was? Part human and part orc? It was as if someone had poured ice water over her as she watched him laboring, his powerful muscles moving under his shirt. Still he wouldn't turn his gaze on her, even as she stared.

Is this what Kargorr was after? More half-breeds?

She'd been watching so long she nearly forgot what he was doing. Her eyes darted to the wall as he began taking down the weapons hung there.

It hadn't seemed that many of the orcs spoke her tongue, but perhaps if he was half-human, he would.

"Don't touch those," she said, and the half-orc froze. "He won't like that."

At last, he turned to look at her, but then his eyes fell to the floor.

"What's wrong? Why won't you look at me? Or talk to me?" She was tired of this, of Kargorr being her only interaction with the outside world.

"He does not allow it," he finally said, stepping away from the weapons. He had no accent when he spoke in her tongue —it was clearly native to him. So he had been raised by a human.

"Kargorr won't let you talk to me?" Cedar stiffened. "Why not?"

The half-orc shook his head, then pressed his lips closed like he was determined to keep them that way. Instead, he turned his attention to all of Lord Kargorr's sets of armor where they hung, and began packing them, along with the racks they were on. He carried it all out the door and deposited it on a massive wooden sledge.

Cedar didn't have much time. She would have to replace the dagger on the wall, or Kargorr would surely find it when he took them all down.

While the half-orc was gone, she dove for the furs to retrieve the blade from underneath them. It took some time for her to locate it, and when she pulled it out, the flap of the tent opened. She tucked the dagger behind her back, her breath sticking in her throat, hoping the half-orc wouldn't see that she had it. He'd certainly tell Kargorr, and then what would he do to her?

She could barely breathe as the visitor shook out the rugs and rolled them up, hefting them over his shoulder. And then, the worst thing possible happened.

Lord Kargorr returned.

Cedar clamped her hand tight around the dagger's hilt,

keeping the flat of the blade against her back. She couldn't attack him here, not with someone else around. Kargorr snapped some harsh words in his tongue, and the half-orc quickly fled the tent, leaving them alone.

Kargorr walked to his wall of weapons, one of the only objects now remaining in the hut besides the bed. He looked over his axes, and she knew any moment now he'd discover the missing dagger.

When she didn't move or speak, Kargorr arched an eyebrow and looked at her from the corner of his eye. The blade of the dagger was cool against her skin.

"Are you anxious, little deer?" he asked, turning away from the weapons. "About leaving tomorrow?"

She shook her head. "No. Why would I be? This isn't my home."

He chuckled at her easy answer. He seemed less stiff now than he had been the last few days. And when his lip curled, it wasn't cruel, but amused.

"That's good, then." He patted the blade of his axe before turning to her. She let out a sigh of relief that he was no longer looking at the wall where the dagger should be. "We've made all the preparations, and it will be a smooth journey."

He sat down on the bed next to her with a heavy, but relieved, sigh.

"In the morning, we'll take out the furs and stow the bed. But until then..." He leaned toward her, and his smell filled Cedar's nose. It instantly triggered a response, her body stiffening, a languid warmth trailing down from her breasts into her hips. She'd already grown so accustomed to that smell, sleeping in his furs, his sweat dripping onto her as he thrust inside her, that it made her skin feel alive.

She shifted away so she could keep her front toward him and her back hidden. The curl fell off his mouth. He cocked his head.

"What is it, little deer?" His eyes landed on her arm, the way it was clasped behind her back, and a stone fell in her stomach. "What do you have hidden there?"

Cedar was left with no choice. Slowly, she withdrew the dagger and carefully held it by the blade as she extended it toward him. It was probably the first time she had seen Kargorr react to something with surprise—which gave way to anger. His breaths came fast and heavy as his glare darted to the dagger in her hand again.

He snatched it by the hilt and examined it slowly, still not speaking. Cedar retreated from him, her arms and legs ready to move should she need to. She wondered what sort of beating she would receive for this. He had promised her lashings for disobedience, and this was certainly a disobedience of the worst kind.

And then his anger faded, too, giving way to something else. Disappointment.

"I'm glad no one else is here," Lord Kargorr said at last, raising those black eyes up to hers. "Or else I would have to have you whipped. In front of the entire *parog*."

She clenched her shoulders tight to protect herself. She thought about running and wondered how far she could get. She had been hit before by many different people over the years, but never whipped.

"Tomorrow," he said in a low voice, running his hands over the smooth hilt of the dagger, "we will pretend this never happened. Won't we, little deer?"

Her eyes flew up to his. Was he going to let her get away with this? With plotting his death?

"Yes," she said, without thinking. "Let's forget it. Please."

But Kargorr shook his head. "I won't forget. I will never forget." He held up the hilt of the dagger to his lips and licked it. "And I will make sure that you don't, either."

12

KARGORR

S he had planned to stab him, perhaps in his sleep. Surely she hadn't thought that would work.

He had fed her. He had cared for her pleasure. He had slept next to her and held her and started to become, much to his chagrin, linked with her. And now, she had betrayed him.

Perhaps this was all a mistake, taking the human as his own. It had been an impulsive decision, and he should have known better than to obey his baser nature when Cedar had first run from him. He should have snapped her neck alongside the old woman's.

The idea made his skin itch like it was too tight.

Kargorr had been sorely mistaken in thinking he could tame her, that he could make her pliant and loyal. She was like a dog that had grown up feral.

Could the dog still learn manners? Could it ever be depended upon?

Her insubordination grated on the sturdy part of him that

led a *parog*, that guided warriors into battle, that killed those who stood in his way. But another, murkier part of him admired it. She had played the supplicant and started to play it well, all while conspiring behind his back. She wasn't a slight woman to be easily cowed.

In a way, she reminded him of himself and the sort of things he had been willing to do to win his own *parog*.

Lord Kargorr was honest when he said he was glad she'd confessed in private. Now he didn't have to punish her painfully and openly.

Not to say that he wouldn't punish her. Now that he had decided not to whip her or cut her throat, and instead, keep her—he would have to be careful with his next move. It would determine how she saw him from then on, and whether she would hide secrets from him in the future. He could not have secrets between them, or it could mean far worse than this.

But she must still be taught a lesson, one that she wouldn't forget easily.

Kargorr slid his fingers along the smooth hilt of the dagger, over the gentle bumps and swells where the carved silver led down the grip to the cross-guard. Cedar's eyes were huge as she remained in a defensive position a good pace away from him on the bed. He needed to turn this around, to use it as an opportunity to invite her in closer rather than to push her away.

"Come here, little deer," he commanded, and instinctively, she obeyed. At least her fear would make her deferential until he could earn her loyalty in other ways. As if summoned, his cock twitched against his thigh.

He knew he could make her sing, and that was a good place to start.

When Cedar was close enough, her shoulders still curled up tight around her neck, he ran his finger down the long blade. Her eyes followed as he stopped at the tip... where he carefully poked through his thick skin. It drew blood, and Cedar flinched.

"Sharp," he said thoughtfully. "Lie down."

Her chest was heaving as she lay back, trying her hardest to appear calm. Kargorr sat in a relaxed posture next to her, his grip returning to the hilt. He lowered the point to her chest, and her breaths came even faster, that red color blooming across her face. He sliced down, cutting through each of the strings holding her tunic together like they were butter. Cedar gasped as it slid away from her breasts, revealing them to him.

With great care, he drew the tip of the blade up her sternum, making sure to never cut her skin. The sharp, cold point brushed over the surface of her, and she shuddered under it. When it reached the hollow of her throat, Cedar swallowed hard, and her brown eyes sought out his. They were so bright and clear, white with irises the color of earth, and wide with her fear.

He kept the point of the dagger at her throat. "You will never hide something from me again," he murmured to her. "Am I right?"

"Yes," Cedar whispered, her throat trembling with each unsteady breath. Kargorr nodded and slid the dagger down her chest, away from her vital veins, down to her belly. She inhaled as he circled the small divot there, leaving a thin red trail on her skin behind it. There, the blade met the laces of her new pants, and he sliced through those laces just as easily. He yanked them down, revealing her round hips and pale thighs, and peeled them off her small feet. He considered in the future he might have to suck on each of those teeny toes, but not right now.

Hilt loosely hanging from his palm, the dagger resumed its path southward from her stomach, which had already started to grow thicker from good food. He was pleased by this development and caressed it with the blade before venturing over the mound at the crux of her legs. She let out a sound then, just a wispy gust of air, and he saw that her hidden lips were shiny under the torchlight.

Good. She *liked* being at his mercy.

Kargorr flipped the dagger in his hand so now the hilt was pointed toward her. Cedar gasped again as he brought it down to her folds, leafing through the pages of her cunt with it. He rubbed it over her sensitive bud and her hips jerked in response—a lovely little reward.

"Stay still," he told her, "while you have your punishment."

The pommel was rounded, making it perfect for easing down into her swollen slit. A mewl fell from Cedar's lips as he pushed it inside her, turning the handle so she could feel all of the silver against her soft inner layer. He thrust it in deeper, watching her face as she took it, and it reminded him of the face she made when he first entered her. She was so slick now that when he pulled the dagger out again, the handle was coated with her, so he pushed it back in, harder.

Cedar bit her lip, trying to hold in her voice, but Kargorr wanted to hear her. So he withdrew the hilt and then buried it again and again, until she was trying her hardest to keep her body from responding. A small moan managed to escape her, and at the sound of it, his control slipped from his fingers like water.

He pulled the hilt out and tossed the dagger to the floor, nearly tearing his own laces as he pulled off his breeches.

"Get up," he ground out. "On your knees."

Cedar hastily obeyed, her eyes dragging over his cock before she kneeled in front of him, dropping her arms to the furs. Seeing her take the dagger had stirred up his need too great, and of its own accord, his thick cockhead found its way to her dripping cunt. There was no choice but to plunge into her, to stake his claim on her again. He submerged himself over and over, remembering the spot that had made her scream just last night, and he worried it with each stroke. Cedar sagged under his relentless pace, so he lifted one hand and whacked her soft, plump ass.

A surprised cry burst out of her, and Kargorr groaned as her tiny channel clenched around him.

"This is what happens to concubines who try to kill their masters," he told her, thrusting into her again, and then slapping the other cheek. Her cry came out sharper this time, and her cunt squeezed even tighter. He pounded through it, forcing her back open, earning harried cries and moans from her lips. She was wetter than she'd ever been, and he took careful note of it, slowing down his strokes as he wound up to slap her a third time.

When he did, she cried out without reserve, and Kargorr almost couldn't bear the clench of her around his cock. How one small human felt so pristine, so maddeningly sublime, was a mystery to him. For the first time, he had to steel himself against ending too soon, even as his balls tightened.

He would make her come. He would force it out of her, make her wallow in her bliss until he filled her up. So he hit her once more with the flat of his palm, and this time her arms gave out and she fell into the furs. He nursed the spot she liked so much, and soon she was shaking all over, reeling from each of his thrusts, sobbing out her penance.

When she hit her crest, it tore him down and sucked him in. Kargorr roared as he shoved himself as deep as he could, until his *sarga* were nearly ready to sink into her, and he pulled back just in time. His seed arced, coating the red cheeks of her ass, her puckered hole, and her dripping cunt. He cursed that he'd wasted it, but he would have another chance.

Cedar fell to the bed, and she would have looked dead if it weren't for the heavy rising and falling of her back. Her skin looked so tender and red where he'd struck it, he ran his fingers over the surface to see if he'd done any damage. When she flinched, Kargorr withdrew, and sat back on his heels.

It was time to repair what was broken.

He found a square of hide and dunked it into a bucket of cold, fresh water, then brought it back to the bed.

"What are you doing?" she asked as he ran the wet cloth over her angry skin, cleaning off the remnants of his spend. He simply grunted, and so she didn't ask further questions as he got more water, cleaning her between the legs. Her small slit had retracted, and he marveled that such a tiny thing could take him.

When he was finished, he applied *kuja*, though she didn't need it now that her body had adapted to him. But it was care and providing that to her would help immensely in turning this betrayal into a bond of trust.

Cedar let out a relieved sigh. After he'd put the washcloth away, Kargorr slid his arms underneath her. She tensed as he lifted her off the top furs, then pulled them aside and lay her under them, instead. Her eyes were half-lidded but curious as he slid in next to her, then pulled her in tight against him.

"Do not hurt me like this again," he said, leaning down to smell her hair. She nodded rapidly, and he exhaled a relieved breath.

"I won't." Though her voice was quiet, he grunted to let her know he'd heard her.

Usually he lay awake at night, considering what he needed to do the next day, what obstacles his *parog* might face and formulating plans to overcome them. But now, the moment Cedar's breathing slowed, Lord Kargorr blew away like snow in the wind.

13

CEDAR

He had forgiven her.

Well. He would forgive but not forget, he'd made that clear enough. She took those words to heart, because she would never forget, either.

She was grateful he hadn't truly punished her. Fucking her with the hilt of a dagger, followed a few erotic slaps on the ass, was the least formidable sentence she could have dreamt up.

He truly did not want to hurt her, she thought, as he cleaned her with a cold, wet cloth. Then he brought her into his arms and crushed her against him, as if she had been the one who terrified him and not the other way around.

In the morning, Lord Kargorr was gone when she awoke, and Cedar was surprised she hadn't felt him leave. She rose from the bed and saw the weapons had all been packed, all except the dagger, which now lay on the furs next to her.

Was it a gift? She got out and put on her clothes, then started rolling and bundling up the furs to make them easier to transport. The half-orc from yesterday returned and dismantled the tent, and many orcs had to work together to lift the main post out of the ground and then topple it into the wooden cart.

Cedar tucked the dagger into her belt, hoping that's what he'd intended by leaving it with her.

That was when she heard a noise that nearly sent her skeleton crawling from her skin: a wild trumpeting that echoed in the frosty air. She wove through the remaining tents of the camp, toward the sound.

It came from a massive beast, taller than the sky, with two scythe-like tusks protruding from beneath its long trunk. It was covered in shaggy brown hair, and certainly it could squash her with one misplaced foot.

Cedar screamed and shrunk back when she saw it, and the massive creature let out another trumpet, alarmed.

Two huge arms wrapped around her, binding her arms to her sides. "Shh," Kargorr murmured into her ear. "Stay still and calm. You don't want us all trampled."

Cedar shuddered but did as he'd ordered, keeping her trembling feet placed right next to one another. With a hum of approval, Kargorr released her, and the beast now stood without any further trumpeting.

She watched as the rest of the tent was loaded into the sledge, and then the sledge was yoked to the massive beast with ropes and wood. Then it plodded away, led by its keeper, another half-orc woman. The sledge was pulled along behind it, over the snow.

"It's time to go." Kargorr still hadn't left Cedar's side. "I have something else to show you, little deer. But you must not shout or scream."

Cedar wondered what other horror he had to bestow on her after that terrifying beast. Still, she followed along behind him as he led her down what used to be rows of tents, but now was bare ground filled with leftover postholes. Up ahead, she could make out a big lump in the snow.

"Liga!" Lord Kargorr's voice surprised her. "Come!"

The lump rose, and what she saw took her breath away.

The creature that appeared was beautiful, in the way swords were beautiful. Cedar knew just looking at this massive animal, with its round ears, soft snout, and fangs that curled a whole hand's length under its jaw, that it could easily kill her. It would barely have to lift a paw. Muscles rippled through its lithe body as it approached them, and Kargorr advanced on it. Reflexively, Cedar grabbed his arm to hold him back, and a grin pulled at his mouth.

"I will be fine," he said quietly. Then he rubbed the huge cat's forehead, and it made a low, rumbling sound as it rubbed back.

"It's *purring*," Cedar said in wonder as Kargorr began slipping a harness on over the creature's head. Just like a pet cat.

He seemed pleased by her reaction and urged her to come forward. After all this, Cedar didn't think he would let her get hurt, so she followed along. Liga—that must be the animal's name—observed her curiously as she approached.

"Hold out your hand," Kargorr said, extending his own palm up. "Like this."

Cedar did as she was told, hoping against hope it wouldn't choose to take off her arm. Her palm was trembling when she held it out, and the cat leaned down to sniff her.

It seemed, mostly, uninterested.

"Come with me." Kargorr gestured for Cedar to walk around the creature's side, where two ropes attached to the harness lay crisscrossed over its neck. Two hands seized her around the hips, and Cedar tried to keep from making a noise of surprise as he hoisted her onto the furry back. Liga danced underneath her, and she couldn't help a little bleat of alarm.

But soon Kargorr was mounted up behind her, and he looped one arm around her waist before picking up the ropes.

"Liga," he said in a brusque voice. It was followed by an Orcish word that Cedar didn't understand.

"Hold on tight," he told her, right in her ear. And then Liga began to move.

Cedar clung to his arm, her only rock in the storm, as the huge beast leapt into a lope. With every step, Liga's spine moved underneath her, and Cedar thought surely she would get hurled off into the air.

"Move your body, little deer," Kargorr said. His hips circled smoothly behind hers, while she bounced up and down with each of the huge cat's strides. "Let yourself sway with her body. Use your hips like you would if you were on top of me."

Her lower body tensed at the implication, and she grimaced as she met directly with Liga's back. The cat hissed with displeasure at her inexperienced rider. But Cedar knew it would do no good if she didn't listen, so she tried to imagine herself astride Kargorr, her hips moving in synchronicity with his as he plunged inside of her. Her thighs loosened, sinking her down onto the creature's back. Soon her legs were no longer fighting with Liga's powerful movements but traveling alongside them, and she found herself undulating in time with Kargorr's firm body. It felt as if all of them were one single creature loping across the snow.

As they made a loop, they returned to find the camp was empty, and in its place stood more of those great, furry beasts with the noses that fell to the ground. Another trumpet sliced through the air as Liga swiftly passed them, until they had reached the front of what Cedar realized was an immense line.

Kargorr brought Liga to a halt, next to an orc she recognized as Orgha, the one who had captured her that day at Lissa's house. If he hadn't caught her, none of this would have happened. She would've escaped into the woods and found her freedom.

She flared her nostrils at him and looked away.

Orgha rode another great cat, with an orc woman astride one next to him. He and Kargorr spoke to one another in their tongue, and then the command was spread down the length of the caravan. Whips were snapped, and all at once, the enormous creatures moved.

Reflexively, Cedar shrank into Kargorr's chest, away from the huge leg that crashed into the ground right next to them. He huffed in amusement and urged Liga on. She sprang forward, nearly throwing Cedar again, and quickly returned to the front of the caravan.

It felt like only minutes had passed when Cedar's hip and abdominal muscles began to tire of the constant movement of Liga's back. Once they were hours in, and the sun was high in the sky, she moaned.

"Can we have a break?" she asked, since all the movement had also dramatically increased her need to pee.

"No," was all Kargorr said. Then, he slowed Liga down to a walk and fell back until they were among the mammoths. He lifted her by the butt, up into his lap, and it was moments like these she became acutely aware of how much larger he was that he could hold all of her weight on his groin and thighs.

"Now relax," he told her, and Liga resumed. Sitting atop him this way, all she had to do was to be carried along, and she wondered where they were going next.

KARGORR

He would have to ride with Cedar more often. He would teach her how to move her body in time with Liga's. Perhaps she could raise a cat of her own someday, when she could be trusted with one.

The idea interested him immediately. If she became attached to a *pet*, that might be just the thing he needed.

She wore the dagger at her belt, as he'd hoped she would. Perhaps if he put the power in her hand, rather than keeping it from her, he could earn some of her trust. Besides, she needed a way to protect herself when he was gone.

A shiver rippled through him. Leaving her alone was unappealing.

Lord Kargorr led the caravan down snowy slopes, toward what remained of a village they had raided a moon ago on the edge of the tundra. For the next move, they would need to build wheeled carts in order to travel, but he had chosen a wooded area that would provide plenty of raw material for the work.

They rested at night, and he was reminded of when he first brought Cedar back with him, and she fought sleeping in his furs alongside him. But this time, on the first night of their journey back southward, she crawled in rather gratefully, and he thought he even heard a pleased sigh when he brought her in close to his body. Cedar sank into his warmth, and quite soon, she was asleep. The steady sound of her breaths slowed his pulse, and the beating of her tiny heart against his chest lulled Kargorr into an easy darkness.

The next day, they traveled hard. When they made camp, Kargorr helped butcher three carcasses so the *parog* would have plenty of raw meat for their cats and more to cook over the fire. He caught sight of a familiar human woman, picking her way through the various sledges and campfires, searching for something.

"Two more down," he called to her, and she spun at the sound of his voice. He gestured onward. "Keep going."

Her brow furrowed, but she did as she was told, and the assembled orcs turned to watch as she passed. There were a handful of humans among the *parog*, but his claiming of one for himself had drawn her some attention—perhaps some of it unwanted.

So far, though, no one had challenged him over it, and he wanted to keep it that way.

When the butchering was finished, Lord Kargorr found himself eager to find her. He weaved among the sledges until he found the one carrying Cedar's pig and her piglets. His concubine sat with two orclings, all of them playing with the baby pigs together.

At the sight of him... a great smile crossed her face, and she held up one of the piglets, who honked and squealed at being displayed in such a way.

"You kept them!" She brought the dirty pig to her cheek and embraced it. "You kept Bread Pudding."

Was that the pig's name? Kargorr wasn't surprised to find she had named it. He simply nodded as he approached, and she put the pig in her lap. The two orclings each had a pig of their own and were feeding them stale chunks of bread—but when they looked up and saw Lord Kargorr, they quickly put down their playthings and ran off into the *parog*.

"Everyone's so scared of you," Cedar said thoughtfully as he crouched down near her.

He nodded. "As they should be." That was the way of things, the *right* of things. Respect and fear were tied into each other. There was a healthy amount of it that kept the *grrosek* in order.

Cedar made a disapproving noise with her tongue, but didn't speak her objection.

"It's time to go," Kargorr told her, rising to his feet.

She replaced the piglet in the sledge, and it scurried back to its mother. She was clearly sad to leave it.

But someday soon, this tenderhearted woman who had tried to stab him in his sleep would be carrying his orcling, attending to it and caring for it, and she would need no further piglets. But perhaps he could give her something to tide her over in the meantime.

14

CEDAR

Cedar's ass was sore to the bone by the time the caravan reached its destination nearly five days later.

They had descended slowly, traveling southeast, until a shallow valley came into view. They were farther west than her own village, at least she thought so. The land was low enough in elevation that snow had not even fallen yet, and the sledges all came to a halt at the top of the final descent, where it became mud, rocks, and dying grasses.

Kargorr cursed something in Orcish. He swung off of Liga, leaving Cedar there alone. The cat shot a glare at her over her shoulder, and Cedar wondered if she was about to be thrown off. But the cat must have understood this little human was important to her master, because she merely licked her paw in a way that Cedar could only describe as affronted.

Lord Kargorr and Orgha chatted nearby, both gesturing with animation. Then Kargorr called out a command, and as before, it spread across the *parog* like wildfire. He stalked back toward Cedar, and all down the line of travelers, orcs began dismounting and pulling objects from the sledges.

"The snow has not come yet," he said with a dissatisfied growl. "Everything will have to be carried in by hand." He lifted her by the waist, off of Liga's back, then fished some meat out of a pouch at his hip and fed it to the huge cat. Blood dripped down the animal's lips as she chewed.

Cedar's arms were stuffed full of furs and leather sacks, and along with the rest of the *parog*, she carried it down the steep hill into the valley. From what Cedar could tell, there had been a human village here not too long ago. The remains of houses dotted the valley, all of them burned to ash. She did not have the bravery to look inside and see what might have become of their occupants.

Had Lord Kargorr burned this village down, planning all along to take it for himself? The orcs were much closer to human lands here, probably a few days' ride from the nearest town.

Cedar wondered what he had planned by occupying this place.

Campsites were staked out, and soon the orcs began rolling their huge wooden posts down the hillside. It was arduous work, climbing back up to the top of the ridge to grab more belongings and then carrying them down again, over and over. By the time the sun was getting low in the sky, Cedar could barely lift a pillow, and her arms felt like soggy bread.

Luckily, Lord Kargorr's tent was the first to be erected, and with ten orcs working on it together, the postholes were dug, the frame went up, and the leather walls were strapped down to the posts.

Suddenly, Cedar had a home again. It was strange to feel that anywhere in particular was *home*. Lissa's house had never been home for her. The hovel where she grew up with three siblings and her parents had been barely enough to contain all of them. But now, she found herself immensely grateful to be inside these familiar walls again, and despite her exhaustion, she helped to dig out the fire pit in the middle of the much bigger, larger tent. Then the bed was put together in the back while Cedar and Kargorr ate dinner. She devoured her bowl of soft gruel, dried berries, and meat. Then Kargorr tore some flesh off his drumstick and gave it to her, and while he wasn't smiling, amusement crinkled his nose as she devoured that, too, and finished by licking off her fingers.

Cedar had never eaten this well in her entire life, and today, after so much laboring, it tasted better than ever.

By the time the initial work of unpacking the tent was finished, she couldn't stand up any longer. She unfurled the furs and spread them out, then fell forward onto them. She didn't know if she could even bring herself to roll over to her side of the bed.

Then a large body lay down on top of her. Kargorr supported himself with one arm, letting the rest of his weight push her into the furs.

"That wasn't so bad, was it, little deer?" he asked in a low rumble, right in her ear. His tusk caught in the hair at the nape of her neck. "You rode well."

The compliment made her chest feel airy and light. She couldn't help it when she let out an exhausted little giggle, feeling she had done rather well despite the fact her thighs and butt would never be the same again. When he lowered a hand there to squeeze, she jolted and let out a whimper.

Kargorr sat up, surprised. He slid a finger into the band of her pants and pulled them down, revealing her like a child about to be spanked. Seeing her reddened flesh, he let out a displeased huff and got up to retrieve a leather bag on the floor. From it he produced a familiar jar, and Cedar watched over her shoulder as he returned with it, scooping out the salve with two fingers. He spread it all over her, surprisingly softly.

It was quick to work its magic, cooling down her skin and soothing the sore muscles underneath. He pulled her pants the rest of the way off, and soon she found him standing at the edge of the bed, his quickly growing cock positioned behind her.

Cedar rolled onto her back, and her hips lifted in anticipation. With a pleased chuckle, Kargorr slid inside her. But he moved in a new way—slower, gentler, as if he was taking care not to inflame her wounds. She tried not to think about the burned houses, instead remembering the piece of meat he gave her, and the way he'd put her on his lap as they rode.

After he had eked one scream out of her after another, he spent himself inside her. Then Lord Kargorr rolled her up in his arm and sighed deeply.

"There will be much to do tomorrow," he said, and Cedar wasn't sure if he was talking to her or himself. "And then it all will truly begin."

A few days ago, she wouldn't have said anything in answer. But Cedar had been thinking about that little speck of light in his abyssal eyes, and what it meant, so she ventured a question.

"What will begin?"

His big head angled down toward her while his hand absently stroked her arm.

"The reclaiming." He tightened his grip around her. "I will take back everything the humans stole from us. I will seize it for my *parog*, and for all of the *grrosek* who awoke to find their land taken."

The words didn't quite make sense. *Stole?* But the orcs were the ones stealing human land—burning down human villages for it. Still, she kept the thought to herself.

When she slept, Cedar slept harder and longer than she ever had before, as if she were dead.

KARGORR

It would take time and work to fully settle the *parog* in this strange place where there was no snow under their feet. But Lord Kargorr felt a new, strange kind of optimism for the future. The snow was their old home. This would become their new one. They would soon move even farther south to take more of what was owed to them, which would mean even more foreign terrain.

While the *parog* labored over rebuilding the camp, Kargorr held a meeting with Orgha in the new command tent.

"The warriors are worried about exposing ourselves in such a foreign land," his right hand said, snatching a piece of cooked meat off his plate and tossing it into his mouth. "They're afraid it puts us at risk to be so close to humankind, *kazek*."

Kargorr didn't like to hear that his *parog* was doubting him.

"They'll soon see what an opportunity this is." Kargorr unrolled the map, which one of his scouts had been slowly filling in as they explored and ruined the nearest villages. "Raids will be quicker."

Orgha nodded, clearly unwilling to contradict Kargorr—to his face, anyway. Who knew what Orgha talked about in the privacy of his tent with his *yapira*?

"Post more guards," Kargorr said after a moment, "and send out patrols to ensure our location remains undiscovered. That should set their minds at ease."

By the time the humans were aware of the *grrosek* presence here, it would be too late.

Rising to his feet, Orgha groaned. He was getting older, and the journey here had probably not been easy on him.

"As you say, *kazek*." He tapped his chest with his fist. "I'll distribute the orders." He paused at the tent door. "When will we attack next?"

"As soon as the camp is in working order again." Kargorr studied the map. "Then we will venture southwest."

"What is your end goal?" Orgha asked. "How far south will we travel?"

Kargorr narrowed his eyes. "As far as we have to in order to wipe them out. When we've secured enough territory here, we will invite the other *parog* to join us."

Orgha's eyebrows flew up. "You don't mean that."

Was Lord Kargorr's second-in-command doubting him? Again?

"I do," Kargorr said firmly. "The humans have built large cities down south, much too big for us to take alone. Once we've shown that I have might on our side, when I have enough human heads to parade around on pikes, morale will be higher than ever. Other *kazek* will see the benefit."

Yes, it was highly uncommon for one *parog* to meet another, not to mention work alongside each other for a mutual goal. They fought over territory when they did get too close. But all *grrosek* held a hatred of humans in common, and Lord Kargorr believed it would be enough to unite them.

Orgha's eyes were still wide, but he gave a nod of understanding.

His doubt wouldn't last for long. Kargorr had a good feeling about this change. Or perhaps it was just the soft, wet, tight cunt of his new concubine talking.

Instantly his cock woke up, and he shuddered under the landslide of need that coursed through him. All it took was thinking about her for his body to want to seek hers out.

But Kargorr had important things to do. He'd worked hard to seed her, and surely it would take soon. The idea sated him, at least for now.

While he patrolled the *parog*, though, taking stock of how

fast things were progressing and where more *grrosek* might be needed to complete the construction, his gaze lingered on his own tent. He would need to assign her guards while he was gone, of course. And a caretaker, too.

He thought on this. Usually older males beyond their fighting years were tasked with such things, but Lord Kargorr bristled at the idea of one coming too close to her, bringing her food and water and emptying the wet basket. He would have to find a female he could trust. A female who was already paired up would be ideal, and who could, perhaps, lend Cedar some guidance on how to better become a part of the *parog*. He considered finding a human for her, but didn't want them scheming or working together.

The number of *grrosek* who fit this new requirement were much fewer and farther between. Then, if he added that they needed to speak the human tongue...

He sighed and rubbed the bridge of his nose. Orgha would probably not like what Kargorr had in mind, but it would be necessary.

Ignoring his tent for now, Lord Kargorr continued his circuit, interfering where needed. He would broach the subject with his right hand later, perhaps when the alcohol was flowing. Beer and wine always tended to put an orc in a good mood.

15

She would have to talk to him about this business of keeping her trapped inside. After days of riding on Liga, Cedar had a deep need to stretch her legs. And even though this tent was much larger than Kargorr's last one, her body craved walking, at least for a little while. And her mind needed to talk to someone else, just for a moment.

Cedar wanted to remember what it was like to be human.

She poked her head out of the tent in the afternoon, when Kargorr had been gone for most of the day already. Usually he visited her around lunchtime to bring her food—and do other things—but today it had been an orc woman she'd never met before, with a mostly shaved head and a pile of braids at the base of her skull. The orc had deposited the food and then left before Cedar could even ask her a question.

There was no one immediately standing outside the tent, not like there had been at the previous camp. Something had changed—perhaps Kargorr trusted her more now.

For a moment, the allure of escape was strong. The camp

was chaotic as the orcs set up their new village, and there was a good chance no one would notice her slip away. The perimeter of the camp, marked with heavy wooden posts, wasn't complete yet. She could cross easily without being seen.

Cedar's heart sped up as she stepped out onto the muddy path. Straw was being laid down on it, and someone was spreading a clay-like mixture over the top. A few young orcs ran through it, and the woman paving it yelled at them. Something about it was so normal that Cedar paused, hesitating right at the entrance to the tent.

If Lord Kargorr caught her, what would be her punishment? It would be public. Certainly it would involve the whip. Were her chances of escaping successfully high enough to take the risk?

She stood there for a long time, weighing it in her mind. She ate better among the orcs than she ever had with Lissa, who only spared Cedar what she needed for the barest survival. Here Cedar slept in a bed of lush furs, and she was warm every night. Bread Pudding was being fed and cared for, much to her surprise.

Why had he done it, when he could have spared himself the trouble of moving the pig and had the sow butchered like the other livestock? Cedar had puzzled over this for their whole journey, but now she wondered if the answer was simple.

Perhaps he wanted her to *want* to stay. And that meant he thought she could run.

Cedar's head was whirling when she heard Kargorr's snarl. He appeared around the corner of the tent and quickly stormed over to her, and she considered running back into the tent at the look on his face.

But she had some demands to make.

Cedar kept her chin high as the massive orc dwarfed her in

his shadow. He grabbed her by the elbow and leaned down close.

"Where do you think you're going?" he asked in a dangerous tone.

All she'd done was step outside, and here he was, behaving like a cretin.

"I'm getting fresh air!" She yanked her elbow away, and his eyebrows lowered even further. "You can't keep me cooped up in there all the time. I'm going out of my mind."

His frown was deep and dark with disapproval, but she knew now that somewhere in there, he wanted her to be happy enough that she wouldn't try to escape. She could leverage that.

"You can't leave without my permission." He glowered at her, trying to cow her, but Cedar stood firm.

"Then give me permission!" She was ready to stomp her foot to get what she wanted. "I have to stretch out my legs. I need to breathe fresh air. It's always smoky in there, and—"

This time he was firm when he grabbed her arm and pulled her into the tent. Once inside, though, he released her, and she crossed her arms over her chest to fully express her displeasure.

"You want freedom?" Lord Kargorr asked, turning his back to her while he began to undress.

"Just enough to go outside and go on the occasional walk. I need to see the sky sometimes."

He grunted to let her know he heard her, but that he was still thinking over the answer. When he had stripped down to only the sling that kept his cock in place, he swiveled back toward her.

"Fine." He advanced a step closer, and all it took was seeing his huge, naked body, with those bulbous pectorals and the powerful belly, to ignite a spark inside her. He was already growing thick against his sling. "But you will not go alone. I will assign you a caretaker who will watch over you when you are not in my tent."

For a moment, Cedar thought he might say *our* tent, but that was expecting too much. Still, Cedar accepted the small victory for what it was.

"Thank you," she said, and found the laces of her tunic on her own. The faintest smirk appeared on Kargorr's face as she took it off, letting her breasts fall free.

"If this is how gifts are appreciated," he said in a low voice, crowding her against the bed, "I may have to give you more of them."

KARGORR

He had been remiss in not posting a guard while he worked today, he knew that now. But perhaps she was telling the truth in simply needing to be outside, and he had been treating her like a piece of livestock that would be happy living in a pen.

That night, after Kargorr had rutted Cedar until she screamed—not once, but twice, because his cock was angry it had been left to fend for itself all day—he left to find Orgha.

His right hand was bent over the great stew pot, giving the cook his personal feedback. Lord Kargorr shoved him out of the way to get two bowls of soup for himself and Cedar.

"As soon as you get on the other side of the table and cook the stew yourself, you can talk," Kargorr said. "Until then, keep your mouth shut."

Orgha laughed a belly laugh as they both walked away from the serving tent. He glanced down at the two bowls.

"When are you going to let your concubine show her face?"

At least Kargorr didn't have to open the door himself. All he had to do was ask for the key to what he needed.

"When I feel it's safe for her," he said.

Orgha thoughtfully bobbed his head. "Do you truly think someone would try to take her from you? From the *kazek*?"

It was an improbability, but Kargorr still hated the idea of her walking around alone, of anyone else so much as looking at her the way he did.

"She needs a caretaker," Kargorr said, in the easy, gentle way one might try to talk to an animal prone to running. Orgha hummed to let him know he was listening, so Kargorr went on. "Someone who is mated. Older, who can give her some wisdom. Someone who speaks the human tongue and can take her on little walks."

Finally Orgha came to a halt, and his eyes glinted like a pair of sharp arrows. "You mean my *yapira*, don't you?"

"Yes."

Orgha rolled his shoulders. "You know I can't refuse you," he said, not looking at Kargorr, likely because he was too irritated and didn't want to be accused of obstinance. "But she will not be pleased." And a displeased *yapira* was a displeased male, generally speaking.

Kargorr didn't have to go home to her, though, so he simply strode on, and Orgha grumbled behind him.

"Fine. She will be there in the morning to take on these..." Orgha rolled his eyes. "...caretaking duties."

"Good."

Cedar was asleep when Kargorr returned, and he liked that he could fuck her into a stupor. She'd taken to him well, he thought. When he was sunk up to the hilt in her, his *sarga* begging to take her, he was sure she had conformed to his shape. It was like she had been crafted in the image of his perfect bedwarmer.

He set down the stew and ate it while watching her sleep.

But she was still only human, he reminded himself. A toy for his pleasure, a nest for his orclings. He gazed around the tent, which now had two central posts instead of one to make room for his future concubines. There was still more seed to sow.

Looking down at the other bowl, he thought he should rouse her to eat, but decided he liked the plane of her face while relaxed this way and let her sleep.

CEDAR

When she awoke the next morning, Lord Kargorr was gone again, and she guessed that he would be busy while the camp was being re-assembled.

Still, it gave her a little chill. She was about to curl up again in the blankets, knowing she had nowhere to be but wishing she did, when someone tapped on the post that held up the entryway. Cedar sprung out of bed, carrying the top fur around herself.

"Hello?" she called out. No one ever came and knocked.

A head of dark hair, streaked with gray, ducked in. The visitor was an orc woman, not nearly as tall as Kargorr but still impressive, with slender but deadly tusks. An elegance followed her movement as she neatly closed the door behind her.

The orc didn't look at Cedar, though, as she set down her things.

"I'm Rathka," she said by way of greeting, her voice thick and her accent heavy. After leaving her bag on the floor, she set a tray of steaming food on the table and then backed away.

Still she didn't raise her eyes to Cedar's. Why would no one but Kargorr look her in the eye?

"Rathka," Cedar repeated. Then the orc chanced a glance

at her, but when she saw Cedar was still watching, she looked away. "I'm Cedar."

"I know." The words hung in the air when none followed them.

Finally, Cedar grew tired of waiting and sat down at the table, assuming the food was for her. The orc woman sat there in silence while Cedar ate, and it was disconcerting to say the least to have a silent companion who wasn't eating alongside you.

"Rathka," Cedar finally ventured. "Why are you here?"

"I'm your new caretaker. I'll be with you at all times during the day from now on."

Cedar stared at her.

"All day?" She'd expected a guard, not a nursemaid. "Why?"

At this, Rathka's head snapped up, and she looked Cedar in the eyes. She was bristling. "Because for some reason, Lord Kargorr has decided you're important." Her tusks curled with her lower lip. "You said you wanted to go on 'little walks.' So here I am, to take you on little walks."

Oh. Cedar's jaw closed so hard her teeth clicked together. So this was how her request had been interpreted: someone to hound her at all times. Now she could go out as long as her warden came along.

Rathka's eyes fell once more, but it was as clear as day that the orc woman wanted to be there even less than Cedar wanted her there.

Cedar wondered if she should apologize, but then a part of her thought that perhaps she shouldn't. Lord Kargorr had talked about orcs respecting a healthy amount of fear.

"Well, then," Cedar said, standing up. She had polished off her breakfast and was ready to walk it off. "Let us go on a 'little walk.'"

16

KARGORR

Assembly of the *parog* was almost complete, much quicker than he had anticipated. Good. Then they could move on to the next part of the plan and refill their diminishing food and supply stores.

Lord Kargorr felt relaxed as he returned to his tent, ready to eat and then fuck, and then likely fuck some more before he slept. He'd never slept better than when he did with Cedar curled under his arm, her small face against his chest.

But when he slipped inside, she wasn't there. His heart stilled, and his body turned cold. He wondered if she'd run off, or if someone had spirited her away.

He stormed out of the tent, searching this way and that for her. His fear had morphed quickly into anger. Kargorr was ready to shout for his warriors when a familiar giggle came from nearby. He'd only heard the sound once before, when Cedar's face was in the furs, but he recognized it.

She came around the corner, a small orcling running behind her. A few paces away, poor old Rathka was following, her lip curled in disgust. His woman paused to lean down and tickle the orcling under the armpits, and he ran away yelling with delight.

She froze when she saw Lord Kargorr there waiting, and must have taken in the state of him, because she approached warily.

He'd forgotten about assigning Rathka to chaperone her. He was so accustomed to her being there, waiting for him—

No matter.

"It's time for supper," he said, taking Cedar by the arm. He shooed away Rathka. "Thank you for your service today."

With a grunt, she waved him off and departed.

"I don't think she cares for me," Cedar said as they ducked through the door.

Kargorr had to chuckle at that. "No, I don't think so, either."

They ate in silence, while Kargorr sorted through the reaction he'd had. It was natural for an orc to grow possessive after coupling, and that they had done many times. But he'd been ready to tear off someone's head at the thought she had left him.

That was not becoming of a *kazek*.

After they ate, Lord Kargorr made sure to take Cedar from behind, so he didn't have to look at her soft face. Still, filling her up with his seed didn't fully slake his need, so he rolled her over, hiked her legs up over his shoulders, and slowly fucked her again while looking right into her brown eyes.

She didn't look away, and he felt himself getting lost in them. It would be so easy to sink his *sarga* inside her right now. He swelled up and unleashed everything he had, his balls squeezing up tight, her sweetly fluttering cunt milking him of all he had to give.

Still, her eyes were riveted to him. As he lay there panting, still sunk deep in her warmth, something even hotter than his bare desire for her began to burn for the small human tangled in his arms.

Her lips were a dark brown-pink, and they looked so lovely spreading apart with each of her labored breaths. Life shone in her bright eyes, and when she still didn't look away after another heady moment, he leaned down closer to her.

Kargorr's relief at finding her safe today, the tiny seed of pleasure he felt at watching her play with that orcling, all built in his throat until he had no choice. He closed the distance between them and crushed his lips to hers.

CEDAR

Why was he kissing her?

Cedar had simply assumed orcs didn't kiss, that it wasn't something they did. It's not as if she'd had much chance to interact with any others outside Kargorr's tent. So when he pressed his lips to hers, she squeaked into his mouth, thinking perhaps he'd fallen on her. But then he circled her head with his hands, bringing her even closer until his tusks pressed into her cheeks, and she was spun up in his whirlwind.

His lips were solid, and they tore into hers with abandon, pulling her apart, his tongue tracing the seam of her mouth. When she allowed him in, his cock twitched inside her, and she answered by flexing her walls around him. Kargorr groaned, then invaded her mouth with his whole battalion, gently reeling his hips back only to glide in once more, his way made easy and slick by his own seed. Cedar didn't realize she had given herself over completely until he was sucking on her lips, nipping them with his teeth, and his cock was sliding in and out in a perfect, humming rhythm. Her back arched, her legs hooking over his hips to bring him in deeper, while her arms wound around his neck.

Their bodies moved as one, and Cedar fully forgot who she was. He was a beast, a monster, a creature of death who had snapped Lissa's neck in front of her, and that meant nothing to her now as he caressed her ass, her hips, her breasts. Still his mouth never relented, and soon she was fully delirious, drowning in him. She couldn't tell one peak from another as she swooped up and down, one tossing her under while another carried her up.

Then, they were both spent, and she shivered as Kargorr finally withdrew.

"I will be leaving in the morning," he said as she curled up under the furs, his arm slung over her waist. His finger absently skimmed over the softened curve of her hip bone.

"Leaving?" she asked, falling still. He had just stolen her and brought her here, and now he was leaving?

"For a few days. There is a village—we will return with fresh supplies."

Cedar knew what he meant, of course. They would raid another town and kill everyone in it, just as they had hers.

She thought she should probably care more. What if they found the village where she grew up, where her family lived? None of them would survive.

Those people sold her away, she was keen to remember. They had turned over their daughter to a wicked old woman in exchange for a single cow. Cedar's own mother, who birthed her and bathed her, who told her old stories and taught her to cook and clean, had traded her away like a few pieces of silver.

"And so I get Rathka instead of you," Cedar said, too tired to cultivate what came out of her mouth.

To her surprise, Kargorr chuckled. "Yes. For a few days. But she doesn't have a cock, so I will not worry."

Cedar snorted at this. As she buried her face in the crook of his shoulder, she wondered if perhaps something was changing—if the wall built tall around him had a top that she could see over. What would be on the other side?

This time when she dreamed of the orc covered in blood, the air filled with the sound of wails, she was no longer standing in front of him.

She was in his arms, her body limp, swaying with the sound of his agonized roar.

KARGORR

He should not have kissed his concubine.

It may not have been the same as using his *sarga* on her, but it was still an act of intimacy he ought to be avoiding. But her lips had tasted sweet and succulent, and they had given so easily under his, pliant and yet eager, letting him invade and plunder her small mouth. The way she had come undone, all of her passion pouring out, her body clinging tight to his as he claimed her over and over—it had almost undone him, too.

Perhaps it had, and he wasn't willing to recognize it.

Lord Kargorr awoke to the low, reddened light of dawn trickling in the top of the tent through the smoke hole. Cedar was burrowed deep into his side, her tiny hands curled up between them into fists. Her eyelids fluttered as she dreamed, and she let out a tiny sound of discomfort that unsettled him.

What was she dreaming about that upset her? He wanted to chase it away, because it had no place in the bubble of quietude that surrounded them in his furs.

Kargorr smoothed down some of her tangled hair, and Cedar jolted awake, her body stiffening in his arms. She let out a few startled breaths, then settled back down so her head rested on his bicep.

It was time for him to get ready, and rolling in the furs with her again was not an efficient way to do that. With a gruff grunt, he disentangled himself and slid out of bed, leaving her curled up there alone.

Cedar didn't speak as he put on his sling, then his pants and undershirt, before pulling down his thick hide armor with the steel shoulders. The dagger he had given her lay out on the table, so he snatched it up and returned to the bed with it.

"Keep this close to you," he said in a low voice, leaving it on the top blanket. Then he slid his axe into the belt on his left, his sword on his right, and left the tent before he could change his mind about abandoning that warm, soft place at her side.

Orgha was waiting outside, along with his *yapira*. She had breakfast in her hands, and when Kargorr emerged, she wore an expression that was clearly displeased. Rathka slid into the tent without another word, leaving them behind.

"Did you sleep on the floor last night?" Kargorr asked Orgha with a chuckle. He probably shouldn't take amusement in his right hand's personal suffering, but Kargorr was in a good mood. There was bloodletting in his future.

The other orc gave him an odd look. "Yes. But Rathka will forgive me when I return with a fat turkey for her." It was customary for a warrior to bring a prize back to their mate, something to show off a strong victory, but Orgha's *yapira* had never been one for trinkets.

At the edge of the camp, Lord Kargorr summoned his cat with a whistle. Liga looked dirty and angry as she approached. He hadn't put too much thought into how she might receive life in the lowlands rather than among the powdery snow of their home. He hoped they wouldn't have to adopt horses, like the humans did, for travel.

The other warriors had gathered, too, luring in their reticent cats with slabs of raw meat. One of the younger *grrosek* was negotiating with a cat that didn't belong to him, and the cat was snarling and quite willing to put up a fight rather than go with an unfamiliar rider.

Kargorr strode in, snarling right back at the big animal, and it instinctively shrank away from him. Then he turned to his warrior.

"What is the problem? Where is your own cat?"

"She gave birth." The orc sighed and gestured to the livestock pens, where the mother cats would build their dens. "I have no way to ride."

This piqued Lord Kargorr's curiosity. "A new litter?"

"A few weeks old. Born right before the move."

Perhaps this was just what he'd been searching for: another reason for Cedar to want to stay. Something to keep her from running, something to keep her from growing lonely. Something that would bring to life her motherly instincts, perhaps, and prepare her for his orcling.

Oh, yes. This would be perfect. And then she would ride her cat alongside his when the *parog* moved again.

He snapped at the stablemaster to retrieve one of the kittens and bring it to his tent while he was away.

"This kitten is young, *kazek*," the stablemaster said with a careful amount of uncertainty. "It will have to be fed."

Even better, Kargorr thought. It would be helpless and small and need Cedar's constant attention.

"Bring my concubine everything she'll need to care for it." He smirked at the warrior, who was now without a cat to ride. "You have served your *parog* well. Stay behind and keep guard. We are still unsure of our surroundings, and an extra set of eyes will be useful."

The stablemaster emerged with a small, snow-white kitten in his arms, the big fangs only just starting to grow. The creature whimpered as Lord Kargorr bid him to take it to his concubine.

He had made a very smart decision today, and it was barely dawn.

"For the taste of blood," he called out, holding his axe high into the air, "and for the spoils!"

When he howled, all his warriors howled with him.

17

CEDAR

L ike yesterday, Rathka did not look at Cedar when she entered the tent with breakfast. It was infuriating, Cedar had to admit, that the orc woman would not engage in even a simple conversation with her when they shared the same language. Though Rathka behaved with deference on the surface, it was obvious to anyone that a mountain's worth of distaste hid underneath. Her very being dripped with insolence, as if serving Cedar was below her—and it probably was.

While Cedar ate, she debated what to do with her time while Lord Kargorr was absent. She should learn her way around the camp, at the minimum. Perhaps then she would learn where its weaknesses were and could plan the best way to make a silent escape. She sensed that her captor would leave frequently for raids now that the camp had relocated into human lands, which meant at least some time where she was free from observation.

Rathka would have to pee eventually.

Unfortunately, Cedar found a guard posted outside the tent. Female, but a warrior this time, with fierce piercings and many small scars. Cedar ducked back inside the tent, sighing. How long would it take for Kargorr to trust her?

Cedar dressed slowly because there was nothing to hurry for. She didn't know how long he would be gone, and her only entertainment, the two little children who fawned over Bread Pudding, were easy enough to find tormenting their mother.

It was rather pathetic that her only friends were two barely weaned orcs, but Cedar took what she could.

A knock came at the entryway post, and Rathka jumped to her feet to see who it was. Cedar heard a quiet whimpering that made her turn around with her tunic halfway laced.

Rathka muttered something in Orcish, then turned to Cedar. "Put your clothes on," she said, finally raising her eyes to Cedar's, as if she had momentarily forgotten the directive. She dropped them quickly.

"Oh, sure," Cedar said, finishing and then turning around so she could receive her guest.

An awkward, small orc appeared in the door, and he brought in with him the reek of animal. In his arms was a small white furry creature that Cedar recognized right away as one of the cats the orcs had ridden on their journey.

Rathka glared at the orc carrying the fluffy kitten.

"What is it you want?" she said in the human tongue, probably for Cedar's benefit. The visitor furrowed his brow in confusion, and so she repeated the question in Orcish, and Cedar committed it to memory. The more she understood what was going on around her, the better she would fare in this strange place.

The orc responded vehemently with a string of words Cedar couldn't understand, then thrust the small animal in her direction. She looked at him quizzically, and then down at the mewling creature.

"It is for you," Rathka explained. "A gift from Lord Kargorr."

"A gift?" Cedar echoed. "For me?"

She gazed at the cat with new eyes. It was a significant present. She would have to take care of it, and who knew what sort of attention it required? But it was so precious with its small, pink nose and big, yellow eyes, letting out sad little noises, that she instinctively reached out and took it into her arms. It had claws, but they were tiny and dull as it scraped her flesh, trying to get away.

"It is not fully tame yet," Rathka said. "You will have to quiet its wildness."

The dirty orc in the doorway reached into his pockets and withdrew a leather pouch that had a nipple attached to it and gestured for Rathka to take it. She did not look happy as she brought the pouch over to where Cedar had seated herself on the bed, the kitten in her lap. It was softer than any fur, as if it was covered in down like a baby chick. The orc spoke again, gesturing something with his hands.

"You will feed it," Rathka said as Cedar took the pouch. It was warm, clearly full of fresh milk, and when Cedar lowered the nipple to the kitten's mouth, it seized it. The orc who'd brought the kitten dispensed more instructions, which Rathka translated as the kitten suckled.

Cedar would need to take it outside to evacuate its bowels regularly, often multiple times during the night. It required exercise, and the orc promised he would return with a leash later. Then he tapped his chest with his fist and departed, leaving Cedar with the small, helpless animal in her arms.

She wondered what this gift meant. Surely it would grow up into a big, fanged cat like Liga. Was she intended to ride it alone, at Lord Kargorr's side?

Or would she be riding behind him?

It was as if Rathka could see the thoughts plain on Cedar's face, because she snickered. It was harsh and disparaging.

"Do not assume it means anything that it does not," Rathka said.

"And what's that?" asked Cedar. She didn't like this woman's attitude.

"You think it means he cares about you." Rathka smirked. "It does not. He is binding you to him. Mollifying you with a cute pet."

But Cedar understood already that it was more than a pet. Liga was Kargorr's companion—she had witnessed that first-hand. He'd always fed Liga himself on their journey and petted her head before bedding down for the night, scratching behind and under her right ear.

Still, it could be a calculated move. She'd always thought orcs to be rather brutish and stupid, but Lord Kargorr was anything but. He thought ahead of her, and around her, and Cedar wouldn't put it past him to try to buy her complacency.

But perhaps she wanted to be bought.

She petted the kitten as she fed him, mulling over how best to handle Rathka. The smartest thing Cedar could do would be to befriend her, to try to make the orc woman her ally rather than her enemy. And yet she couldn't lose sight of the fact that in the hierarchy of the camp, Rathka was lower than she was, and that appeared to be of great importance to orcs.

"I'm not misunderstanding," Cedar finally said as the kitten turned its head away from the nipple and coughed. "I know where I am." She was a bedwarmer, he'd made that clear enough. Cedar held up the kitten under its front legs. "What sort of name should I give it?" she asked, to change the subject.

The question took Rathka by surprise, but then she narrowed her eyes and looked away again. "Whatever you want. It's your choice."

"Hmm." Cedar endeavored to not let the dismissal get

under her skin. "I thought it might be nice if it had an Orcish name, though."

This earned another reaction. Actually looking thoughtful for a moment, Rathka studied the little cat in Cedar's arms. Unlike Liga, it had smatterings of black spots in a smoky gray.

"*Kiya* means 'smoke.' You could name it after its spots."

Cedar smiled at this. *Smoke* was a good name for a creature who would grow up to be lethal and lithe, and Kargorr might see it as a symbol of her willingness to integrate.

"Kiya," Cedar repeated, and Rathka actually smiled when she said it. "That's a nice name. I think I'll call him that."

Rathka nodded. "Then it is so."

Cedar returned the smile and brought the kitten up to her nose so she could look in its eyes. Milk dribbled from his little mouth, which she wiped off with her tunic. Then she bundled Kiya up in the furs, where he languidly stretched, contented now that he had a belly full of milk.

It was a good gift. Despite Rathka's words, Cedar felt rather warm herself. Kargorr had thought of her, wanted her to have companionship. Whatever the reason, she was glad he had.

KARGORR

Lord Kargorr had always loved the scent of blood. While he was the orcling of a simple warrior, he had quickly fought his way to one of the most feared orcs in the *parog* where he grew up. Even as a youth, older orcs fell to him in sparring matches, and it was known by most then that Kargorr would challenge the lord or leave to start his own *parog*.

He had wondered what the blood of another orc would taste like splattered across his face. But taking what belonged to someone else, rather than building it himself, felt lazy and unearned. No, even then he'd planned to create his own *parog*, and continue the *grrosek*'s mission of spreading across the land as they had done once upon a time.

That taste for blood had led many to leave with him, warriors and their families and children alike. He had traveled to other *parog*, challenging their *kazek* to sparring matches when he was accused of poaching. Every time he demonstrated his power, more *grrosek* saw a better life under his leadership and chose to leave with him.

Not since the Melting had an orc so brazenly built his empire. Orgha had been one of his earliest followers, with no orclings of his own given his *yapira* couldn't bear them. While the older orc wasn't the strongest, nor the most capable in battle, he was loyal and quick-witted, which Kargorr found more useful in a right hand than an orc who was good with a battle-axe.

And Orgha, too, yearned for blood. He could almost smell the nearest human village, tasting the fresh flesh on the wind.

They headed to a larger outpost than the village where Kargorr had found Cedar, but now that his *parog* had moved south, he had a large enough force with him that it presented no real threat. It would be burned to the ground like all the rest.

When it was time, he and his warriors sent their cats away. The animals would return to the *parog* and let the others know to expect them home.

They attacked as the sun crept up above the distant mountains, while the air was still cool and wet. Lord Kargorr charged into homes, killing every human he encountered with a wide swing of his axe. When the scent of death hit his nose, the blood rage began.

Now his vision was narrowed to a single point: the battle in front of him. He roared with his fury as he tore into another house, and screams rose in an orchestra from all around the village.

Never had his blood run so hot and fast in his veins as it did now. All those nights burying himself in Cedar's sweet cunt had poured hot oil on the fire that burned inside him until it was a raging frenzy. He was fury incarnate as he sliced his enemies in two, leaving nothing living in his wake. This was the power of the *grrosek*, his blood sang. This was what befell those who had taken what was his.

It wasn't until the entire village lay dead that he remembered his plan. He had intended to acquire more humans like Cedar, someone else to bring to his bed and fill with orclings. He'd gotten too caught up in the glory of it, in the sheer exuberance of victory, that he'd forgotten all about it.

That wouldn't do. He ought to be encouraging his warriors, too, to take concubines, but the blood rage had taken over all of them. A reddish hue pulsed in their eyes, as he imagined it did in his, and they roared with each fresh kill. It was time to return home with their spoils.

"Round up every horse we can find," he called as they gathered in the town square. Only one of his warriors had suffered an injury, but she cleaned off her blood with a hand and licked it, then bellowed in honor of her new scar.

Once they had yoked the horses to wagons and filled them with every last bit of food, gold, or clothing they could find, Kargorr's party mounted their new prizes and began the trip home.

All the while, his blood rage filled his ears with the pounding beat of his heart, his cock throbbing in time. After riding hard for hours, the *parog* came into view, and he urged his horse on at a gallop.

There was only one way to slake his rage, to quell his need, and her name was Cedar.

18

CEDAR

The sound of tearing awoke her.

Cedar blinked her sleep-filled eyes as a great, dark shape entered the tent, his face lit only by the torch in his hand.

"Kargorr," she murmured as the massive orc dumped the torch into the fire pit. The leather of the tent door had ripped and now hung limp behind him. There was an eerie glow in his eyes, much like the moment Lissa's dead body fell to the ground at his feet.

Kiya hissed when he woke and scrambled off the bed as Kargorr approached. The massive orc's teeth were clenched, the fire now swelling up behind him as the torch's flames caught on the coals in the firepit, bathing his face in shadow while the point of his ears and the tips of his long hair glowed bright red. Cedar felt compelled to flee, to scrunch herself up small in the back of the tent like a rabbit looking into a wolf's mouth. And yet her body was fiercely, wildly awake now, stirred up by the curl of his fingers, how his black claws reflected the firelight. His tusks looked especially sharp and cruel, like scythes protruding from that heavy, jutting lower jaw.

He grabbed the fur on top of her and flung it aside. Cedar was naked underneath, as he insisted she sleep. A dark growl rumbled in his throat when he saw her exposed. Kargorr yanked down his bloodstained pants to reveal that monster between his legs, the one that was bigger and fuller than she'd ever seen it.

Lord Kargorr didn't bother with his armor. He kept it on as he pinned her down, his huge hands swallowing up both her wrists at once as he held them up over her head.

A whimper escaped Cedar at the scent of him, so familiar and yet tinged with another smell, something more sour.

Blood. It covered him, even his face, and when he smashed his mouth to hers, she could taste it on his lips. His claws buried themselves so deep in her soft flesh he almost pricked her skin. With a jerk he lifted her hips, his eyes wilder than she'd ever seen them, and his cock sought her out.

"Mine," he grunted, the head dragging over her clit as it searched for her entrance. "Mine."

That seemed to be the only word he was capable of uttering. Then he found his prize, and Cedar gasped at how wet she was already, how that broad head slid into her. But he'd spent no time preparing her, so his first deep thrust was brutal, forcing her open. A cry slipped out of her as he yanked his cock back and then plunged it in a second time. He was merciless, and her body devoured it. Still her wrists were trapped in his hand as he took her, claimed her, fucked her into oblivion. His cock scoured every last inch of her for pleasure, squeezing it out of her.

Cedar almost didn't notice when he finished inside her because he barely slowed his pace, but the sound of each of his thrusts grew wetter and more obscene.

"Soon," he growled between pumps of his hips, "you will be fat and ripe with my orcling. And you will never, ever leave me."

These words seeped into her slowly, hovering on the fringes of her vision as her entire body began to squeeze tight. She cried out again and again as he sank into her deeper with every stroke, until those lumps at the base of his cock were urging her even wider.

Kargorr hissed, and suddenly shallowed his movements, snarling something in his tongue that she couldn't understand. Abruptly he pulled out of her, then flipped her over with very little effort, so her face was in the furs. Then he slammed into her with abandon, and that tiny dot of light in front of her exploded, blinding her. She was at the mercy of her body, of its culmination, and behind her, Kargorr roared as she clamped down around him. And still he kept fucking her, using her until she had given herself over to wave after wave of excoriating bliss.

But those swells at the root of his length didn't prod at her again. When he jammed himself deep, she could feel the hot rush of his seed inside her, but it made her feel cold.

She wished she could have seen his face as it happened, but he had turned her away—intentionally.

He hadn't wanted to look at her. Why?

As Kargorr collapsed to the bed behind her, all his muscles twitching, unease prickled Cedar's skin. Soon, he got off the bed and opened the tent flap, roaring some command for anyone who could hear. Someone returned, and gave him a mug full of beer, and he sat in his chair to drink it.

Kiya shivered in the corner of the tent, clearly frightened by the activity, so Cedar crept over to the kitten and picked him up, soothing him with soft strokes on his head. Lord Kargorr's eyes remained steadfastly looking nowhere as she returned to the furs, Kiya in her arms, and curled up with him.

When Kargorr lay down next to her many hours later, he didn't touch her before he fell asleep. Cedar drifted off, wondering what she had done wrong.

KARGORR

She'd been so beautiful with her head tossed back, her hair fanned out behind her, her mouth open and her pleasure streaming from it. As Kargorr's blood rage faded, as she sapped the fury and violence from his body through his cock, he had wanted nothing more than to sink himself fully inside her, for his *sarga* to find their home in the soft squeeze of her cunt.

He almost did, against his will.

What was it about this little fleck of a human woman that made his *sarga* ache to fill her? He had almost truly coupled with her, and at that moment, he understood what he'd been doing wrong.

Lord Kargorr had grown too close to her, much too close. He had let Cedar inside himself, and she was burying her claws deep. If he wanted to achieve his goal, he had to hide her away from his own eyes.

In the night, Cedar awoke frequently to dress so she could take her kitten outside and feed it. Each time, she returned to the pile of furs, keeping a safe distance away from him. How was she so soft and yet tough, so sharp-edged but also sensitive?

She understood what he had said with no words, and it had hurt her. She had seen right through him. It was unsettling.

But she had her place, and she would learn it. He would make sure of that from now on.

Lord Kargorr left the next morning before she awoke and set out to begin the unloading. They had brought home more goods than the *parog* could possibly use, but he had been high on his victory and his blood had been hungry. Perhaps they could trade their extra goods to another *parog* and work toward earning their trust. Trade was rare, but it did happen from time to time, particularly where steel and iron were concerned. The *grrosek* didn't waste their time mining ore from the ground, but stole it when they needed it, making it valuable and desirable.

As Kargorr and his warriors worked, he spotted Cedar with her new kitten on a leash, taking it from one place to the next while a pair of orclings followed her. The pet had been a smart decision on his part. Now she was occupied and had a place to direct her attentions while he was gone. He watched them for a moment longer, until one of his warriors approached him with a concern about how they planned to butcher the cows.

Lord Kargorr turned away. He had business to attend to.

That night, there was a great celebration for the raid's success. Everyone ate until they couldn't eat any longer and then danced and sang into the stars. As the ale flowed, the rutting began. Cedar remained seated on his lap, as she was supposed to, but she didn't lean back and settle into him, as he had expected. She stayed still and straight, never looking at him, and Kargorr supposed it was for the best. It would make it easy to distance himself from her, to put her in the place she belonged. Occasionally she took a drink or reached down to pet her cat where it lay at their feet, but that was all.

Kargorr shook his head and downed more mead. But as his head grew fuzzy, all he wanted was *her*, and he couldn't banish the thought from his mind. Soon he grew tired of the revelry and leaned in to Cedar's ear.

"It is time for bed, little deer," he said, keeping his voice soft for her. She removed herself from his lap, picked up her kitten, and walked on ahead of him to the tent without looking back. Somewhere in his gut, it stung.

He wandered into the tent behind her, noting how he had damaged the door last night. He would have to have that fixed.

Inside, Cedar was putting her pet to bed, and he approached her from behind to place his hands on her shoulders. She fell completely, perfectly still, like a figurine.

"Have you named it?" he asked, hoping he could find a crack in her hard armor. If there was one, it would be here, at the juncture of his gift.

She nodded sharply. "Yes. His name is Kiya."

Kargorr furrowed his brow. "Kiya?" he asked, truly befuddled. It was a familiar word, one that meant... "As in, excrement?"

Cedar whirled around and gaped at him. "No! It means 'smoke.' That's what Rathka told me."

He couldn't help it. Kargorr snickered at the woman's gall. She had lied to Cedar, and his human had eagerly believed her.

"Smoke is *sikida*," he said, shaking his head. "*Kiya* are the droppings we leave behind when we've had too much to eat."

His amusement faded when Cedar looked down at the sleeping kitten and her lips pursed together. She had tried to give it an Orcish name, and he felt honored. His gift was appreciated, and the animal's name was her way of showing it. Now she looked like someone had stomped on her favorite toy.

"He will be a fine steed regardless of his name," Kargorr said at last, and kneeled beside her over Kiya's sleeping form.

"I'm keeping it," she said with a stubborn jut to her jaw. "I think it's pretty."

Lord Kargorr kept his laugh to himself. The beer and the mead were swirling in him now, though, and the sight of his people making merry, their cries carrying throughout the *parog*, made him want to join in.

"That will show Rathka," he said at last, and finally, she rewarded him with a smile.

When Kargorr took her that night, he gave in. He looked in Cedar's eyes and drank them up as he sank himself inside her, again and again. When she came around his cock, she didn't look away, as if beckoning him and daring him at the same time.

He matched her, keeping their gazes locked as he released himself deep in her body, and he wondered if any of his spend had found its way to her womb.

He stayed encased in her, rolling onto his side and bringing her in close. He didn't let her go, even as he slept, in case she blew away with the wind.

CEDAR

She forgave him much too easily.

Kargorr had firmly put her in her place, and so she had become committed to that place, to keeping him at arm's length. She couldn't let him gain even more of a foothold, couldn't give herself over to a fantasy where somehow, things were different between them.

She could be helpless here to his unpredictable push and pull, or she could take control instead. There were two possible outcomes: she found the right moment when she was out with Rathka and succeeded in putting the camp behind her.

Or he caught her and punished her, to never let her out of his sight again. Either option was better than slowly dying on the inside and bearing the brunt of each of his capricious whims.

But then, as if an east wind had taken over a southern one, Lord Kargorr let her in. A hidden trap door opened as he looked into her eyes, as he pumped his cock ever-so-slowly in and out of her, and Cedar wondered just how far she would fall if she stepped through it. Would that dark void inside him swallow her up whole? Would it be warm and soft like the furs, or frigid and harsh like the ice plains from where he'd come?

Uncertain, Cedar let herself put in one foot. Perhaps she could give him a little of herself and watch what he did with it. She would keep her heart hard but her mind open to him, to the idea that perhaps there was something here for her amidst the orcs.

The more she explored the camp with Kiya and Rathka, the more often she saw other humans, men and women alike, toiling like their orc counterparts. They were quiet and meek, and none of them had tried to speak to Cedar so far, but their existence here suggested that she, too, could have a future among the orc horde, if she wanted one. She would need to learn more of the language and the culture to fully ingratiate, but Cedar could do it.

What would that future be like?

19

KARGORR

T he *parog* was settling in to their new home rather nicely. He had sent off eight scouts, one in every direction, to map out the closest human settlements. They would go farther if they could, marking on leather with charcoal where they had gone and the landmarks they'd found along the way.

Just as important, though, was his selection for the small delegation he would send to the closest *parog* to start the process of diplomacy. He didn't want to go away himself for so long and leave his own people without a leader at such a pivotal moment, so he thought carefully about who he would send in his stead.

Eventually he settled on Orgha, who would represent him well, along with one of his esteemed warriors, a half-orc who could match—and even surpass—a full orc with his skill in battle. If their envoy was challenged, Samrak would be a fair fight for anyone put forward.

A week after the raid, Kargorr gathered together a wagon

full of goods, and even some gifts of iron and steel on top, with the promise of more in the future. It would be a long journey back into the snowy tundra for Orgha and Samrak, right into the mouth of another *parog*'s territory. He hoped Cedar wouldn't bear the brunt of Rathka's strained bond while Orgha was away. It was difficult, Kargorr had heard, to be separated. But Orgha was his best choice for the effort, and Rathka would not be allowed to go with him while she had duties here to attend.

As expected, Orgha took the news well, saying he was honored to be chosen and carefully hiding any displeasure he might have felt at being given such a task. He would be gone a long time, but he only tapped his chest and agreed to do whatever Kargorr asked.

When the sledge was prepared and Orgha mounted his cat, he stopped to lean down and kiss Rathka. He ran his hand over the tooth necklace that hung from her neck before he nudged his cat into a walk. The mammoths were yoked to the sledge, and they set off, back into the north.

There would not be another raid until Orgha returned, in case something went wrong. The weather was cooling, the earth preparing for winter, but Kargorr had begun to look forward to it. The snow would be welcome and familiar to his *parog*, and then he could spend plenty of time in the furs getting warm again with his concubine.

The last of the leaves on the trees fell, creating a carpet on the ground. Cedar's kitten was growing stronger every day and had already become rather tame. She even taught it tricks, something a *grrosek* had never thought to do. She would cut up tiny pieces of meat and then encourage Kiya to follow her, feeding them to him as he did what he was told. He could sit, and jump into the air, and even walk around in a circle.

Cedar poured all her love into the little creature, and Lord Kargorr was surprised by how much she had to give.

"How did you come to be a slave?" he asked her one night as they lay in the furs, covered in each other's sweat. "I have always wondered."

Cedar tilted her head up curiously, like she didn't understand the question. Rarely had he asked her about her life, because before, it hadn't really mattered to him. But the more times the sun set and rose, the more often Kargorr thought about what had made her who she was, how she had come to be at the farm in the village, running off into the woods.

"My parents sold me," Cedar finally said. "We were starving. Lissa brought a cow to our village to sell for meat, and all my parents could talk about was how long a cow would last. When they took me to her, I assumed it was to help bring the cow back."

She paused a long time, but Kargorr didn't speak to fill the silence. Then she said, "I went with her, and my family kept the cow. I thought it was my responsibility to make sure they could eat, even if it meant I never saw them again."

This was how Kargorr learned the way humans treated their offspring. Her parents had been hard on her as a child, making her work to earn her keep even as little more than a girl. This was not how the *grrosek* did things. Orclings were orclings and must be given room to go wild and play, to not have to worry about where their next meal came from. That was how a strong warrior was grown, not by cheating them of care and affection and forcing them into labor.

It surprised Kargorr even more, then, that Cedar had so much of her own tenderness and warmth to dole out to Kiya, lavishing him with it, when she'd had none as a child.

She would make a fine mother.

That thought, after so many weeks of enjoying her body and conforming her to his shape, triggered him to ask the *shosek* for the leaves. He had nearly forgotten with how deeply he had fallen into the crevasse of Cedar.

The *shosek* was in her dim, smoky tent, burning some kind of incense, when he arrived. Only a weaver of medicine could get away with ignoring him as she did, dragging the incense through the air in a serpentine shape with her eyes closed even as he sat across from her. When her meditation was completed, she paused for a moment to breathe deeply before acknowledging him.

"Lord Kargorr," she said with a long exhale. "What brings you to me?"

"The leaves. I want to know if my concubine carries my orcling yet."

He sensed disapproval in her expression, but she carefully schooled it. Not everyone believed as he did, of course, that sowing half-orcs in a human concubine was the way to grow an empire. But he was *kazek*, and not her.

"Of course." She slowly rose, and Kargorr could almost hear her old joints creaking. Her hair was wild and gray all the way through, like a tundra bush. She rummaged through trunks in the back of her tent, then emerged with a handful of dry leaves.

"You know how to use them?" she asked pointedly.

Lord Kargorr's *shosek* had been with him since the beginning. She had helped with his very own birth when she was a much younger woman. She knew he'd never had need of the leaves before; he had always been careful with his seed, and it wasn't until he saw Cedar fleeing that day that he'd ever yearned for orclings of his own.

But he understood how they worked from his own warriors trying to grow their families, so he said, "Yes. Look for them to change color."

The *shosek* held the leaves just out of his reach and narrowed her eyes.

"Not just any color. You are looking for bright red. You understand, *kazek*?"

Kargorr grunted. Only this old woman could get away with speaking to him this way.

"Yes, I understand," he said, and she put the leaves in his open palm. But then she grabbed it, hard, before he could go.

"You know, don't you?" She dug her claws into him. "That an orcling born without the bond, without the use of your *sarga*, will be weaker in life?"

Every muscle in his body went rigid. These were old traditions, ancient superstitions that did not come anywhere near reality.

"*Shosek*," he warned.

"Do not talk to me like I'm your concubine, too," she hissed. "You are opening a door that could help you rise to the power you seek..." The weathered orc leaned forward, her cracked tusks bright in the firelight. "...or it could take all of it away."

Kargorr snatched the leaves from her and stood, shivering with his anger.

"I did not come to my *shosek*'s tent for fortune telling," he snarled, the very hair on his skin bristling. How dare she threaten him? "I will grow fine, strong orclings, who will inherit all of this when you finally crumble to dust."

With that, he swept out of her tent, clutching the leaves in his hand.

CEDAR

Kiya was getting bigger by the day, and Cedar had spent many hours stitching together a new, larger bed for him with the extra blankets, clothes and furs that had been pillaged in the last raid. Lord Kargorr had suggested a craftsman would do it for her, but she insisted on doing it herself. She'd learned to sew as a girl, and often did it for Lissa, trying to put together old clothes so they looked new again. Cedar enjoyed building the outer layer of the bed and then stuffing it with torn-up bits of skirts and potato sacks, trying to make it as soft and cozy as she could.

Lately she'd been collecting other furs, one given to her as a gift by the family of one of the orclings she played with. They did not look her in the eyes, the same way the rest of the orcs wouldn't, but they were friendly and kind and seemed to see her as their superior, which sat strangely with her. Cedar had never stood in a station above someone else, and it was pleasant and discomforting at the same time. Not even the other three or four humans scattered about the camp would speak to her, as much as she wanted them to.

How had they ended up here? There were two men and two women, who all seemed to speak in the orcs' language fluently. One woman had a half-orc child, but when Cedar attempted to speak with her, Rathka shot her a warning look.

Kargorr must not want Cedar mingling with them. Well, that was fine. They all appeared to be concubines, too, and thus were not much use to her.

Cedar paid more attention now to what Rathka said to the other orcs as they walked around the camp, still annoyed at the *kiya* incident. One afternoon, they came across an old orc man out in front of his tent scraping leather. When Cedar stopped to see what he was doing, he summoned her over to show her. He could speak bits and pieces of the human tongue, saying his daughter had taken a human man of her own.

The old orc had a bounty of cured hides and furs in his tent shop, which he showed off to Cedar happily, proud that someone was taking an interest in his work. Cedar left Kiya with Rathka as she browsed his collection, and she paused on a pelt she'd never seen. It was small and pitch black, with white spots dotting it.

"A good eye," he said, stroking the pelt. "From a rare deer. I have only ever seen one in my life. A faun."

That explained the spots. Cedar ran her hand over it again, thinking how sad it was this unusual creature had been killed before it could even grow up.

"Take it," the old orc said at last, slipping it off its rack. He slung it over her arms. "Perhaps the lord's *yapira* will enjoy it."

Cedar had heard this term before but was unsure what it meant. Still, after she had refused the gift twice, he insisted a third time, and she accepted. The leatherworker looked pleased with himself as she exited carrying the fur, and Rathka only clucked in disapproval as they returned to Kargorr's tent.

The more furs Cedar acquired, the higher she piled them around the bed, and at night, she kept the faun's fur under her head.

Kargorr never remarked on them, but when the latest black fur appeared, she thought for a moment she saw him smile.

He always looked at her now as he rocked his cock in and out of her, nursing her flames ever bigger and brighter. He had learned how to make her sob, how to make her beg, how to make her scream. He would hold her down and slide only the throbbing, wet swell of his cockhead inside her, over and over, until she said, "Please, I need it."

"Very good, little deer," he would answer, then he would plunge inside her, giving her everything she wanted.

It was curious when he returned one evening with a handful of leaves, and Rathka made herself scarce. He also brought a large clay bowl and then made his request.

"Urinate in it," he told her in a surprisingly firm tone.

"In there?" Cedar asked, having only gotten used to the wet basket a few weeks ago. "Why?"

"I will use it." He set the leaves on the table, spreading them out.

"For what?" She didn't like the direction this was going.

Rather than answering her question, Lord Kargorr said, "Come now. Just some." He held out the bowl again. "Then I'll get you that syrup-coated bacon you like."

He was a wily one. If she could, Cedar would eat that crusted bacon until it killed her.

"All right." She took the ceramic pot and shooed him away. Instead of leaving, Kargorr sat down at the table and watched her.

She saw the dagger and remembered what he had said about there being no secrets between them. With a sigh, she squatted over the pot and closed her eyes, thinking much too hard.

"You must relax," Kargorr said in a quiet voice.

Finally, it burst free, and Cedar let out a stream into the pot. When she was finished, she awkwardly shuffled away, humiliated that she'd done that in front of him.

Kargorr kneeled next to the pot and dropped in one leaf, then two, then three. Curious at what he was doing, Cedar crouched beside him and watched.

Before them, the leaves began to change color. They went from pale brown to yellow, to orange, and then bright red.

Bloody red.

Cedar gasped and turned to Kargorr, and saw his eyes were alight, his mouth parted in surprise.

Suddenly, he was upon her, dragging her into his arms, crushing her against his body. His tusks framed the crown of her head as his breathing came heavy, and his claws curled around her waist.

"What is it?" Cedar asked against his chest, finding it rather hard to breathe.

"I've succeeded." He gently released her, keeping his hands on her shoulders. "I've planted an orcling in you. It grows even now."

Her mind went blank as the winter snow.

Cedar knew this time had been coming, but now that it was there in front of her, it barreled into her, plowing her over.

She was with child. With the offspring of an *orc*.

It would grow up to look like one of those half-orcs, with the fine features and sturdy frames. And Cedar would be bound to Kargorr.

Forever.

20

KARGORR

Cedar had been nesting without realizing it. Lord Kargorr almost hadn't needed to read the leaf colors. She was gathering more soft things for their bed, carving out a warm place for her to lie and rest while she grew his orcling inside her.

The leaves weren't just red, but a dark, blistering red, like they'd been steeped in blood.

Not only was she carrying his orcling, but it would be a strong one. A powerful one. Lord Kargorr could smell it on her as much as he picked up his own scent coating her skin. He breathed her in deeply, memorizing the size and shape and color of her aroma. He imagined her now, swollen up thick and heavy, and his cock thrashed in its sling.

But Cedar was still motionless in his arms, her expression unreadable. He had hoped she would be elated, but instead it was as if she was in a trance.

Kargorr sat on the floor and pulled her into his lap, her

head tucked under his chin. His hands encircled her, lying loosely over her thighs and under her belly. He curled one there, imagining where his orcling would grow from a small bead into a living, breathing thing, and when she had given him one, he would plant another one there. His cock pressed at her rear where it sat on his groin, but she didn't react.

"Little deer," he murmured in her ear, petting her soft belly. "You know I will always take care of you. I will keep you fed and warm and provide every fur or tunic you desire."

She nodded slowly, the first movement he had seen from her since the leaves' revelation. Kargorr kept speaking, hoping to lure her out.

"All your needs will be attended to," he said, tracing his lips over her hair, stopping to nibble on the shell of her ear. "They will have a powerful father, and a strong and willful mother." He felt victorious when the edge of her mouth quirked. "And they will likely always be getting into trouble, just like she does."

As he talked, her body slowly relaxed, until she had settled back into his chest. He slid his hand up over her breast, weighing it in his palm, teasing the nipple until it peaked. His other ventured downward, between her legs and over her leather pants, pressing the fabric into her cunt as he dragged his fingers up and down. It only took a few moments for him to feel her moisture there, as wet as she got for him. No cunt had ever wept for him like Cedar's.

But Kargorr took his time with her anyway, though his cock ached to be inside her, to fill her with his pride and pleasure. He peeled away her clothing, then lathered her up, chewing off his claws and filing them down so he could stroke his fingers inside her. He whisked over her nub with his palm until she was gasping and arching in his lap.

When at last he slid inside that warm, soft cunt, its rippled walls flexing and squeezing him, he finally felt as if this new place in the lowlands was home. Here was where everything began, right in this tent. Cedar's breasts bounced as he thrust into her, pushing her voice higher and louder. She reached out for him in the throes of her ascent, and he held her close, driving into her as he clutched her tight to his chest. He couldn't help wrapping his lips around hers, sucking them into his mouth, lavishing attention on her tongue. He wanted to taste all of her.

His *sarga* ached the tighter she held onto him. They burned. They longed to open her wide and bury themselves inside her. It made no sense, as he had already filled her with an orcling—and yet he wanted nothing but to fully encase himself in her.

Still, Kargorr held himself back, fucking Cedar more and more ruthlessly as she rushed to her peak again. He imagined how full she would get with him and then he let off, his cock swelling to fill up every last crevice of her.

When she had wrung the last drop from him, he gently rolled them to one side so he could stay buried in her. He could taste the salt of her sweat on his tongue, and he could have simply licked her clean.

If he had felt protective of Cedar before, if he had hated the mere idea of anyone looking at her like *that*, it was not even a simmering charcoal to the bonfire that raged now.

Now he would burn to the ground anything that got between them.

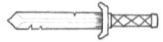

CEDAR

Kargorr was... *pleased.*

Cedar hadn't known he was capable of it. A smirk played at his mouth as they ate breakfast, like he was guarding a special secret. When they were finished, he announced there would be a celebration that night, one to honor his future son or daughter. Immediately he set about barking orders around the camp. There would be a whole pig roasted in a pit—not Bread Pudding, he promised.

When she arrived, Rathka's demeanor was darker than ever. But Cedar refused to let the old woman's foul temper bother her. Something was changing right there. She was carrying the lord's child, and he had made it clear when he was on top of her, inside her, what it meant to him. What *she* meant to him.

A picture of her life here among the orcs grew clearer every moment, and for the first time, she thought staying might be better than leaving. It was warm here, and she never wanted for a meal.

Cedar had never considered having a family. When she lived in the house where she grew up, crammed in with so many brothers and sisters, the idea had seemed ludicrous. Having children meant you had even more mouths to feed when food was already so scarce. And then, living with Lissa, Cedar had known she would never even get the chance to meet a partner—not until Lissa died, at least.

But suddenly, now it was in front of her, already in her future.

A pocket of resistance still lingered, though. Lord Kargorr had made it clear once upon a time that Cedar was intended to be one of many, that she was merely another garden bed to sow. Was that still in his plan now?

Cedar tried to tuck her doubts away, to hide the question from herself because she didn't like the fierce surge of jealousy it inspired. No, every signal she was getting from Lord Kargorr said his course had changed. He wouldn't have kissed her, wouldn't have looked her in the eyes the way he did, if he still intended to have others.

She had to believe that if she were to stay.

When the sun set, wood was gathered and stacked in the fire pit. The pig had been roasting all day, and Cedar salivated at the smell as she and Rathka passed.

"Let us hope you don't lose it," the old orc woman said as they surveyed the tables being set up, the barrels of mead and beer rolling out.

Cedar fed Kiya another treat. "Lose what?"

"Your offspring. It's foolish to hold a celebration when these things are so tremulous early on. The *kazek* is too eager."

A dark, icy dread washed over Cedar. That couldn't be true. Now that she was with child, surely it wouldn't be taken away so soon. She remembered Kargorr's hands caressing her belly, and her mouth tasted of ash.

The tension in her body remained as the orcs drank and cut into the roast pig. Was Rathka right? Would Kargorr be disappointed in her if, after all this pomp and circumstance, Cedar lost their baby?

Lord Kargorr sat in his immense chair as the bonfire swelled, spitting sparks and smoke while Kiya found his place at their feet. Kargorr lifted Cedar into his lap, and she was surprised to find a lump already growing underneath her.

Food was served on immense trays, and she devoured all of it, feeling a hunger she'd never felt before. While the potatoes tasted odd, the pig was divine. As Kargorr emptied his mug, the sound of orcs talking and laughing grew louder. Other orcs would stop at their table and tap a fist to their chests.

"Congratulations, Lord Kargorr," each of them said, and he thanked them with a vigor that surprised Cedar. He was pleased, that much was clear, and in an unusually good mood.

One half-orc approached the table, tentative, a small object tucked in his hand.

"I hope that my *yapira* might conceive soon, too," he said, setting it down in front of them. It was a small animal carved from wood—a beautiful piece of dark mahogany shot through with a light grain. "Perhaps tonight. So I bring you an offering in hope you will bless our chances."

When Cedar glanced over his shoulder, she saw another orc standing behind him, also carrying a gift.

"I hope that you, too, find the joy of creating your own orcling," Kargorr said amiably. "And that your efforts tonight are successful."

The half-orc wasn't the only one to make a request like this. Soon there was a pile of children's toys lying out in front of them, and in the background, the music began. Orcs emerged with drums, with fine lutes pillaged from some long dead musician, and even great wooden tubes they could blow to bring out a variety of deep, booming sounds. Orcs rose from their seats and began to dance, and Cedar was once again stunned by the beauty of it. They were not elegant, but they were filled with life and energy. She had never seen a human behave with such wild abandon as more and more bodies danced before the flames.

The hours passed as everyone ate and danced and drank. Cedar was startled by the sound of moaning, and she turned to find at one of the closest tables, the half-orc from earlier had his full-orc woman bent over the bench, and his cock was thrusting in and out of her. It dribbled with his seed, and Cedar shivered at the heat that immediately blasted through her at the sight.

She heard Kargorr chuckle behind her. He smoothed over the soft curve of her hip with one palm, applying enough pressure that the space between her legs ground against the object in his lap. Rather than a tunic and pants, Cedar had worn a dress for the occasion, one that the seamstress had assured her would continue to fit nicely even as her belly grew. It was the only barrier between her orc's hand and her bare center, and he quickly crossed it, sweeping up under the dress to trail his fingers along the insides of her thighs. Cedar shifted, wishing he would bring it just a little closer, but he merely circled her sex, stopping to curl his fingers in her thatch of hair and then moving on. He traced the lips of her pussy, and even as Cedar pushed her hips into his touch, he resisted giving her what she wanted.

Then he untied his laces, letting his heavy dark green cock free. More orcs had joined in, and nearby, one orc had his partner spread over the table, teasing his ass, and then shoving his cock deep into it. Cedar gasped at the sight, and a bright spark lit in her belly. As she watched, Kargorr's cockhead, slick with seed, slid across her. Still he teased her, finally thumbing over her sensitive pearl, and Cedar arched into him.

"Do you need my cock, little deer?" Kargorr murmured, leaning down to watch the show over her shoulder. "Has the party gotten you dripping for me?"

Cedar nodded rapidly, knowing she should be ashamed at how her body begged relentlessly for his. With a hum of approval, he lifted her up, positioned himself in the wet divot between her legs, and slowly lowered her.

Cedar moaned as he worked his way inside, slow inch by slow inch, his hand holding her belly as if he could feel himself inside her. Maybe he could with how far he stretched her open, how he demanded her body to give in to him. When she had settled fully on top of him, those lumps at the base of his cock prevented her from taking him any more deeply. He took a ragged breath, stilling himself, before he lifted her up and dropped her down again.

He took her on his lap that way, in front of every orc in the *parog*, claiming her as his. As her cries rose, so did those among the orcs around the fire, until the sound of ecstasy surrounded her. Still Kargorr stroked her clit, taunting her with every thrust of his hips, until she shattered around him. He milked her climax, and then, with a powerful roar, unleashed everything inside her.

While she was limp and boneless, he swept her up into his arms and rose to his feet. The orcs cheered and howled as he held her up like a trophy for everyone to see, his seed leaking down her legs and dripping to the ground.

21

KARGORR

Yes, he was proud of his new concubine for taking to his seed so well. Sometimes it took many moons, but for his Cedar, it had only been one. It made him confident he could keep her round with orcling for some time. Perhaps she had even been made for him, made for this purpose, the way her body spoke to his, called to his, and swallowed him up like he belonged there.

The first snows fell earlier than they had expected, but the cats were pleased and even ran around in the falling flakes. Cedar's pet—he still could not call it *kiya*, as much as she loved that name—frolicked in the soft, powdered snow until it was so tired it collapsed in the bed Cedar had lovingly made for it.

Every morning, Kargorr awoke to her curled into him, his arms wrapped around her. He would lie there and look at her sleeping face, and not only did his cock ache, but so did another part of him, somewhere even deeper and more forgotten. It warmed him thoroughly, even as the winds blew colder, and sometimes he would remain in the furs far longer than he should just so he didn't disturb her. Cedar liked her sleep and tended to be ornery if she didn't get enough of it.

Other things about her were changing, too. She ate more than ever, and she would ask for strange foods, like cold milk or barely cooked beef. Sometimes she craved things he had never heard of, or perhaps he didn't know the word in the human tongue—like something called *chocolate*, which he gathered involved sugar, butter, and some sort of fruit.

"I've only had it once, but it stuck with me," she said morosely. "A merchant had come through town when I was younger, and I managed to buy a piece after selling some gloves. I haven't thought about it much since then, but now..." Cedar groaned with just her desire for it, and Kargorr's cock twitched, thinking it was being summoned. "If only I could have chocolate."

He described the dish to the cooks who worked in the serving tent, and, rather baffled, they tried to make something that matched it with a late fall fruit that was yellow and hard and sweet. The concoction it yielded, though, did not please Cedar, as much as she tried to pretend it did.

Kargorr had begun to notice these things about her, like how her left eye would squint when she tasted something bad, which was often now. Sometimes she would feel sick, and her cheeks would blow out when she was trying to keep it inside her.

"It's better to let it out," he'd told her, and she ran from the tent to empty the contents of her stomach into the wet basket.

All good signs, he knew, but he still didn't like how she would crawl into the furs afterward and curl around her belly, muttering that she would never touch her favorite syrup-covered pork again.

She always did the next day.

One night, Kargorr returned from a long talk with the armor craftsman to find Cedar lying under the furs with her cat curled up next to her. As usual, Rathka tiredly rose to her feet and departed when he stepped in with their dinner.

Cedar wasn't usually sleeping at this time of day, not now that her pet was getting older and needed constant exercise and attention. Kargorr sat on the bed and shooed the animal away, a creature which, unfortunately, did not respect him. Kiya stretched out languidly before hopping off to find his way to his own nest in the corner. Cedar let out a dissatisfied mutter under the blankets, but otherwise did not emerge.

Even though their food was hot, Kargorr found himself very much distracted by the sight of Cedar's chest rising and falling under the furs. He never stopped hungering for her, like a cat that hadn't eaten for months. Every time it felt as if he'd been starved, and still afterward, he wasn't sated. No matter how many times he took her, he craved more.

Kargorr lay down next to her, and at last she peeked out from her hiding place under the blankets.

"Are you an orcling afraid of the snow giant?" he asked, surprised to find his own tone rather playful.

"Snow giant?"

"A big, frightening monster that we use to threaten orclings into behaving."

Cedar snickered, then groaned. "I'll take the ice giant."

He plucked the end of the fur and peeled it away so his hands could slip under it, around Cedar's small body. How such a little woman could carry his offspring was a mystery and a marvel. Usually, she fell into his arms easily, and then he would breathe in the sweet smell of her arousal. But instead, she stiffened, and her breath came out as a moan—not the sort he would like to hear from his concubine in bed.

"I feel awful," she muttered, curling tighter around herself and away from him. "I think I'm going to be sick again."

And then she leapt out of the furs and ran to the door of the tent, groaning as she emptied her stomach.

When she righted herself once more, Cedar looked pale and shaky. She waved away food and returned to the bed, much to Kargorr's dissatisfaction. But just as you couldn't lead a horse to water, apparently you couldn't lead a woman full of orc spawn to food.

That night, he pressed his body to her back, his cock eagerly nudging at her ass, but she just groaned in displeasure again.

He very much disliked this turn of events.

The next day, Lord Kargorr asked his *shosek* for a remedy, and she begrudgingly offered one. When he brought it to Cedar, she confessed it tasted terrible, but it helped ease the unruliness of her stomach.

In the meantime, he had begun to worry about something else, too. His delegation to the neighboring *parog*. Orgha had not returned yet, and without him, Rathka grew more irritated by the day. Kargorr didn't like that she brought her poor spirits into the tent with Cedar, so he had a firm talk with her outside the door.

"He is gone on *your* errand," Rathka had said, doing her best not to look her *kazek* in the eye, even while speaking impertinently. "What if my *agsan* never returns?"

"He will," Kargorr said. "Orgha would never fail at this."

And then, when the snow had stopped falling and a good foot of powder lay on the ground, the mammoths appeared on the horizon.

159

CEDAR

It was, apparently, a major event that the party Kargorr sent away to meet with another clan had returned safely. There were whoops and cheers as they arrived outside the camp.

Cedar followed Kargorr out to greet them, Kiya at her side. Rathka rushed ahead, toward Orgha's great cat, and rose up onto her toes to kiss her returned husband... or whatever he was. As much as Cedar disliked Rathka, the sight of their reunion stirred her heart. How would it feel to get old alongside someone you loved, and still love them when your hair was all gray?

The wagons they brought back were mostly empty of everything they had left with, and Cedar gathered from Kargorr's reaction that this was a good thing. The other clan had accepted his gifts, and a tentative peace was brokered.

Kargorr and Orgha embraced, which took Cedar by surprise. They patted one another on the backs as the rest of the party reunited with their families after so much time away.

While the camp came out in force to greet the new arrivals, Kargorr brought Cedar in against his side. He looked simply delighted with this development.

"They will be willing to work with us now," he said, and she wasn't sure if he was talking to her or to himself. "Their *parog* is interested in what I have to offer."

"Which is what?" She was interested in this door that he was letting her peek inside.

Kargorr's lips peeled back over his tusks in a cruel smile. "Power."

The camp had a celebration that night, and when the dancing began, Rathka dragged Orgha into the fray. For being much older, Rathka could still move her body with an almost mesmerizing ease. It was clear that Orgha still lusted for her by the way they twisted around each other, their hands every which way.

Cedar almost wanted to dance herself, but as she sat on Kargorr's lap at the head of the gathering, she didn't know if he would ever let himself be seen doing something as common as dancing.

"Do you know, little deer," Kargorr began, a thoughtful look on his face, "why this is all so important to me?"

Cedar startled. He never gave her *reasons* for things. He simply did them and provided no insight into his decisions. He did not ask her opinions, certainly, though sometimes she desperately wanted to offer them.

"Why?" she finally asked, curious where he was leading her.

"What I'm doing now, it's the beginning." He tightened his arms around her, rubbing his thumb across her belly. "The beginning of something great. Something..." He searched for the right word, cursing under his breath in his own tongue. "Ah. Magnificent."

She wondered if he meant his successful delegation, or the creature growing in her belly. Perhaps both.

"Something that will allow me to shape the world, to take everything for the *grrosek*," Kargorr said, his voice turning low and dangerous. "I will lead all of us, in one unified front, into the south."

Into the human lands. So that's what he was doing—gathering the other clans to his side so he could expand his territory even further.

"And you will be king?" Cedar asked, rather boldly. But Kargorr simply laughed.

"Kings are petty rulers," he said with a snort. "It is a title passed down with nothing to deserve it. No, I will be chosen. I will lead us to victory, and when we have driven the humans out and ground them to bits under our heels... we will become one great *parog*." His eyes narrowed. "And they will ask me to lead them."

He sounded so certain that Cedar didn't doubt him for a moment.

KARGORR

He would have to be careful with his next move.

Now the eyes of the other *parog* were watching. He needed to prove his worth, show the might of his own warriors, and take one of the larger human settlements. Then, perhaps, he could call on his new ally and march even farther southward.

With the heat of victory in his veins, he looked harder at his future here in his own *parog*. Perhaps in the next raid, he would find his future concubine, another soft human to warm his bed and carry more orclings for him, as his first one had taken to him so well.

The thought of putting his cock inside a different woman, though, made his guts twist. How did he know she would feel as good, as soft and wet as Cedar? How did he know she would wrap her legs around him and cling to him like she was caught in a storm, and he was her only salvation? It had taken some time to earn Cedar's obedience, and more recently, her affection, and he loathed the idea of teaching another stubborn human woman how to live alongside the *grrosek*.

Perhaps, in a larger human town, he would find the right match. Perhaps he would find a woman who triggered his desire the way Cedar had, and his instinct would guide him. Then, in some years' time, he would have his own orclings to join him in battle. He would create an army that was loyal to him.

Though he did not like the uneasy shudder that ran down his spine.

Now that Orgha had returned, the planning began in earnest. Kargorr had gathered reports from all of his scouts, and together he and Orgha began assembling a map of the surrounding area. There were a few larger settlements within a few days' ride. They needed to choose the best target based on the force they could bring, but it was difficult to estimate from just reports.

"East is better," Orgha argued. "Closer to farmland. From there, we can cut off their supplies."

But Lord Kargorr didn't want to anger the powers that be too soon and earn their attention. Picking off small villages was one form of aggression, but taking out a large settlement was a much bigger threat that might demand action.

"We isolate them first." Kargorr narrowed his eyes at the map. "Begin by knocking down the smaller outposts."

It would be a longer campaign, but it would yield much greater results. He could control the spread of information, and reports would be much harder to follow back to the *parog*'s location. Above all, he needed to keep his people—and his concubine—safe from attack.

Orgha nodded, having heard and understood the command.

"We will leave in two days," Kargorr said. "Plan to be gone for at least two weeks." He frowned. "And make sure to take care with your *yapira*. She carries a dark cloud around with her that I don't want near my orcling."

His right hand opened his mouth as if to speak but then stopped himself. Instead, he nodded in understanding.

"I will ensure she takes care with your concubine," Orgha said, but something about the way he said *concubine* made Kargorr's hair prickle.

"Do you mean something by that?" Kargorr asked,

crossing his hands behind him in a way that Orgha would certainly perceive as a threat.

The other orc took a step back. "No, *kazek*." He tapped his fist to his chest. "It's just that you treat her as less of a concubine and more of a..." Orgha trailed off.

"A what?" Kargorr prompted, not enjoying the direction this was taking.

"A *yapira*."

A frigid wind blew into the command tent then, whipping back the flap that hadn't been tied. At first, Kargorr wanted to tear into his right hand and show him the folly of talking back.

But perhaps he was right, too. Lord Kargorr found himself thinking of Cedar more and more often, not just of her body, but of her comfort. Her care. He brought choice cuts of meat for Kiya, as he had unfortunately given in to calling the kitten, because it pleased her.

"You know," Orgha said in a tentative voice, as if speaking to a reticent animal, "that may not be such a bad thing."

Kargorr reflexively snarled. His plan did not involve taking a *yapira*. It was to sow plenty, far and wide, and create an empire. Binding himself to one woman, orc or human, would make him look weak. A *kazek* with a *yapira* was not as feared, not as trusted to have the requisite bloodlust.

"It brings balance to your life," Orgha went on when Kargorr did not respond. "It soothes the soul when it spins too fast, and brings warmth when it gets cold and stale."

Kargorr wondered which soul his was.

Perhaps Orgha was right. Kargorr hated to consider it, but maybe sinking his *sarga* into Cedar's supple body at last would finally slake this impossible thirst of his.

He shook his head. A *kazek* did not have such luxuries. Kargorr was trading that sort of life for one where the *grrosek* reigned over this land, and he would need his rage to conquer the humans and achieve his mission.

That thought was fresh in his mind as he chose not to respond to Orgha's suggestion and instead bid him a tight goodbye. Kargorr stepped out of the tent into the freezing night, thinking he might take a walk before returning to his tent.

That was when he heard Cedar shouting, angry and shrill, and on instinct, he ran toward her.

22

CEDAR

Cedar thought the party's return would have improved Rathka's mood, but it only seemed to make her more irritable, as if this was an ugly chore that stood between her and time with Orgha. When Cedar slipped and called him her "husband," it worsened an already dark mood.

"He is my *agsan*," Rathka corrected sharply, clutching the tooth that hung on a string around her neck. "Mine. For always."

Cedar considered this as she walked Kiya toward the tent where they served the most delicious food. The orcs, she had found, made good use of what they pillaged. They utilized herbs and spices in generous quantities, and they loved salt. She had rarely eaten so much salt, and it was heavenly.

Up ahead, some orclings laughed and jostled each other as they carried bowls of stew alongside their parents. This dish smelled like apples, and Cedar thought it was an unusual but not unwelcome flavor for stew.

Kiya pulled on ahead, drawn by the smell. He was growing bigger every day, and nearly rose to her ribcage, and soon he would be stronger than his mistress. Up ahead, one of the children laughed, elbowing the other in the side—which made the smaller one trip.

The stew flew out of her hands, splattering meat and vegetables across the ground. Instantly, Kiya dove for it, and Cedar jerked with the leash. He scrambled to eat up as much as he could while she pulled him back, trying to keep him away from the spilled stew.

Rathka roared something in Orcish, lunging toward him. She kicked the cat's head away from the spilled stew, knocking him across the jaw.

He let out a sharp, pained howl. Then he stumbled away, whimpering, his ears pinned back.

A flash of searing-hot fury lanced through Cedar's body. Rathka snapped something else in her own language that she couldn't understand—but she didn't care.

"How dare you!" Cedar's voice exploded out of her. She seized the much taller Rathka by her hair and yanked her backward, away from Kiya. Rathka cried out as it was pulled from her scalp. "You kicked him!" Cedar shouted again. "You bitch!"

Her rage poured out of her, something she'd never known existed until she heard Kiya's helpless yowl. When Rathka begged Cedar to let her go, Cedar flung her away by the hair and then shoved her hard, knocking her to the ground.

Rathka landed on her hands. Her head jerked up, and she glared at Cedar with hard, black eyes.

"It is just a cat!" Now there was no mistaking the obstinance in her. "How dare you? You are not even a *yapira*. You are a *concubine*!"

When Rathka moved to stand again, Cedar pushed her down once more.

"No." She had seen how Kargorr treated those who disobeyed him, who talked back to him, and if that was what it took for the orcs to respect her, then she would do what was needed. "Stay down there. Where you belong."

Behind her, she heard a chuckle. She spun around to find Lord Kargorr standing nearby, taking in the scene before him. Cedar stepped back, putting some distance between herself and Rathka, wondering how much he had heard.

Would she be lashed for this? Rathka was Orgha's *yapira*, and Orgha was Kargorr's right-hand man.

But then, Cedar found she didn't care as she stooped down to the ground to check on Kiya and make sure he wasn't injured. She would do it again if she had to. The kitten flinched back at her touch, and Cedar growled anew because now Kiya was afraid of her.

"What's happened here?" Kargorr asked, hands tucked behind his back.

Cedar stuck out her chin. "She kicked Kiya. And I won't let anyone hurt him."

When Cedar got to her feet again, Kargorr advanced toward her, and she thought he might hit her. He'd never raised his hand to her before, but she knew Orgha was important to him.

Kargorr took her chin roughly in his hand, pulled her up onto her toes, and snatched her into a kiss that could have drowned her. It was almost vicious in its power. Cedar gasped against him, but he only kissed her harder and deeper, invading her mouth with his tongue and clutching the back of her head.

When he was finished, Kargorr pulled away and rounded on Rathka.

"Go back to Orgha," he said in a low voice, one that reminded Cedar of a snarling wolf. "Go back now, before I decide there should be a greater punishment for you than sending you home."

Rathka flushed a deep green and turned on her heel, running from the scene. Only then did Cedar notice how many other orcs stood around watching, and her face burned.

But Lord Kargorr didn't appear to notice them. His eyes were focused only on her, as if everything else in the camp had ceased to exist.

He swept one arm under her knees and the other behind her back, lifting her into his arms. In front of everyone, he carried her down the pathways back to their tent. When she gave a startled objection, because she had left Kiya behind, Kargorr ground out a quick, "Someone will care for him," and shut the tent flap hastily behind them.

Cedar yelped as he tossed her onto the furs. There was a red tinge to Kargorr's eyes, the same as the time he had returned from a raid and mercilessly fucked her. He crept onto the bed like a predator, and the expression on his face would have sent most humans running. But Cedar remained still, watching him just as steadfastly as he crossed the furs. Soon he was on top of her, boxing her in, his knees straddling her hips and his arms curled around her head. He leaned down close, so his mouth was only breaths away from hers.

"You are so fierce," he said, his voice rolling the words like stones. Then he dove down to her mouth, bruising her lips with his, plundering her for everything she had. Cedar's blood felt too hot and too fast. Rage at what Rathka had done to her beloved animal still coursed through her, and she attacked Kargorr with just as much fervor. He rewarded her with a groan, and his groin rubbed urgently against hers, showing her just where he wanted to be.

Cedar tugged at his thick, fur-lined leather tunic, and with a pleased chuckle, Kargorr disposed of it. Once their clothes lay scattered on the floor and the bed, and Cedar was sprawled naked before him, Kargorr descended once again. He worried her lip with his teeth, then moved to her ear, nibbling her lobe while his clawed hands cupped her breasts. When he reached them with his lips, he licked a trail around each nipple before clamping down on it, sucking hard until Cedar was whimpering and arching into his mouth.

"These will nourish my orcling so well," he said, squeezing her breasts together and thrusting his hips against her. There was a new breathless hunger in his voice. "They'll grow so fat with your milk, and I'll keep them that way."

Why did his words spark a flame in her belly? She couldn't help her moan.

While he smothered her nipples in his affection, his fingers trailed down between her thighs, where he found her already weeping with her excitement. He buried his fingers in her.

"Always so tight for me." That red hue to his eyes grew brighter. "Perfect for taking my cock."

Cedar wanted more than just his fingers. She whined as he pumped them in and out of her, searching out the sensitive places inside her.

"It fits so well inside me," she managed between moans. "Please. Please, I need you."

The demand seemed to strike a chord somewhere deep inside him, because Kargorr let out a monstrous growl, then yanked his hand free of her. He slathered the head of his cock in her wetness, and he bared his teeth as he crouched over her. Spreading her legs wide, he dragged himself through her wet petals, over her clit and back again, his hooded eyes watching her as she writhed and moaned and snapped her hips up to urge him inside her. Still he ignored her body's pleas, just teasing her with the anticipation of him.

There was a new look in his eyes, something wild and fearsome, like he would eat her whole. Then he allowed the soft head of his cock to nudge at her entrance.

"You are mine," he said, fisting his hand at the root as he started to push it inside. "You will always be mine."

She wanted him, of course. She yearned for nothing else but to be filled by him. But he was saying something else this time, though perhaps it was hope that made her believe it.

Kargorr thrust inside her in one smooth motion, as if he could no longer hold it back. There he rested for a moment, settled where he belonged, panting. His huge body, the scar that rent his face in two, all of it came to rest in her heart.

As if he could hear her thoughts, her massive orc dropped onto one elbow so his heaving chest was flush with hers, his tusks brushing her cheeks. When he began to move, he remained deep inside her, simply rocking his hips back and forth to stay fully enveloped. Harder and harder, those lumps at the base of his cock pressed at her taut opening, pulsing against her. He began muttering in his tongue, something guttural and thick with need, as he thrust again and again. Cedar whined and thrashed as the two swells urged her open, demanding she give even more.

Kargorr pulled away enough that he could look at her, *truly* look at her, and in his eyes, she saw a version of him she'd never seen before. Something softer, with none of the same cutting edges and high walls. He was, at last, exposed to her, and his truth...

It was not what she expected to find. He was more than just a beast, and inside him lay a soul as hungry for nurturing as hers.

Then, her body finally relented, and Kargorr eased the rest of the way inside her—those twin bulges stuffing her as full as she could take.

Cedar cried out, her arms lashing around his neck like a collar and her fingers tangling in his hair. She felt something shift in that moment, and she only wished she knew what it was.

KARGORR

She had been magnificent, his Cedar, giving Rathka a rather firm dressing-down. The orc woman looked just as shocked to see so much fire in her, to feel her fierce protectiveness and stern pride. It warmed him from his throat to his groin, to witness Cedar standing up for her pet with such fury. She knew her place and demanded others bend before it.

Kargorr would shed his own blood for her. He would *bathe* in it for her. Now, inside her, her huge brown eyes gazing up into his, her soft eyebrows slack and her pink mouth round with her pleasure, he knew it in a place even deeper than his gut. His whole being vibrated with the need to finally take her, to claim her—and so, at last, he gave in to his every longing and sunk his throbbing *sarga* inside her.

Cedar's whole being bucked underneath him as he shoved his cock deep, where it was meant to be. She whimpered his name, and the sweet sound of her voice nearly sent him off the edge. But he had more to do.

She was his. Fully, completely, and utterly his. It was time to show her, with every muscle and drop of blood in his body. She would never lie underneath anyone else. She would never be far from his thoughts. She would bear him many orclings and grow old with him, her supplicating body always giving, her sore but fiery soul resting close to his.

Kargorr moaned with the rush of euphoria that flooded him as his *sarga* were fully embedded in her. This was where they belonged. But he was also intent on teaching her what they were for—and the heights of pleasure to which he could bring her.

Gritting his teeth, Lord Kargorr reeled his hips back, his *sarga* popping free of her, only to thrust them in once more.

Her cry was louder this time, so he summoned all of his willpower and buried himself in her, over and over, making sure his *sarga* slicked in and out of her impossibly tight cunt. Soon tears were breaking free from her eyes as she clenched harder and harder, squeezing his cock like Liga's huge jaws around a rabbit.

When he finally wrenched her climax from her, it streamed out of her in a scream. No longer could Kargorr resist the wet pulse of her around him. He plunged into her, fully seating his *sarga* inside her, and at last he burst. Cedar gripped his arms so hard her nails bit into his skin as his cock swelled up, filling every empty space she had left. Her cunt had fully surrounded him, locking him in. He groaned as his seed streamed out of him in wild force, her glorious body wringing him for everything he had.

It was difficult not to simply collapse on top of her, so Kargorr twisted to one side so he could remain lodged in her. Cedar gasped and wriggled, and he clutched her hip tightly to stop her moving.

"Stay still," he murmured into her hair, stroking that perfect softness. He inhaled her smell, so fragrant with her satisfaction, and a lightness he'd never felt before settled on his shoulders.

He knew who she was. At last, he had found his *yapira*, the one intended for him—and in such an odd place.

But telling her so, giving into it so fully, frightened him. Kargorr was never afraid, not of anything, until now. He could not yet give her that weapon, not until he was certain he had fully won her loyalty and her heart.

And not until he had achieved his mission. No one could know, not yet, not until he had secured the other *kazek*, and built the army he needed.

Here in their tent, though, where they were alone... he could at least know that he had found her.

His one, his only.

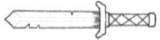

CEDAR

It took many minutes for the swelling in Kargorr's cock to recede. When it did, he slid out of her, and a torrent of his seed followed. Cedar gasped as her body released him, and she curled tight against his side at the slight ache it left behind.

Kargorr hummed, smoothing a hand down her shoulder and cupping it around her back. Cedar felt warm and weightless, like a bird peering down at the wide world beneath, knowing nothing could reach it up in the trees. While Cedar was exhausted, a new part of her felt *awake*, alive in a way it had never been before. It was as if she could feel Kargorr's heartbeat thrumming through her, huge and slow like a steady, beating drum.

"Kargorr," Cedar asked in a hushed, weak voice, her vocal cords still upset from the way she used them earlier.

"Yes, little deer?"

"What was that? That... on your cock."

His muscles stiffened under her hands, as if it was the one question he hoped she wouldn't ask.

"Nothing important," he replied at last, drawing her closer against him. He lowered his head to whisper to her. "Did you enjoy it?"

It wasn't commonplace for him to ask something like this, so she hastily answered, "Oh, yes."

He grunted, and she thought it was a sound of contentment.

Cedar didn't notice when she fell asleep. Her dreams were soft, like her bed, like her heart at this fragile moment.

23

CEDAR

When she awoke, though, the furs were cold, and Lord Kargorr was gone.

Cedar hastily climbed out of bed, threw on her tunic, pants, and boots, then went to the door. Kiya slept peacefully on the floor, as someone must have let him in during the night.

When she peered out and found no one around, she slipped out into the morning. The camp looked emptier than usual save for a few orclings and their mother. The air was cold, so she went back inside to get the cloak the leather craftsman had made for her.

"He left, you know," came Rathka's voice from behind her. Cedar spun around, reflexively clutching the cloak to her chest. Kiya growled where he lay in his bed, and Rathka eyeballed him, making sure to keep a wide berth between them.

"Left?" Cedar echoed. She didn't understand it. He hadn't said anything about leaving.

"On a long raid. He gathered up all the warriors before dawn. They hadn't intended to leave until tomorrow... but he had a fire inside him." She arched an eyebrow. "Did something happen?"

Cedar's mouth opened and closed, but no sound came out. Something had happened, she thought, but not something that would send Kargorr running at first light without saying goodbye.

Though she supposed he'd never said goodbye before. Why would she expect it now? Because they'd had amazing sex last night, like always?

The warm brightness that had surrounded her when she awoke fully dissipated. Rathka observed her face as Cedar cycled through one possibility after another. He must have changed his mind abruptly in the night about which day to leave, probably because of the weather. He didn't want to disturb her, so he left quietly.

Still, she couldn't help wondering if she'd done something wrong but was utterly oblivious to it.

"Nothing happened," Cedar finally answered after sifting through her options. "I expected him to go." It had only been a matter of time after the delegation returned. He'd let her in on his plan—she had to remember that. Kargorr had probably assumed she would understand what was demanded of him next.

She wished he'd told her how long he would be gone. Now she couldn't possibly ask Rathka, or the old orc would figure out the perfect way to drive the needle into Cedar's belly.

But Rathka almost seemed to pity her. She didn't object when they went on a long walk with Kiya, or stopped to play with the orclings near the leatherworker's tent, or even when Cedar ventured out of the camp to let Kiya run.

"You're going to get cold," Rathka grumped, sliding Cedar's hood back on over her head.

Perhaps the orc woman was making up for what she'd done. Perhaps this was her deference, the one that Cedar had demanded yesterday.

She didn't mind it.

That night, though, Cedar found she'd grown so accustomed to Lord Kargorr's presence that she felt awkward eating her dinner alone. Then she made the cat get on the bed with her, though he was no longer interested in snuggling.

Cedar ran her hands over her belly, hoping she hadn't misunderstood everything.

KARGORR

He'd awoken early, before the sun rose, his blood alight.

He had taken his *yapira*. He had pleasured her and filled her with his *sarga*. He had a new energy he'd never sensed before, as if he could lift a mountain himself.

After a life-mating, almost always the *grrosek* remained holed up for days on end, wild with their newfound bond, fucking again and again until an orcling was made—or the need was sated and the demand fulfilled.

But Kargorr did not intend to claim Cedar, not yet. He would certainly not go into a wild rut and delay his trip. He could not be perceived as attached while he was still courting the other *parog*. Not only was a mateless *grrosek* naturally more aggressive, more driven to explore and take and ruin, but sometimes mate bonds that crossed a *parog* could bring them together. Other *kazek* needed to think Kargorr was an option for their own unmated warriors.

And so, instead of curling himself around Cedar and pleasing his *sarga* with her once again when he awoke to the sunrise, instead of giving in to the urges of the bond and staying for days to fuck her into the bed, he'd risen and demanded his warriors rise, too.

He wanted to destroy.

Most everything had already been prepared for their journey. They were traveling light on the assumption they would find goods and supplies in conquest. They brought only what they needed for the next few days, slung over their cats in leather bags, and ran away into the morning.

Orgha had not asked Lord Kargorr his reasons for the schedule change, and the dour look on Kargorr's face led his right hand to remain silent.

It didn't please him to be leaving right now, when all he wanted in the world was to curl up in Cedar's nest with her and fuck her until she knew she was his—but this was the right thing to do if he wanted to succeed.

They rode long and hard that day, pitching their camp in the dark. Kargorr was glad for it because his *sarga* ached, almost worse than before he had used them on Cedar, and he was forced to ejaculate two times before they were finally, though temporarily, sated. He tried to argue to them that his *yapira* was already carrying his orcling, and so there was no need for them to desire her, but in this matter they were unconvinced.

Another day of riding later, and Orgha suggested stopping early for the night so their mounts would have time to eat and rest. They were making good time, and Kargorr wanted to keep beating the sunlight, but he knew his right hand was correct. He needed his warriors fresh.

When they reached the first outpost his scout had discovered, they rode in without preamble. Lord Kargorr swung his axe from Liga's back, so filled with his lust that he wanted to move fast, to demolish his enemies quickly so he might return to the *parog*. To Cedar.

But he had other things to do first.

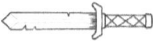

CEDAR

When less than a week had passed, Cedar's pride finally eroded enough that she asked Rathka, "How long will they be gone?" She thought surely Kargorr would have returned by now, or at least soon.

But the knowing smugness she had expected didn't appear on the orc woman's face. Instead, Rathka frowned, like the question worried her.

"You don't know?" She sighed deeply as they sat on some high rocks above the camp, watching Kiya playing with one of his siblings. "It is at least four days' march to their first destination. Orgha was not sure how many destinations they had. 'As long as our strength holds out,' he told me."

Cedar was surprised to hear Rathka share anything personal from her life with Orgha. Most of the time, she refused to speak a word about herself or her own preferences.

"It could be a month," Rathka said thoughtfully. "Maybe many months. Who knows?"

It landed like a heavy, sharp stone in Cedar's belly. *Many months.* She hugged her middle, purely out of instinct, thinking how much would change and how quickly. She expected he would leave on campaigns from time to time, as he had before. But not for whole months.

Cedar rose from her seat, endeavoring not to let her surprise or her disappointment show.

"It's time for Kiya's dinner," she said, turning to hide her face as her lip trembled. "Let's go back."

Rathka followed along without her usual objections,

which she always made when Cedar attempted special trips for her pet. Cedar whistled and Kiya came running, and the cat received a nugget of dried chicken liver from her pocket for his obedience.

When Cedar went to bed that night, for the first time since she'd been stolen, she let herself weep. It was quiet and slow, but it was enough for Kiya to hear her and hop onto the bed, concerned. She pulled him close, wishing it was Kargorr there with her instead, and fell asleep with her head in his fur.

The following days were some of the longest of Cedar's life. The feeling that something was missing gnawed at her insides, as if she was hungry but her stomach was in her soul. At night she could almost sense Kargorr there, a ghost separated from her by a hundred miles.

She hated it. She hated how helpless she felt, waiting and watching. If she was going to keep her mind intact, she needed to find some way to occupy herself.

As they did every day, Cedar and Rathka wandered around the village. The sky was empty of clouds, and though it was bitterly cold, the sun was welcome. Cedar asked every orc she came upon if they could use her help for something, but most of them were too surprised to give her a straight answer, and some gave her dirty looks, aimed carefully at the ground.

There may be a few humans in the village, but a new one, a strange one, was clearly not trusted.

The only orc who entertained her was the leatherworker who had given her the faun's pelt. He had been brought a fresh kill, a massive bear, and wanted to save and use the hide.

Rathka strongly disapproved of Cedar stepping in to learn

the work, saying it was below even the lord's concubine, but Cedar ignored her and listened to what the old orc had to teach her. It was disgusting, truly. Perhaps that was why she ended up enjoying it so much. She couldn't think of anything else but the tear of the flesh away from the hide, the stench or the endless scraping. It occupied her fully, and when the day was through, her arms were sore and the leatherworker was pleased she would come back.

"You smell foul," Rathka had said as they ate their dinners. "We ought to visit the bath tent."

After Cedar had some time to digest, they walked to the baths at the other end of the camp. Cedar came here as often as she could, but they glared at her if it was too frequently. This time, the tent was empty, and she and Rathka each filled a tub with hot water from the fire.

Kiya stuck up his nose at the sight of the tubs and sat irritably in the corner, as if he feared one of them trying to pull him in.

As they undressed, Cedar saw Rathka had some scars of her own. The orc woman noticed Cedar taking inventory and her eyebrows rose.

"I was going to be a warrior," Rathka said as she sank into the hot water. Cedar tested it with her leg first, then submerged herself in the next tub. "I trained. But my leg isn't good, and I was denied when I came of age."

Perhaps that explained some of her bitterness.

"I'm sorry," Cedar said. Rathka did always seem rather restless. "Could you have trained other warriors instead?"

Rathka looked at her like she'd sprouted antlers. "Only a seasoned warrior trains younger warriors. Don't be ridiculous."

The orc slipped under the surface of the water to wet her hair, and Cedar followed her example. Then Cedar soaped her body, but as her hands grazed over her nipples, she instantly thought of Kargorr, and her muscles went tense.

That old question came back to her, again and again. Did he still plan to take more concubines? Had anything really changed between them if he could leave without saying goodbye?

The silence drew out as Cedar was lost in her thoughts.

"You grew too attached."

Rathka's soft words startled her. Cedar glanced up from where she'd been staring into the dirty water.

"You think he cares for you, don't you?" Rathka went on. There was no judgment in her tone. It was mostly sympathy.

Cedar couldn't trust herself to speak. In truth, she did think that. Kargorr had led her to believe it. She hadn't imagined the night before he left, and it had all been plain to her then how he felt.

Right?

Finally, Cedar decided to set her foot in the sand. To carve out a space for herself. To insist that she had one.

"He does care for me," Cedar said matter-of-factly. She didn't follow it up, because she had no need to explain herself to someone like Rathka.

"Hmm." The orc woman washed her hair thoughtfully. "But has he taken you as his *yapira*? No. He would have, if he cared for you the way you think he does."

It was true that he'd made no commitments to her. As far as they were concerned, Cedar was nothing more than a concubine to be sown. But perhaps humans couldn't be *yapira*s, and he wanted her anyway. Could that be enough?

Cedar didn't want to argue about it with Rathka. The old woman could believe what she wanted, but only Cedar knew what had transpired between them, and that was what mattered.

So she remained silent, and Rathka appeared to understand the message. They both bathed in the quiet, no sound but an owl hooting beyond the leather walls. Soon the water grew cold and Cedar stepped out, pulling down one of the furs left out for drying to wrap herself up.

Rathka still did not emerge from the water. Her eyes were closed, and her head was leaned back on the edge of the tub, as if she was asleep.

"He has not taken you as his *yapira* because he plans to have others." She turned her head slightly toward Cedar and opened one eye. "Surely you know that by now."

The words pierced deep. Cedar was already soft, already vulnerable, and Rathka had found the perfect dagger to slide into her chest.

You are mine. You will always be mine. Kargorr had clearly staked his claim on her, but that didn't mean he belonged to her in return. He had said this was the beginning—could he have meant she was simply the first?

"The tent," Rathka said. "It's much bigger than his previous one, is it not?"

Cedar froze as she hovered over her pile of clothes.

The tent was bigger. Much, much bigger. One whole side remained empty, which Cedar had simply assumed was for the baby. Or perhaps Lord Kargorr's spoils.

Did he really intend to share that space with another concubine?

"You are carrying his orcling," Rathka went on, and Cedar wished more than anything the old orc woman would stop, but she didn't have the voice. "So you serve no further purpose for the next year. Lord Kargorr will want many orclings. When he returns with his next concubine, she will take your place." Rathka closed her one eye and turned back to the ceiling, exhaling with relaxation. "You will be relegated to the bed in the back."

Cedar's chest burned. Her throat closed, so her breaths

came fast and shallow. She struggled to put on her clothes, her hands trembling as she tried to slip on her pants and tunic.

Rathka was wrong. She had to be wrong.

But that had always been Kargorr's plan. She knew his ambitions, how he sought to create an empire. What made Cedar think that would change now?

24

KARGORR

His muscles swelled with blood as he swung his axe. Another man fell, and the sound of screaming all around him filled his veins with fire.

Cedar had taken to his seed so quickly that his warriors now spoke often of finding their own human concubines, so Kargorr resisted his instinct to finish the job whenever he came upon a young man or woman. The band had horses now, and many wooden wagons, so they could bring as many prisoners back with them as they chose.

Lord Kargorr gave every youthful body a cursory look, but no one spoke to him. No one stirred him. His *sarga* knew who his true mate was and wanted nothing but to return to her.

This was their third outpost. Soon, he thought, they would be ready to move on the settlement.

He had been gone for nearly two weeks now, and the ache for his *yapira* was undeniably powerful. Whenever he thought of their orcling, nothing more than a tiny pebble inside her, he longed to call off the rest of their quest and return home.

No. He would have his way with Cedar when he returned, but for now, he had something to prove.

When everyone was dead save for two human women, who his warriors had chosen for themselves, the *grrosek* took what they could and loaded it up into the new wagons. Kargorr left the farm animals, having plenty of supplies already, and then they burned the village to the ground to the tune of the women's sobs.

Odd, he thought, that his Cedar had never cried. But that was why his *sarga* had chosen her. He had known from the first moment he smelled her who she was.

After two more days' ride, they reached the settlement. From scout reports, they would have to ride through a significant amount of farmland before reaching more densely populated areas. But Kargorr's force was significant, as he'd brought almost every single capable warrior with him, hoping that the *parog* could fend for itself.

That night, he held a long discussion with Orgha as to the best path inward.

"Make them think we are larger than we are," Orgha said. "Split into groups and approach from multiple directions. Let them believe they're surrounded. Leave fire everywhere we go to confuse them."

This was why Kargorr had chosen this orc to be his right hand, after all.

With a swift nod, Lord Kargorr agreed. They gave out troop assignments, and two of their number would remain behind to guard the women and supplies.

They waited until night had fully fallen before creeping out from the trees. Kargorr had not yet sent Liga home—he wanted his best warrior, the cat's huge jaws, to help him on this mission. They had never attempted an attack as bold as this. And though he knew the humans didn't stand a chance, he still didn't want to lose a warrior when he didn't have to. Not when they had family waiting at home for them.

Not a concern he'd particularly cared about before, he thought. It was an odd thing, a new thing, to worry about going back alive.

They raced silently toward the village, mounted on their cats to muffle the sound of their footsteps. Kargorr lit his torch, then held it out as they passed fields of wheat, letting the flame touch everything it could. Smoke rose into the air elsewhere outside the settlement, where his second troop was spreading the flames.

Two guard posts sat at the edge of the settlement, and already men were shouting up in the tower. But it was too late. Kargorr and his warriors streamed past amid arrows falling. He circled the guard post, trailing his torch along the walls, as Liga snarled at the volley dropping from above them. His cat was too fast to be caught by human arrows.

Men screamed as the fire spread. Kargorr spun and followed his warriors into the settlement, where people had fled their homes. He cut and sliced, rent and tore, leaving a trail of bodies in his wake. His blood sang, his muscles swelled, his veins pulsed.

He heard one of his warriors roar a few houses away, and he quickly urged Liga to follow the sound. A band of humans had gotten one of Kargorr's number alone, and he was run through with a sword, his cat snarling and hissing as the humans backed it up against a wall.

With a powerful shout, Kargorr ran at them from behind, sweeping with his axe to take off a head, swinging down to remove an arm. When the humans had all been summarily executed, Kargorr swung off Liga's back and went to kneel by his comrade, who was bleeding out on the ground. He exchanged a nod with the other orc, who tapped his chest with his hand one time. Then Kargorr ran his axe through his comrade's head to end his suffering.

Once his warrior was dead, he mounted up and continued his path, holding his torch high over his head to catch fire to the thatch roofs.

It was a long and bloody night, and Lord Kargorr had never felt his purpose so clearly laid out in front of him. Someday, he would come here with his *yapira*. It would no longer be a *parog* of tents, but a whole city as their number grew and other *parog* came to join them.

Kargorr howled his victory as he speared a fleeing man through the chest, and his warriors howled back, scattered as they were. Soon, the sun began to rise, and the settlement fell quiet again save for some whimpers as one of his warriors dragged back a human man, ashy from the flames.

He nodded at Kargorr. "My conquest," he said, and the warriors all tapped their chests.

As they strode out of the ruined settlement, smoke drifting into the orange morning, Orgha stopped next to him. "No one for you?"

Kargorr arched an eyebrow. He doubted the question Orgha asked was the one he really meant.

"None that caught my interest," Kargorr finally said.

"Hmm." Orgha knew better than to pry more, but Kargorr had a feeling his right hand had already seen through him.

CEDAR

When Liga returned, hope swelled in Cedar's chest that Kargorr might finally be on his way home. The enormous cat was surprisingly pleased, so much that she rubbed her nose up and down Cedar's chest. She hoped it meant Kargorr was all right.

It had been nearly three weeks now, and though it worried Cedar that they hadn't received word from the raiding party, Rathka rolled her eyes and said, "They'll return when they return, and no sooner."

The silence was most deafening at night. In it, Cedar could hear every beat of her heart, a single drum thumping, while something inside her told her that Kargorr's bigger, heavier, slower one should be beating right next to it.

She helped the leatherworker as often as she could to keep her mind off of Rathka's words and had quickly become his valued helper. He allowed her to toil away on her bear when she had done some of the drearier work, and as she hollowed out and cleaned each part of it, she thought of that heavily beating heart.

Now, Rathka would leave Cedar there alone to attend to her own matters, seemingly unconcerned that Cedar might try to run. And never did anyone look askance at the human woman in their midst as she left for the evening and walked back to Lord Kargorr's tent alone.

It would be so easy. No one would give Cedar a second look if she headed toward the edge of the camp and walked out into the snow.

The huge tent loomed even larger around her, now that she knew what it was for. The emptiness made her ache, and so did the specter of another bed filling that space.

If Cedar had to watch Kargorr take another woman, she would claw both their eyes out. She knew it as surely as she knew her own name.

But he wouldn't. Things had changed since he built this tent. Hadn't they?

Cedar slept less and less, sometimes lying awake for hours

as she stared up at the gap in the ceiling, where she could just barely make out stars. Now, instead of eating too much, she ate too little. Rathka would put more food in front of her, but to Cedar, it all tasted like nothing.

"You have to feed yourself as well as your orcling," Rathka would say, pushing the bowl closer again, and Cedar would eat enough that she was left alone.

Late one evening, while Cedar lay in bed with the fire dying in the pit, a horn blasted. The sound pierced air like a knife.

She covered her ears, wondering what could have happened. Were they being attacked?

Kiya pinned his ears back as she passed him and peered out the tent door. Now she heard... cheering? Orcs streamed out of their tents, down the pathways toward the gathering area. Another horn sounded, and she heard a familiar roar of victory.

Lord Kargorr had returned.

Her body lit up like a flame. He was alive. He'd come back to her.

Cedar ran along behind the other orcs, trying to get ahead of them so she could see him first. Horses were assembled at the entrance to the camp, orcs mounted on them, blood covering their bodies. They pulled wagons full of goods. At the center rode Kargorr.

Her orc. Her monster. Half of his face was brown with dry blood, bisecting it once again. His tusks curled cruelly up over his lip. Her single beating heart jumped, sensing his was nearby.

And then she heard the sobbing.

She knew that sound. Women. Cedar's eyes searched until she found them: two human women and one human man, being led out of the wooden cart where they were held.

Horror descended on her. Rathka was right.

The flame went out like ice water had been poured on it. Kargorr *had* brought home new concubines. He planned to replace her with these meek, sobbing women. To spread his seed, like he had once promised her.

Cedar stopped where she was, and then backed away as other orcs passed her.

She was nothing, after all. Just a warm body to be used and thrown away, as she'd always known she was.

How could Cedar have been so foolish to think anything else?

Her arms wrapped around her middle as she turned and bolted back to the tent. She had to be fast. She would get her baby out of this place, far away from him. Cedar would never, ever watch as he took another woman. She would never lie there and listen.

Her chest was impossibly tight as she snatched her cloak and boots, shoving them on as fast as she could. This was her only chance, while everyone was distracted. Kiya circled her, clearly concerned at her sudden frantic packing. She threw some food from the table into a bag and turned to leave. Kiya followed her, as he always did.

She couldn't bring him with her. She couldn't feed him if she could barely feed herself. Who knew how long it would take for her to find a human settlement?

Taking his leash, she tied him to the post, kissed his forehead, and then fled the tent.

She wouldn't let Kargorr do this to her. She would rather die.

Cedar walked the opposite direction of the gathering at a normal pace, trying not to attract attention to herself. But everyone was enraptured with the new arrivals, so she burst into a sprint, running past tent after tent. The cheers and cries of other orcs rose into the air as the party was welcomed home.

She felt sick to her stomach, like bile was already burning its way up her throat.

Finally, Cedar was out in the snow, running away from the light of the torches mounted around the camp. It was a dark night, but the stars glittered brightly, lighting her way. She had held in the heaving misery until now, until she finally reached the woods, and then it crashed over her.

Cedar sobbed into a tree trunk, pausing just long enough to get her breath back. He cared nothing for her and their child.

Then she stilled her tears, knowing she needed to put as much distance as she could between herself and the camp. She remembered how Kargorr had threatened her with the whip, and knew that if she was caught, she would be lashed while his new concubines watched.

So Cedar ran, summoning all the buried strength in her legs, into the woods. She didn't know what lay ahead there, but it was better than what lay behind her.

25

KARGORR

Where was she?

How he hungered for his Cedar. He had pushed his warriors hard to return to the *parog* so he could claim her again, finally. He had even brought her a gift, an offering, as only mated orcs did.

He couldn't avoid it, not any longer. He had to have her.

Kargorr dismounted his horse, the big, stupid creature, and handed the reins off to whoever happened to be standing nearby. The *grrosek* parted for him as he stalked through the crowd, searching for her, sniffing the air just to catch her smell. His *sarga* throbbed thinking about her, imagining how warm and soft and tight she would be, relishing how she would taste, how her eyelashes would flutter as he held her, how she would curl up close to him as she slept. He needed to find her, now.

When he didn't see her among his *parog*, who all tapped their chests as he passed, his throat tightened. Ravenous, he barreled toward their tent. Surely she hadn't slept through this.

Unease rose in his belly as he reached the door and snatched it open. He expected to see her inside, perhaps naked on the furs—oh, that would be ideal—but instead, the tent was empty. Empty save for her cat, who was tied up, whimpering and whining.

Kargorr stared at her beloved pet. Where had Cedar gone without Kiya? Why would she have left him tied up?

The realization hit him like a sword through the chest.

She had *run*.

The swell of rage that overtook him was unlike anything he'd felt before. Never, even in the heat of battle, had he experienced such blistering fury.

His *yapira* had run from him. Carrying his orcling. She intended to abandon him, forever.

The shout that erupted from him shook the ground, and Kiya hunched into the corner of the tent. Kargorr nearly took the place down as he searched for an article of her clothing, finding one scattered across the furs. Clutching the garment tight, he stormed out. His eyes darted left to right as he considered which way she had gone.

How could she do this to him, after all the battles he'd fought to come home to her? How could she leave him after what he'd shared with her?

He thought of the orcling they'd created growing up without him, and he was nearly blinded by rage as he charged into the snow. He howled, "Liga!" and his cat came running, thrilled to see him again. Grabbing her scruff in his hand, he leapt onto her back and leaned down to whisper in her ear.

"Find her," he growled. "Find her for me, Liga." He held out the clothing so she could smell it, then tucked it away while she sniffed the air. Liga paused, ears flicking forward, and then all at once she sprang into motion.

It was as if Liga could sense Kargorr's urgency the way she flew through the snow, one huge bound after another. She dove into the trees, weaving between trunks, following her nose.

Kargorr's arms swelled with his fury, and he gripped Liga's mane even tighter. His *yapira* was leaving him, taking their offspring with her. He had given her his *sarga*, and she dared run from him?

He ground his teeth together, his vision clouded. He was glad for Liga's eyes as she made her way deeper into the woods, because all he could see was her betrayal.

Liga snarled, and up ahead, Kargorr made out a shape with dark hair sprinting through the snow.

Cedar.

He roared as he jumped from Liga's back, landing in the snow behind her. She spun around, her cloak flying, and her eyes went huge when she saw him. For a moment, their gazes locked, and the whites of her eyes were shot through with red.

Then she turned and ran off again, even faster.

All of Kargorr's predator instincts took over as he watched his woman flee into the branches. Running from *him*. A wordless shout ripped itself from his throat as he took one step for every three of hers, easily gaining on her. When he was close enough, he threw himself at her, tackling her to the ground.

Cedar cried out as they both landed in the snow. Kargorr was on his feet instantly. He seized her by the wrists and hauled her up into the air, trapping her arms at her sides like she was little more than a toy. Her face was flushed bright red, and tears had frozen on her cheeks.

"You run from me?" he snarled, jerking her closer to his face. Her huge, brown eyes were wild as he stared into them, his vision narrowing to the single point of her face. "You would steal my orcling from me?!"

Her fear gave way to her own fury. Like she had done so long ago, Cedar spat on him.

"And *you* would replace me!" she snapped back, wriggling to get free of his iron hands. "You would throw me away!"

If his anger had been aflame before, it now erupted into a forest fire. He slammed her against a tree, and she gagged as the air was knocked from her lungs.

"I would never," he hissed between closed teeth, "*never* throw you away. Not like you have me."

It was the most acute sting he'd ever felt, to find his tent empty and his true mate gone. His hands tightened around her arms, and she whimpered when his claws bit into her flesh. But he was too deep in his blood fury to notice how he hurt her.

His body had ached for her while he was gone, his chest empty and hollow. Now the thrill and pleasure he'd felt at returning to her had dried up into sand, and all that was left was his despair and rage.

Before Cedar could answer, Kargorr smashed his lips to hers, crushing them, forcing her mouth open so he could wind his way inside. Her tongue fought with his, but he easily overpowered her. All his fire boiled up and over until he had not one of his senses left.

He had to punish her, his *yapira*, who had so brutally maimed him—far worse than the scar across his face. So he conquered her mouth as he reached under her cloak, finding her round breasts with one hand while the other kept her pinned. She writhed, whimpering as she tried to push him away. But Lord Kargorr only snarled, no longer capable of words.

He had become the manifestation of wrath itself, an animal driven by its instinct to hunt, to devour, and to claim.

CEDAR

He was a demon. A beast.

A monster.

When Lord Kargorr pulled away from his bruising, demanding kiss, there was nothing left in his black eyes—they were empty save for the red that glowed around the edges. This was surely how his victims saw him, covered in dried blood, his face contorted in his thirst for the kill.

Cedar's tunic split open with an audible *rip* as his claws tore it from her body. The bitter, icy wind hit her bare skin, and she tried to cover herself, but he had both of her wrists clutched tight in his one huge hand. His chest heaved, and the air filled with steam from his breath as he traced her breast. Then he slid further down, snapping the laces of her pants, and Cedar's pulse sped up. He was truly terrifying, and how she could ever have thought he cared for her...

She was a fool.

When Cedar was at last exposed to him, the bitter chill whipping over her skin, she gave up fighting. There was nothing she could do to escape him, not now. She had left her dagger behind—another stupid mistake.

He had told her to always keep it with her. She wondered if it was because he thought she might need to use it on *him*.

Lord Kargorr snarled as he yanked down the front of his breeches, and that huge, familiar dark green cock of his emerged. Cedar had tried to hold in her fear, but now she sobbed knowing what he planned to do with it.

"You are *mine*," he thundered, his voice shaking her bones. "Only mine. Forever."

All she could do was nod in understanding as her limbs fell limp. Cedar would never be free again.

Keeping her arms above her head, Kargorr hooked his hand under her ass and lifted her off the ground. Her body cried for his, but her heart was quiet. He lined himself up, and she closed her eyes as the head of his cock made its way inside her.

Her mind rebelled at how good he felt, how she grew slick and wet for him as he finally buried himself inside her. A moan escaped her lips as he reeled his hips back, then plunged into her again. And again.

She moved like a doll as he took her, owning her, claiming her over and over. Those lumps at the base of his cock pressed harder and harder against her opening, and she cried out as she started to give way to them.

"Never forget," he said as he thrust in again, deeper. "Never forget who you belong to. My *yapira*."

The word startled her. Had she heard him right? His *yapira*?

His cock dragged along the sensitive lining of her channel, the pleasure she fought winding higher and higher. Tears slipped free from her eyes at how her body betrayed her, how it sought the rest of his cock to fit inside her.

And then it did. The bulges on his shaft slipped through, spreading her as wide as she could go, and her tears flowed even more freely as her peak took her. It catapulted her into the flames, and then dragged her back out again, right into ice water. He fucked her harder, those lumps slicking in and out while her pussy clenched down around him. Kargorr groaned, his black eyes burrowing into her.

"My *yapira*," he muttered, over and over, until he began to swell. Cedar felt as if her body might simply squeeze down to a dot and then vanish.

Kargorr roared one last time as he jettisoned everything inside her, and she felt the hot rush of his seed filling her. The swollen bulbs at the base of his cock had lodged in her again, and to her horror, she felt his huge heart beating next to hers.

They were reunited now. She was forever tied to a creature of pain, destruction, and death.

When at last Kargorr was finished with her, Cedar fell to her knees in the snow and wept.

KARGORR

He shook his head again, trying to clear the red haze that had taken over. He could hear Cedar crying, and he longed for nothing more than to stop it.

But he had done it. He was the reason she kneeled helpless on the ground before him, her gentle sniffles filling the night air.

He pulled up his pants, then reached down and lifted her out of the snow, fully naked. She didn't object, simply shivered in his arms as he brought her in close to his chest. She stayed with her head turned away from him, her eyes focused on nothing. He bent to snatch up her cloak and lay it across her in his arms, hoping to stave off the frigid chill.

Her clothing was in ruins. There was no hope for them, so he left them there, like a grave marker. The place where he had reclaimed what was his; the place where any innocence left between them had died.

Cedar didn't speak as he carried her back on foot, Liga following at a safe distance behind. When Kargorr entered the camp, the other *grrosek* turned to stare. Perhaps it was obvious what had happened; perhaps his authority would be questioned for not keeping his woman on a leash. But he would not have his *yapira* whipped, so he ignored them until he reached their tent, and then stepped inside.

Kiya growled as Kargorr passed. Perhaps the cat didn't recognize him anymore. He laid Cedar on the furs, and she remained where he put her. Kargorr untied Kiya, then returned to the bed, where his *yapira* still had not moved. Tears slid over her nose, dripping down to the blankets, but she made no sound as he lay beside her.

He combed back through his memory, trying to remember anything outside the fog of his rage. Why had she done this? Why now?

You would replace me! You would throw me away!

Kargorr dropped a hand to her side, simply seeking her warmth. She flinched, but didn't move. She was shivering, he realized, so he pulled over an extra fur and covered her with it.

"Why did you run?" he asked at length.

There came no answer, but he waited anyway.

It could have been minutes or a whole hour later when Cedar finally answered.

"The women." She closed her eyes. "More concubines. More... *orclings*." She spit the word, and curled away from him, wrapping her arms tight around herself.

Kargorr tried to think what she meant. What women? What concubines? There was no one but her.

At last, he remembered: the humans the party had brought back with them from their conquest, with their loud and pitiful crying.

It all unraveled in front of him. The moment he understood was like a blow to the side of his head.

Cedar *had* waited for him. Not only was she loyal, but she was jealous, too. There was only one reason why she had left his side, why she had fled tonight of all nights, at this moment of all moments.

The truth settled in, ugly and dark in Kargorr's belly, of what he'd done to his *yapira*. She was his only. The one he had been destined for. The woman who carried his orcling, who had moaned so sweetly under him when he pleasured her, who ate too much and had once thought about killing him with a dagger in the night.

Kargorr had hurt her. He had hurt her in a way no *grrosek* should ever hurt his chosen one.

"No, little deer," he said quietly. "It is only you."

Kargorr wrapped his arms around her, trying to bring her in close—but she was as stiff as a stone, and he hoped against all hope that he hadn't broken her.

26

CEDAR

His *yapira*. That's what he had called her.

Rathka had led Cedar to believe this meant something. That it was a special bond, a sacred bond.

Just words, Cedar thought. They were all just words.

In the morning, she awoke to the strange sensation of warm arms locked around her, keeping her rooted to the bed.

"It's early, little deer," she heard Kargorr's voice say when she moved away. She had forgotten what he sounded like while he was gone, but the familiarity of it washed over her like a warm blanket—which quickly turned cold. It was a very different voice from last night, when he had roared like a bear driven to madness. "Get some more sleep."

But Cedar had become an early riser in his absence, and she found she couldn't bear being so close to him. It made her heart squeeze tight, like a curled fist, protecting itself. She tried to worm away, but he held her fast.

"Don't go yet," he murmured, lowering his face to her hair.

So she lay there, quite still. As much as her body longed to mold into his, to take him inside her now that he was here again... she could also feel the scratches on her back where he'd pushed her naked body against the tree trunk, and her soul hardened.

At last, Lord Kargorr let out a sigh and released her, sitting up with his thick legs hanging off the bed. She crawled out, put on her clothes, and patted Kiya on the head. It was time for his breakfast.

Usually Rathka would be waiting outside the tent, but Cedar had a feeling that this morning, she wouldn't be.

Kargorr remained sitting, watching her with unreadable eyes. She wondered if perhaps she wouldn't be allowed to leave the tent anymore. Perhaps he intended to fulfill the promise he made her once upon a time.

"Are you going to whip me?" Cedar finally asked.

Kargorr's head jerked up when she spoke, and his eyebrows rose, lips parting around his thick tusks.

"Whip you?" he repeated. He searched her face for a long moment, the silence building louder and louder between them, until he lowered his eyes and shook his head. "No, I will not whip you."

Her shoulders relaxed, and she thought that at least she had that much. She wouldn't be marked on the outside to match the fresh scars she bore on the inside.

Kargorr's lips were anchored in a hard frown as she pulled her cloak tighter around herself.

"Can I go and get breakfast?" she asked, trying to determine whether she was a prisoner again or not.

His dark eyes studied her, and then he rose to his feet in a slow, heavy motion that made him look like he was made of stone.

"I will."

Cedar's whole body slumped. She should have expected it. She *did* expect it. But the misery that came upon her at the idea of being trapped here again, unable to leave the tent with only Rathka for company...

"Come," he said, and she realized Kargorr was now standing right in front of her. Cedar tilted her head back to look up at him, and he took her chin in his hand. "We will walk there together."

It looked like he might try to kiss her, but then he hesitated. When she gave a faint nod, he let her go and stepped out of the tent.

Cedar followed behind him, Kiya at her side. Usually the cat strayed away, sniffing things as they went, but today he remained close to her with his eyes pinned on Kargorr, a curl in his lip.

Other orcs greeted Lord Kargorr as they passed, always keeping their gazes down, tapping their chests and nodding with respect. There were many smiles as families had reunited the night before, and the good mood floating around the camp made Cedar want to disappear.

Once they secured food and the cook handed over some raw meat for Kiya, they made their way back to the tent and ate together in silence. Cedar only finished about a third of her portion before pushing it away.

Kargorr looked down at the mostly full bowl, and then up at her face.

"You must eat more than that," he said, sliding it back toward her. "You are thinner now. It's not good for the orcling."

She clenched her teeth together, lips pursed.

That's all she was to him. A body. A host for his offspring.

Cedar took the bowl back, and shoulders tight to her neck, she forced the rest of the food down.

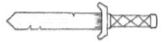

KARGORR

He had hoped that mentioning their orcling would bring out Cedar's maternal instinct. Surely, if she didn't care for him, or herself, she would care about their young. She would take care of her body in order to ensure its survival.

Instead, Cedar had hardened even further, like an animal retreating into its den to hide.

Kargorr had matters to see to, but he was reluctant to leave his *yapira* without at least bandaging the wound between them. But leading the *parog*, and the success of his mission, was paramount.

After Cedar had forced down the rest of her breakfast, she sat there quietly, not speaking. Kargorr leaned out of the tent and called someone over to fetch Rathka so his *yapira* would not be alone. When the old orc woman arrived, she simply nodded to Kargorr in deference, without a shard of obstinance on her.

Cedar did look up as Rathka arrived, and her eyes narrowed. She seemed even more wary now, more closed off, so Kargorr leaned down to whisper in her ear.

"She's only here to be your friend, little deer," he murmured. When she gave no response, he sighed into her hair and left.

The new concubines still cried, his warriors told him as they began the long process of unloading goods and dividing them up. He had no advice for them, because his *yapira* had never been such a weak thing.

A stash was made for further gifts to neighboring *parog*, and everyone was thrilled at the prospect of so much fresh meat and produce. Some of it had gone bad on their journey, but most survived thanks to the cold, and the cooks were thrilled to have new ingredients to work with.

Orgha found him that afternoon, out in the sparring field, dueling a pair of younger orcs at the same time. Kargorr couldn't bring himself to return to his tent, not yet. He hoped that perhaps Cedar's anger would fade if she was given time and space.

But what she felt toward him now, was it really anger? Or something worse?

Kargorr was sweating as he tossed away his weapon and walked to greet his right hand. Orgha tapped his chest.

"There are rumors that your concubine ran in the night," Orgha said quietly as they began to walk.

It was inevitable. The right thing to do, the correct thing to do to maintain order and reinforce his authority, would be to punish her—publicly.

But then he would never, ever have her back.

"She is my *yapira*," Kargorr hissed. "You will address her as such in private."

Orgha's eyes widened, but then he nodded in understanding. "I thought so. And you used your *sarga*?"

Kargorr didn't need to speak it. He had bonded to her in every way. Now he just had to find some way to repair that bond.

A drawn-out sigh fell from Orgha's lips. "And your mission?" he asked in a pointed tone.

"We will keep it between us for now," Kargorr commanded. "Until the time is right." He narrowed his eyes. "Do not tell Rathka."

Orgha shrugged. "I would not be surprised if she already knows."

With a grunt of dissatisfaction, Kargorr led them both away from the training field and toward the serving tent. He would find something good for Cedar to eat, perhaps request a food he knew she liked. Syrup-encrusted pork, maybe, as long as he assured her it wasn't her beloved pig.

"Why did she run?" Orgha finally asked, keeping his voice low so others couldn't overhear.

Kargorr tensed. While he often treated Orgha like they were on equal footing in their partnership, in truth, Kargorr still had to maintain his right hand's respect. His authority was important.

But Orgha would also see right through him if he lied.

"She believed I had brought back other women to take as my concubines." Kargorr's teeth ground together. If only she had simply asked him. But if she felt the bond as strongly as he did, perhaps the fear of it breaking had been too much for such a small creature to bear. "I found her fleeing into the woods."

Orgha sucked in a tight breath. For a concubine, the penalty of running should be enormous.

"And did she come back willingly?" Orgha asked.

Kargorr set his jaw. "No."

The word hung in the air. For once, Kargorr rued his blood rage, the very thing that kept him alive, that granted him the strength to fell his enemies. It had led him so far astray that the damage might never be undone.

After a time, Orgha nodded with understanding. "It will take time to heal," he said. "Rathka and I have fought many times, but still she remains at my side."

But this was no argument, what had happened between Kargorr and Cedar.

"You have not hurt her as I have hurt my *yapira*," Lord Kargorr said, grinding out each word. "I do not know if it can be fixed."

They approached the serving tent, and Orgha stopped to study him.

"Don't underestimate the power of the soul bond," he

said. "Do whatever you can to bring her back to you, or the gnawing in your belly will only get worse. You may have to... make some concessions."

Kargorr growled at what he was asking. "I will not claim her in front of the *parog*. Not yet. There is too much left to do."

Orgha simply shrugged. "I wish you luck in your quest, then." And with that, the older orc left him standing there to retrieve his servings of roast beef.

That was not a concession Lord Kargorr could make. But what would it cost him if he didn't?

Then he remembered. He'd returned to the *parog* with a trophy from his conquest, one which he'd intended to give to Cedar last night. It wouldn't fix what he'd done, but perhaps it could form the first step of a bridge over the chasm between them.

CEDAR

Rathka was quiet as she sat down at the table where Cedar remained with her empty bowl in front of her.

"That's good," the orc woman said gently, piling up the dishes on a tray. "I'm glad you ate."

Cedar had been forced, but she didn't say it aloud.

"Has the *kazek*'s return improved your mood?" Rathka asked, with a hint of good-natured mockery. Usually, Cedar would fire a barb back at her, but she found she didn't care to tell the old woman anything.

After minutes of silence passed, Rathka suggested they go for a walk to return the dishes, and Cedar nodded without answering. She rose to her feet and put Kiya, who was already much bigger than even the biggest dog, on a leash. How long would it be until the cat was no longer allowed in their tent and would have to sleep in the snow with the others?

Then she would truly be alone.

They strolled without speaking. Cedar watched orcs busying about, sorting through the spoils of the raid and delighting in what had been brought back. Without asking, Rathka stopped them in front of the leatherworker's tent and gave Cedar an apprehensive look.

Perhaps the familiar stench of the workshop and the steady, mindless scraping of leather would be a good distraction. Cedar wondered if, now that Kargorr had returned, she would be allowed to continue her work here.

She stepped inside, and the old leatherworker, Carn, turned to greet her. There were piles of new furs littered about, and the smell of carcasses almost overwhelmed her. Cedar had become sensitive to many smells, and things that used to please her now made her stomach churn, but the odor of death here made her feel strangely grounded. It was familiar, and that was all she wanted right now.

Carn must have noted her mood because he didn't speak to her further, gesturing instead to where he'd already skinned a cow and had the raw hide stretched out. She began the work of preparing it, and it came as second nature by now. She lost herself in the monotony of the task, in the steady movement of her hands as she scraped and applied the foul-smelling mixture and scraped some more.

She had learned all the words she needed to get by in the leatherworker's shop and picked up new ones every day, listening while she worked as he conversed with other orcs. Perhaps Cedar couldn't speak more than a few words of their language, but she could understand much of what went on around her now.

After a few hours, Kiya came and insistently buried his claws in her shin, reminding her that he had needs.

"I'll come back soon to help with all of this," Cedar said, gesturing at the work that lay ahead of them.

"Only if you wish it," Carn said. "I can handle it alone."

He probably thought he was doing her a favor. Perhaps it was just a sign of his deference now that Lord Kargorr had returned. But knowing she wasn't needed made Cedar wither. She liked helping here because she could feel useful, and Carn always appreciated her contribution. But now he was making it clear that he was merely humoring her. So she withdrew, leaving wordlessly with Kiya.

Rathka waited outside, and they walked quietly to the edge of the camp, where Cedar unclipped Kiya's leash and he went running. She threw snowballs at him the way he liked, and he leapt off the ground, trying to eat them out of the air. He only ever ended up with snow all over his face, but that was part of the game.

A few times, Rathka opened her mouth as if to chide Cedar for something, but then she would close it again and look out over the land, instead. Cedar wondered how much the old orc knew.

Soon, the sun had drifted low and it was time for dinner. When Cedar rose to her feet, Rathka caught her elbow.

"What is wrong with you?" Rathka asked, her brows drawn together. "You haven't said a word all day, and usually I can't make you shut up."

Cedar jerked out of Rathka's grip. "It has nothing to do with you," she snapped, surprised even at herself and how sharp her voice came out.

The orc woman studied her with even more interest. "You did run away last night," Rathka said thoughtfully, more like she was speaking to herself than to Cedar. "That's why Lord Kargorr left." She laughed darkly. "I had assumed you were *occupied* with your *agsan*."

It felt to Cedar like a sharp spike to the heart. That's not who Kargorr was. He would never let her be that person. She knew where she belonged now, and it would never be at his side.

Cedar leaned close to Rathka. "Shut your mouth," she said in a low, quiet voice. "What happens in my tent stays in my tent. It is for me alone to know."

Rathka watched her even more carefully, as if trying to decipher what it was Cedar wouldn't tell her. So Cedar schooled her face into a mask of neutrality and called on Kiya to return to her. He'd gotten so big now that he nearly bowled her over. Cedar still ended up stumbling backward, almost falling over until someone caught her.

"He's going to be a big cat someday," she heard Orgha say. Cedar righted herself quickly and put space between them, remembering how those same hands had once grabbed her as she fled for the woods and dragged her back, sentencing her to this fate. "Perhaps he will be bigger than Liga."

"Sorry," Cedar said. "He doesn't know his own strength yet."

Orgha's eyes connected with hers, and though they were just as pitch black as Lord Kargorr's, there was a smattering of concern in them.

"A common occurrence when gifted with great power," Orgha said carefully. "To not have full control over it. It can lead to many mistakes."

So he knew. She was merely a *mistake*. What Kargorr had done to her—a *mistake*.

"Kiya would never truly harm me," she said, reaching for the cat's head to pet him, to try to cool her blood. "Humans—and orcs—can harm in a way Kiya couldn't dream of."

But all Orgha did was nod, and then he passed her, stopping in front of Rathka. His fingers tangled in his *yapira*'s silver hair, then he drew it to his nose and sniffed it, his body relaxing as he brought in her smell. It was obvious when

Rathka felt it, too, because her stiff shoulders softened and she leaned into him, probably without realizing it.

Cedar's resentment froze into ice in her chest. She snapped on Kiya's leash and turned away, leading him back to the tent, with or without Rathka.

27

KARGORR

Perhaps for the first time in his life, Lord Kargorr was nervous.

If he had learned anything about Cedar in his time with her, it was that she'd never been allowed to have things that children should have. She worked instead of playing and slept on a hard floor with all of her siblings. Since she'd begun living in his tent, Kargorr had seen how she loved the luxury of the furs. But it was *grrosek* tradition to pile a bed high with wolf and bear and fox. He knew after enough raids of human homes that this was not how humans did things.

He carried his gift rolled up under his arm, back to his tent as darkness fell over the camp. He found he liked how much later the sun set down in the lowlands, and during the winter, it would grant them even more time to work. And there was much work to be done for the next stage of his plan.

Once again he would send Orgha away, this time with a different missive: *come and join me*, it would say. Kargorr also planned to offer gifts to yet another *parog*, one even farther afield, and had to choose another of his warriors to represent him.

Samrak, the half-orc, would be perfect. He was an emblem of what Kargorr sought to create. He had the strength and dedication of an orc, but the agility and eyesight of a human. It made him deadly on the battlefield, skilled with a hammer, and clever with his tongue. He would make a perfect emissary.

Now that the plans had been made, it was time for Kargorr to present his token to his *yapira* and to try to earn her back.

When he slipped inside the tent, he found her on the floor, sewing together Kiya's bed. The cat had outgrown it again, so she must have torn out the stitches to make it bigger. Soon her beloved animal wouldn't be able to sleep in their tent anymore and would have to start integrating into the group that lived outside the camp.

Cedar looked up when Kargorr entered, and for the briefest moment, he thought she looked pleased to see him. Then her eyebrows lowered, and she dropped her head once more to continue her work.

"I brought you something," he said, settling down next to her. Her hands stilled as he set the blanket in his lap. It was a bright color—many colors, woven together—and rather bulky. Kargorr unrolled it so it swept over her knees. She dropped her hands to the fabric, and her eyes went wide.

"What is this?" Cedar asked, sampling it with the pads of her fingers. "Some kind of wool? Or alpaca, maybe?" Her eyes were big and her lips had parted in surprise.

Yes. This was a good gift.

"It's a blanket that will keep you warm," Kargorr said. He took the end and carefully slung it over her shoulders, tucking it neatly under her chin so she was wrapped up in it. She petted it softly, and pulled it even closer, like she was hiding inside it. Kargorr looped his arm around her back, intending to bring her to his side so he could smell her, but she stiffened underneath him.

"It's lovely," she said, clenching the ends of the blanket. "Someone with a lot of craftsmanship made this."

Kargorr nodded slowly. It was certainly finer and more delicate than anything he owned.

Silence passed between them. Kargorr placed his chin atop her head, wrapping his other arm around her, too, but she did not soften to him.

He hated this coldness between them. It wasn't right for an orc to be so detested by his *yapira*. He wondered if he could ever make right what he had done.

CEDAR

It truly was a beautiful blanket, with a swirling pattern Cedar knew must have been difficult to weave. How many hours had someone labored over this blanket? She turned the question over in her mind as she felt along the soft fabric. What was it made of that it was so smooth under her fingertips?

But Kargorr did not know the answer to these questions. Whoever had owned this blanket, whoever had known its story, was gone.

Still, he had brought it back with him from his raid, thinking of her. A tiny spark of warmth flared in her heart, knowing she'd been on his mind while he was away, just as he'd been on hers. But then she thought of last night, how poisoned his return had been, and squeezed the blanket tight in her hands.

"It's time for bed, little deer," Kargorr said to her, smoothing down her hair with one hand. He rose to his feet and peered down at her when she didn't move. She found herself trapped for a moment in time, in a different world where she hadn't run away, where he hadn't chased her in a rage, where everything was as it should be rather than the tangled mess it was now.

He stooped down in front of her, and Cedar couldn't resist looking up into his face. She took in the brutish, jutting jaw that held his big tusks, that strange nose, the pure night of his eyes and the puckered scar that crossed from his temple to his chin... it was all so familiar to her and yet now, completely foreign.

Slowly, Kargorr reached out and slipped one finger into her palm, and it was big enough that he could sweep up all her fingers. He lifted her hand until her knuckles rested on his chest.

Cedar had to look away from his dark eyes as they burrowed into her.

"Please sleep in this bed with me," he said, leaning down to brush his lips over the back of her hand. "You are safe here. I promise you."

Whether or not that was true, Cedar didn't know, but she doubted she had a choice. She got to her feet at last. He carried the blanket to the bed, and when she was settled, he covered her with it. Kargorr removed his clothes, climbed in beside her and drew her into his arms. Cedar wondered if he might try to fuck her, so she held all her muscles tense.

Kargorr let out a heavy breath. "Not tonight, little deer," he said, leaning down to brush his nose over her hair. "Just sleep."

And after a time, wrapped in the soft gift he had brought for her, she did. But now in her dreams, the blood was every-where, swallowing both of them—and they were drowning.

When Cedar awoke, she was surrounded by warmth. The blanket was tugged up to her chin, and big arms were wrapped tight around her, pressing her close to Kargorr's enormous body. There was something long and thick nudging at the space between her thighs, caressing her ass. Instinctively she rolled her hips back against it, and she heard a soft grunt. Lips touched the crown of her head, working their way down to her ear, where she could feel his hot breath.

It was only then, when he rubbed himself against her back and her scratches burned, that Cedar recoiled, remembering what had transpired the night before last. Kargorr's grip on her loosened, letting her move away.

His resigned sigh filled the air, and Cedar cringed, wondering what he might do if she refused his advances. Instead of encroaching on her, though, Kargorr sat up in the furs, his bare chest exposed. She couldn't help the rush of heat that raced down into her belly at his familiar form, at the bulk and size of him. He sniffed the air, and his dark eyes narrowed.

"You want me, little deer," he said quietly as the morning light spilled in through the roof of the tent.

Cedar curled in further on herself, embarrassed by how her own body betrayed her. He moved toward her, and she thought surely he would push her down and pry her legs apart. Instead, he ran one huge hand, with its sharp, black claws, down her arm in a soothing gesture. When she finally turned her head to look at him, she found an unfamiliar expression on his face—something like sadness, perhaps, or regret.

Carefully he traced lower, smoothing over her skin, then the fabric of the tunic she'd worn to bed. She shuddered involuntarily as it crested her hip before sliding back up to her shoulder. He simply petted her that way, deepening his touch with every pass, kneading her with his strong fingers. He moved up to her shoulders, continuing those sure, steady touches, and only barely digging into her flesh. Cedar couldn't help but groan at the sensation of her tight muscles giving to him as he slowly worked them over her back, which faced him still. Once he had finished with her upper body, he spread his exploration of her lower, across the curve of her spine, where he continued his methodical manipulating. She couldn't help sagging into the bed as he unraveled more and more of her tense edges, forcing her body to relax into his touch. When he reached her ass, she didn't feel that same sense of lust radiating off of him that she usually did when he rubbed this part of her body. No, it was with a distanced precision that he continued downward, massaging the hard, strained flesh of her hips. It was a combination of pain and relief as he expanded his reach to her thighs, finding all the places where she didn't even realize her body hurt.

Gently, he put a hand around her belly and encouraged her to roll onto her back, and Cedar reflexively obeyed. Now she could see him as he focused on his work over her clothing, his brows furrowed in concentration as he performed the same motions on her thighs, her calves, her ankles. Her heart beat faster as he trailed his hands up again, and his forehead smoothed as his fingers edged to her thighs, slowing their ascent at the laces of her pants.

His eyes shifted slightly to look at her as he unfastened them, and Cedar remained very still, wondering what he would do. Would he insist on putting his cock inside her? Her heart rebelled at the idea, but the lower half of her twitched instead. They remained, holding eye contact, as he slid the pants down her hips, over her feet. After he'd freed her from them, he even held her feet, rubbing them as he had the rest of her.

Now that her skin was bare, Cedar could feel the callouses on the tips of his fingers as he trailed them back up her legs to her thighs. But he did not demand she open them. Instead, he resumed those firm dips into her flesh, following a path that led him closer and closer to the mound of her pelvis. There, he paused and waded through her dark curls with his claws, twining them around his fingers.

That was when, of their own accord, her thighs parted. She wanted that touch, *needed* that touch, as much as it pained her to admit. It would be a welcome relief to the growing heat that left her tingling and wanting.

Kargorr gave only the barest nod as he ventured farther down to the hood of her sex. He spread his fingers and slid them deeper between her thighs, one on each of her lower lips, merely brushing the swells of them. She was surprised to find his hands cold, which must have meant that she was quite hot, and Cedar hated this, too.

It only grew worse, and her folds became more engorged as Kargorr traced the outside of her, refusing to gratify her. Soon, her body was rising of its own accord, desperate for his touch to travel inward.

Abruptly, Kargorr moved, climbing over her to position himself between her legs. Cedar tried to snap her thighs shut, alarmed at his abrupt movement and what it meant, but he kept them splayed in front of him. This time, the rush that went through her was not pleasure, but panic, remembering the last time he had forced her legs apart.

Kargorr sat back on his knees and rubbed her calves in soothing circles.

"Be still," he said, a phrase that would normally have come out rough, but now was softer than his voice had ever been. "Please."

Please.

Cedar could not think of another time he had ever uttered this word to her, when he had ever asked for her agreement. So she obeyed.

28

KARGORR

The scent of her fear was sour. The light cloud of pleasure that had settled on them vanished in a moment, and then Cedar was sliding up the furs to put distance between them.

It made Kargorr's chest ache, his throat close up. His *yapira* feared him. She cringed at his touch, and each time it was like a needle being driven deeper.

He could not rinse away what he'd done with words. Cedar would never believe them, anyway. Instead, Kargorr would show her. Besides, he had been nursing a hunger for what felt like an eternity, ever since he left the *parog* on their long raid. Now that he had claimed his *yapira*, he wanted to completely consume her, every part of her. He wanted to suck her fingers, lick her sweat, taste her soft, wet cunt. Now that he had used his *sarga* on her, when the smell of her arousal wafted up his nose, behind his eyes, it spread across his body like flames licking up grease and became a bonfire of visceral need.

When he pleaded with her to stay and she did, it gave Kargorr hope that he could coax her out like a shy animal. His cock throbbed for her, but he willed his mind away from it as he bent down between her legs, lifting her thighs so her knees were slung over his arms. Cedar wriggled, clearly uncomfortable at being so exposed, but he would soon quiet her objections.

His mouth descended on her, his big tongue swiping over her reddened, exposed skin. She trembled under him as he licked the other way, barely glancing over that tiny, hidden bead. Kargorr marveled, always, at the smallness of her body compared to his. How could she take him so well? Despite how impossible it seemed, she had once moaned and screamed as his cock slid in and out of her, and it had fit perfectly.

Cedar didn't make a sound as he dragged his tongue over that tender spot again, and again, though her body had already begun to shiver and quake with this small taste. Kargorr wanted more. He wanted to lick up all of her, to suck down the liquid that dewed on her cunt like the sweet marrow from inside a bone. But he had to move slowly. If he devoured her with nothing but hunger, nothing but raw need, she would still only think herself an object. A tool.

Cedar was no longer a means to an end for him, though. She *was* the means—and the end.

So he went slowly, his hands returning to their work of stroking her skin and pressing rhythmically into her thighs to loosen all the taut muscle there while he lapped her. Slow and steady, Kargorr passed his tongue back and forth, merely hinting at what else he could do.

And then, she released a little whimper. It was the pleasurable kind, and a tenseness drained out of him he hadn't realized he felt. As a reward, he was firmer with his tongue, concentrating it around her hidden bud. Her hips rose off the furs and he chased them, gently sliding up his hands so he could press her down to the bed. He applied just the barest pressure, so if she wanted to escape him, she could.

It railed against every instinct he had to give her freedom now when he had so recently lost her, but caging her, strapping her down tighter, would not yield the result he wanted.

He circled her sweet button, changing his patterns and angles to surprise her, and every so often his tongue leapt down to her cunt to drink up all the nectar gathered there. This was the power of the bond, he thought, swallowing her up and feeling his cock grow ever harder. She tasted like everything he'd ever craved. His control fractured as he drank more and more, as she squirmed and her gasps morphed into reluctant moans, but Kargorr gripped tight to the remains of it.

How he needed his cock inside her. How he longed for nothing but to reunite with his *yapira* and remind her how he could make her sing. Instead, he slipped his tongue down and pressed it into her hot cavern, and she let out an unwilling cry.

Instead of fucking her with his cock, he fucked her with his mouth, and it was better than any dessert. Now he shifted between her two tender places, lavishing attention on each, and her moans rose steadily higher and higher. He knew she needed more, but he held her there, languidly wandering his path, never speeding or slowing in his torment. Soon Cedar was grinding her hips into his face, her legs tensing over the hooks of his elbows.

It was when she uttered a helpless cry of pleasure that Lord Kargorr nearly lost control. His breathing came heavy as he tore his lips away, gazing down at her bright red, dripping cunt. It would be so easy to take her right now. Already a drizzle of white seed ran down his length, dripping onto the bed.

No. He would show her his mastery. His tenderness. Perhaps, even, that deeply buried thing in the oubliette of his soul.

Instead of his cock, as he craved in the pit of his belly, he had something else he could put inside her. He sat back from the bed and hastily trimmed his fierce claws until they were smooth at the tips. Did he mistake the eagerness in her expression?

Eagerness was good. Very good.

Lord Kargorr wetted his fingers in her leaking juices, and she gasped at this new sensation. Cedar watched him intently as he dragged them through her lower lips, over her most sensitive place and back again until he could feel the pulsing of her cunt as it awaited him. With intention, with the most gentleness he could muster, he eased his finger inside her. She was tight, so tight, even around something so small as this that he had to bite hard on his lip, leaving the tang of copper on his tongue.

As he tested her, keeping his exploration shallow, he returned to the task of licking and tormenting her clit, simply offering the pad of his finger to her as an appetizer. Her body answered, a helpless moan falling from her lips as she ground against him, trying to take it deeper. He offered her even more without making her fight for it, sinking his hand in further, moving his tongue just a little faster.

Cedar couldn't hold in her sounds any longer. She finally broke when he wriggled a second finger into her, and a heady cry escaped her lips. More languid strokes, more flicking and sucking, nursing her slowly to a flame... and he was rewarded.

She shattered around him, utterly and completely. Her whole body sagged, her moans coming out mangled as her channel clutched his fingers tight, and Kargorr shivered with his own aching need. But he remained, licking and teasing, until she had come all the way back down to the ground.

He drew away, his balls tight and his *sarga* begging to be with her again. But he took deep breaths as Cedar lay panting on the bed, her limbs splayed like a fallen doll. Kargorr petted her belly, thinking of his—*their*—orcling growing inside, and his cock twitched with how desperately it needed her.

Instead, he leaned down and kissed there, and Cedar's breath halted in her lungs.

"I will get us breakfast," Kargorr said at length, rising from the furs. The confusion on her face didn't escape his notice as he tugged on his breeches, then hung a thick bear cloak over his shoulders and stepped out of the tent.

Yes, he would get breakfast. In a moment.

Lord Kargorr stumbled away from the tent, his groin so searingly painful that even walking was difficult. He propped himself against one of the posts along the edge of the camp, yanked out his cock, and stroked it roughly, squeezing as tight as he imagined Cedar's cunt to be. It took only two moments for him to reach his conclusion, and then he jettisoned it all into the snow. The force of it nearly stole his legs out from under him.

When, at last he was under his own power again, Kargorr left to do what he promised. He would feed her and pleasure her and hold her close until she returned to him.

CEDAR

She lay there panting for whole minutes after Kargorr left, unsure of what had just transpired. Cedar had seen his huge, green cock drooling for her, thick and fat and pushing at the limits of his skin. And yet he had only... licked her. Devoured her, really. Sucking her up and lavishing attention on her, seeing only to her pleasure and nothing else.

She'd never heard of such a thing, putting a mouth on a pussy the way one would put a mouth on a cock, and it had been utterly marvelous.

And then he'd left without demanding more. That puzzled her most of all. Cedar had expected it, certainly. Perhaps she'd wanted it, too.

Now she felt strangely unfulfilled. What did it mean?

When he returned, Kargorr brought with him some of that syrup-crusted pork to go with her meal, and she thought perhaps something was changing. They ate in quiet, but not an uncomfortable one, and for the first time in ages, she felt hungry. She devoured it all, and then when he stood to attend to matters around the camp, he leaned down, took her face in his hands, and kissed her.

It wasn't the ferocious, demanding kind she had grown accustomed to. It was slower and sweeter, precise and yet soft. And then, after brushing his forehead against hers, he left.

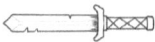

When Rathka appeared, she found Cedar still sitting at the table, brow furrowed.

"You will have to forgive him sometime," the orc woman said, sitting down across from her, "if he is your *agsan*."

Cedar stood abruptly. "I have no interest in discussing this with you."

She went to Kiya and woke him, and the big cat stretched as he yawned. Once she had his leash attached, she gave Rathka an impatient look, and together they left the tent.

It was a sunny day, despite the cold and the snow, and it was probably as good a time as any to let Kiya socialize with his own kind. Cedar knew her time keeping him as a pet was almost over, which made her deeply sad. She liked that he needed her, that he sometimes still slept on the bed when Kargorr was gone to keep her warm, that he offered good company when she was alone.

But soon, she thought, she would have a baby instead.

Kargorr's child was growing inside her. The picture of it was met with as much trepidation as hope. It would be something of her own, but also a reminder of Kargorr whenever he was gone, for better or worse.

When Cedar approached the great field of snow beyond the camp, Kiya went and ran in it like he always did, leaping in the fluff and sprinting in circles. She led him to where the other cats tended to assemble and the stablemaster fed them their meals. He stayed close to her side as they approached a few of the much larger adult animals relaxing, but she encouraged him to go and investigate.

"You have coddled him too much," said Rathka with a click of her tongue. "Now he doesn't know how to be a cat."

Cedar hoped this wasn't true, but then she thought of what Kargorr had said about the way she was raised—how children needed love and affection as they grew up, and she thought he would be all right.

After some coaxing, Kiya finally walked out into the snow, approaching the group of cats gathered there. A big one got to its feet as he approached: Liga, Cedar realized. But she resisted the urge to greet Kargorr's companion, and waited while Liga slowly, carelessly slinked toward Kiya. He lowered his body, as if in respect, and Liga stepped around him in a circle, sniffing him all over.

Then, nearby, some of the younger cats appeared. They had spots and stripes like Kiya did, and when they all began to greet one another, she realized they were his siblings.

Soon, he was chasing the others around, and they were chasing him in return. He forgot all about Cedar as he played wildly with the cats his own age, leaping and tumbling and rolling over each other.

He needed this, she realized. He couldn't be cooped up all day with her.

She'd thought she'd be taking him back home that night,

but when she moved to leave, he was utterly distracted by his playing. If Cedar called to him, he would come, expecting his treats—but what would be kinder to him? What would be wiser?

Rathka stood watching while Cedar debated with herself.

"Shall I say something, or will you bite off my head again?" the orc woman asked.

Cedar hadn't forgiven Rathka, either, for filling her head with doubt and fear. But Rathka was, unfortunately, the only one who Cedar spoke to besides two little orclings and the old leatherworker, who she wasn't sure she would see again.

"Say it."

Rathka gave a curt nod. "Be selfish a little longer. It will not hurt him."

Cedar's gaze jumped to the older woman's. Was she really saying something kind, something helpful? There must be some sort of blade hidden inside it.

"I have heard Lord Kargorr will be leaving again soon, and you will want your pet with you," Rathka added.

There it was. Cedar nodded, understanding. She had expected as much. All of this had been preparation, she knew, for his plan.

"Kiya!" Cedar called, whistling. The cat halted in the snow, then turned to her with ears pricked forward, and she reached into her pocket. He flew toward her, stopping right at her feet to wait for his treat. She held it out and he licked it up out of her fingers, then rubbed his cheek against her hand.

"Come home now," she said to him, scratching his head. "We'll return tomorrow, I promise."

29

KARGORR

"I think you should go yourself," Orgha said as they both stood hunched over the map, trying to determine how many days' ride it would be to the next *parog*. "I will take Samrak with me and lead the gift envoy. I already negotiated once with another lord who wanted to take off my head before I explained myself. I can do it again."

Kargorr didn't like it. But he also knew that, as always, Orgha was right. Convincing another lord to join his mission was something he ought to handle himself. He just didn't want to leave his *yapira* so soon, without fixing what had gone wrong between them.

But perhaps it wasn't something that could be fixed with a nail or a length of rope. There was, he hated to think, a chance she might never forgive him.

In that case, she would need time to forget. Perhaps Kargorr could return from this mission successful and have the reunion with her he had hoped for, and it would be good for both of them.

"Two days' time, then," Kargorr said, nodding. "We will load a heavy cart with goods for the eastern *parog*. That lord is a more finicky orc, so you will need to be gentle with him."

Orgha snorted. "If I can handle you, *kazek*, I can handle him."

Kargorr barked a laugh. "Spend your day tomorrow with your *yapira*," he said. "As I will with mine. And then we ready to leave."

The other orc looked at him thoughtfully for far too long.

"Yes, I will remind her of our bond for when I am away," Orgha said at last. "So that she will be thinking of me as I'll be thinking of her."

Kargorr furrowed his brow. It was an odd thing for Orgha to say. He never discussed his relationship with Rathka, nor had he ever shared anything about his life with her before now. With a significant nod, Orgha turned and left the tent.

Right. If Kargorr could remind Cedar of what they once had, and perhaps create a good memory together before he left... that would be in her heart while he was gone.

The sun hung low in the sky, casting long bands of orange among the poles holding up the *parog*. Kargorr studied the bustle of activity as he walked, before word had spread of the upcoming journey. Families ate together with their doors open or sat around fires. Off in the distance, he heard a drum beating.

Someday, Kargorr thought, that would be him and his own orclings. But they would have a new world, a different one, one that he had hewn for them from solid stone. His departure was necessary to create that world. Then, he could claim Cedar as his *yapira*, once the foundation of it was steady under his feet.

She was not in the tent when he arrived, and for a moment, panic washed over him, wondering if she had run again. But Kiya was not there, either, and he spotted Rathka's bag on the chair, which meant they had likely gone out together.

Perhaps Kargorr could discover what had been keeping his *yapira* busy while he was away. The more he could learn about her, the better it would solidify their bond.

He walked with his hands tucked behind his back, peering into doorways as he looked. At first, he intended to avoid the leatherworker's, which always had an unpleasant odor around it—until he saw Kiya sleeping on a mat in front.

Kargorr paused and quirked an eyebrow. Is this where she'd been spending her time? He found it odd that Cedar would choose the foulest place in the *parog*, and yet also not surprising. She did love her furs.

He hummed as he approached, and Kiya's head snapped to face him. The cat's lip curled in the beginnings of a snarl, and his back arched. Kargorr was glad that Cedar had a creature so fierce to protect her.

"What are you upset about, Kiya?" came Cedar's voice. She appeared in the doorway, and her face went slack when she saw Kargorr there. "You're early. Or, I mean, earlier than usual. I don't come here often, I promise. Just, when you were gone, there was nothing to do, so I—"

He touched a finger to her lips, quieting her, and her eyes went round.

"Hush, little deer." He took her shoulders in his hands firmly and turned her around. "Show me what you've been doing."

When Kargorr stepped inside, his leatherworker, Carn, let out a surprised yelp. He quickly put down his tools and kicked away the basket of supplies at his feet.

"Lord Kargorr," he said, tapping his chest. "I didn't expect you here. It's quite messy—"

Kargorr held up one hand, and Carn fell silent. He took in the state of the shop and was amazed by the array of leathers in various states of curing. On the floor was a gorgeous white fur, perhaps some sort of northern fox, and that looked like where Cedar had been seated before he interrupted, her tools scattered about.

"You should be neat with your workstation," he said to Cedar, tilting up the side of his mouth so she would know he was jesting. She had a look on her face like she'd been caught doing something wrong and hurriedly gathered up her supplies. He kneeled and put a hand on her back. "Are you upset that I found you out?"

She froze under his touch. "You're not angry?"

"Angry? That you have been making yourself useful?" His brows drew together. "No. I am not angry. As long as you aren't making more work for Carn."

The old orc hurriedly came to her rescue. "Not at all," he said in her tongue, reaching for a fur that was hanging up overhead. Cedar tried to stop him, but he gently pushed her out of the way. "She is a fast learner," Carn added in Orcish, holding out the fur. "I believe she made this for you, but then she changed her mind. I think she was afraid you wouldn't like her craftsmanship."

Kargorr turned to Cedar, who was watching this unfold with her mouth open. She glared at Carn.

"You're not giving that to him, are you?" she demanded.

Carn shrugged.

Now Kargorr was deeply curious. He took the fur, the massive thing, and lifted it off the ground until he reached the end, where the bear's head had once been. Cedar had kept the upper jaw and left the teeth attached. She'd also retained the claws at the tips of the arms and legs.

"You did this?" Kargorr asked, lowering the huge fur. It must have taken hours upon hours.

Cedar nodded, clearly ashamed. Kargorr dipped his head to Carn in thanks for letting her work on a massive animal like this—one of the great big bears of the north—and for giving her a way to occupy her mind and her hands.

"Take this to our tent," Kargorr said, returning the massive pelt to Carn. Cedar furrowed her brow, but Kargorr simply took her by the hand and led her to the door. When they stepped outside, he waved down the closest orc. "A bath in my tent. Now."

Kargorr turned to her, and while Carn busied with bundling up the pelt, he dragged his hand underneath her hair. Cedar stiffened, but didn't recoil from him.

"You smell terrible," he said, shaking his head. "I need to get you clean before I can appreciate your gift."

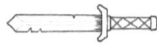

CEDAR

She hadn't meant for him to see the bear's pelt. It was an experiment, one that Carn had gifted to her when the bear's body was brought to him.

But Kargorr did not appear to be upset that he'd found her in the leatherworker's tent, doing menial labor. In fact, she'd seen pleasure in his eyes as he surveyed the pelt, examining the head she'd left on, running his fingers over the sharp teeth.

She followed him back to their tent, where a tub had already been brought in. It reminded her of the very first night in the previous camp, when Kargorr had demanded that she clean him. She wondered if that was the night they had conceived the child she carried now.

How things had changed and also stayed the same.

The bear pelt was brought in while the bath was filled one bucket at a time until steam curled into the air above it. Kargorr stood before her, immense as always, as he traced his fingers down her collar to the laces of her tunic, which he pulled open slowly, intentionally. He lifted it up over her head and arms before tossing it away. Then came her pants. Soon she was revealed in front of him, and her nipples were so hard in the cold air that they hurt.

"Get in, little deer," he commanded her, and reflexively, Cedar obeyed, climbing into the tub. The hot water enveloped her, and she couldn't resist letting out a sigh of pleasure as it covered her cold skin. She watched as Kargorr undressed himself, revealing that big chest with the full pectorals, his strong belly, the line of muscle that trailed from his hip bones to the massive cock at the apex of his groin. His thighs were dense and thick, and when he turned to peel his pants off his big feet, Cedar found herself admiring his carved ass. No wonder he could fuck with such abandon when he looked like that.

At last, he stepped into the tub and settled in front of her, placing his legs on either side of her hips. She remembered this position, too, and how neatly she nestled between his calves. With his added bulk, the water rose nearly to overflowing the tub, and Cedar sighed as it covered her collarbone. She felt Kargorr's eyes on her as she tilted her head back and sank even deeper, letting her hair drift under the surface of the water. Her knees floated up, and she felt his hands wrap around them, gently tugging her closer. Soon she was fully spread, her feet in his lap and her head leaning against the back of the tub. Perhaps she ought to have hidden herself from such exposure, but she was too tired and pleasantly warm to care.

Her eyes did open, though, when Kargorr's calloused hand wrapped around her foot. He kneaded it with his strong fingers, forcing his thumb through the stiff muscle, and Cedar couldn't help the low gasp of pleasure she let out. His body shuddered at the sound, but otherwise he gave no indication that he'd heard her as he continued his thorough rubbing.

When he'd finished at her heel, he took her other foot and repeated the motion, digging his hands into her strained muscles, which she hadn't realized were quite so hard until now. She couldn't help sagging deeper into the water, her hips sliding toward his in the tub. When he finished with her other heel, he let it drop to his lap, and then she heard shuffling. Cedar glanced up to find him holding soap, and he took her legs once more, lifting them out of the water so he could lather her feet, then her calf and knee. His hand slipped down her thigh to her rear, where he ever-so-gently urged her to lift her hips.

Her body lit up like a flame at the touch. It remembered him so easily, how he felt around her, inside her, and suddenly all it wanted was to return to that place where they were joined together. Cedar crushed her eyes closed, hoping that if she simply didn't look at him, at his square face and deep-set eyes and bulky, scarred chest, she could stave off how much she needed him.

And yet, she obeyed his unspoken command, her thighs spreading and her body rising with his hands. When he had her above the surface of the water, he continued soaping her, from her thighs to her belly. He leaned forward as he set her down once more, then continued upward to her chest. He spread suds liberally over her breasts, but never stopped on them for too long, only brushing his palms over her nipples as he worked the soap across her warm skin. When he reached her throat, he paused underneath her jaw, and Cedar couldn't help peering up at him.

Kargorr's brows were drawn together in thought, his lips curved down at the sides. Was he unhappy with her? Had she done something wrong without realizing it?

He leaned closer to her, his broad hands gliding up to cup her face. Cedar realized her legs were slung over his thighs, so now his prominent cock was rising in the water between them, and she shivered at the sight of it.

"Look at me, little deer."

Her eyes jumped to his. This time, underneath the impossible blackness of them, Cedar thought she saw something else —something softer, warmer, sweeter. But was that simply her imagination? Her vast well of pathetic, hopeful thoughts?

He didn't care for her. He didn't love her. She was an object, a vessel, as she always had been. He wanted her complicity and thought he could buy it from her with affection, by rubbing her feet in the bath and looking deep into her eyes.

At last, Kargorr spoke.

"I meant what I said." He stroked a thumb across her cheek. "You... are my *yapira*. The one I was supposed to find."

Cedar frowned. He had called her this, and yet while he did it, he had stolen from her. He had ripped away any trust they might have built between them out there in the snow. What did he hope to gain now by telling her?

There was no destiny here, no intention. She was simply the unlucky girl who lived in the village Lord Kargorr destroyed, that was all. Perhaps his backward, brutish beliefs wanted it to mean more than that, but she knew the truth underneath.

It was all luck, or in her case, the lack thereof. When Lissa was murdered in front of her, Cedar knew there were no gods, no force of fate. She'd always suspected, but Kargorr had cemented that knowledge.

His hands slid under her hair, down her neck, around her back, so he could draw her closer. His frown deepened.

"You do not believe me."

She couldn't stand the expression of hurt that crossed his face. Surely he didn't have feelings that could be injured. He pressed his lips to her forehead and held her there, his arms curled loosely around her.

"If that is really who I am to you," she said finally, clenching her hands, "then why does Orgha treat Rathka as his partner, his equal? They have no children, and still, he loves her. He cares for her. He kisses her goodbye before he leaves. He doesn't steal away in the night."

Kargorr's arms stilled around her.

"It is different for Orgha," he said. "You know that I am trying to build something. Create something. Take back what is mine."

It only took a breath for her to understand. So he would not treat her as Orgha treated Rathka, not while his work continued.

All that he offered her now was what he *could* offer her. She would never be more important than his mission.

Kargorr said nothing further when she didn't answer. After a time, he drew away and gently turned her in the tub so her back faced his chest, then tipped her into the water to wash her hair. The intimacy of the gesture bewildered Cedar, but she allowed it, sinking into his hands. When he finished, he slid her into the triangle of his crossed legs, and while he was hard there underneath her, he did not attempt to put it inside her. No, his fingers trailed down to her breasts, circling her nipples, refusing to touch them. He explored her belly, her hips, her thighs. His tusks brushed the back of her neck as he brought his lips to her flesh, gently pressing them there before moving across her shoulder. While he touched every inch of her body with his hands, he covered the rest with his kisses, curling himself tighter and tighter around her until she thought she might vanish inside him.

30

KARGORR

Though her heart was conflicted, her body knew him. She leaned into his touch without realizing, pressed her hips down into his while she sat in his arms, let herself drift into his chest as he kissed along her shoulder. Kargorr curled his hand around hers and drew it over her head, so he could continue leaving the imprints of his lips up her arm. She trembled under him, but still wavered, reluctant to give in to what she really wanted.

And so he continued languidly, balling up her fingers in his palm and cupping them like a small, tender thing. He brought her hand back down to her chest, then curled it around her waist, his atop hers. Instead of his fingers sliding over her hip, it was her fingers. As he guided them back up to her chest, it was her hand that traveled over the swell of her breast, across the taut nipples just barely above the surface of the water. She shivered as he rubbed back and forth, from one breast to the other. Her round ass ground perfectly against his cock, and truly, all he wanted was to bury his *sarga* in her again, to be one with her at last.

Instead, he nipped the lobe of her ear, letting his breath fall over her skin. A gasp escaped her lips, and he guided her hand down, over the soft swell of her belly. Though his cock nudged urgently at the space between her legs, Kargorr ignored it, caressing her elbow inside of his as he guided her everywhere except there. She shifted in his lap, and he knew her body was aching for more.

But no, he planned to take this slow. Now that she was clean and the water was cooling down, it was time to explore the gift she had made for him.

Gently he released her, then slid his arms under Cedar's small body. She let out a squeak as he lifted her up and stepped out of the tub. He pulled down one of the warm furs hanging near the fire, then wrapped it around her as he set her down on the bed. Cedar blinked up at him in surprise as he used it to whisk the water off her, trailing it down each of her arms and then her legs. When he was finished, Kargorr used another one on himself, then retrieved both and hung them back up to dry.

When he returned to the bed, Cedar sat with her arms over her chest like she had the very first night they were in his tent together. She was hiding herself from him.

Instead of demanding that he see her, as he wanted, Kargorr sat down near her with his legs hanging off the bed. He pulled the bear's head into his lap, examining the nose, the ears, the empty eye sockets.

"You thought of me while I was away," he said at last, not looking at her. He continued petting it, feeling the soft fur.

After a time, she answered with a soft, "Yes."

He nodded. Just as he had thought of her while he was gone.

"Thank you, little deer." He held up the pelt, admiring the craftsmanship. "This is beautiful."

She was silent. When he looked up, her eyes were red and wet around the edges. She gritted her teeth together as she met his gaze. He had never seen such hardness, never such searing, bare anger in her.

"You ruined everything," she ground out, and the harshness of her words startled him. "You ruined it all!"

Her honesty took him aback. Kargorr studied her, how she covered herself, how she tried to hold back her tears, and knew she was right.

He brought in a deep, calming breath. Seeing his *yapira* with such misery and hate on her face... it made him ache, like a wound that wouldn't heal.

"I know." That was all he could say. He wanted to ask if he could ever undo what he'd done, but he already knew the answer.

She might forgive him, perhaps someday. But she would never forget, and there was no apology that could mend this scar.

CEDAR

Lord Kargorr watched her for a long time, the bear pelt in his arms. Then, without answering, he set it aside at the foot of the bed. He turned to her, his brows drawn tight, and reached out to curl his fingers around hers. Then he brought her hand to his lips and pressed them there, fervently, as if he hoped she could feel what he felt through them.

She was warm, so warm inside from their bath, from the way he'd held her in his lap. Just this touch set a fiery blaze to her skin, and all the hairs on her exposed body stood up on end. Slowly, he kissed further up, on her wrist, turning her arm over so he could pepper another one on the inside of her elbow. Cedar felt helpless, unable to move or speak as he leaned forward, leaving another on her shoulder, and then her collarbone. When he reached her jaw, he was still clutching her hand tightly in his, the tips of his claws pressing gently into her wrist.

He stopped just before touching his mouth to hers. There, Kargorr looked at her, long and hard, his black eyes seeing through her like she was a brook of crystal-clear water. She bit her lip, resisting the need to bridge the gap between them. The ghost of a smile touched his cheek, and then he pressed his mouth to hers.

But he didn't devour her. No, Kargorr took his time, sampling her, taking her lip between his and sucking on it gently, his hand never letting hers go. He gripped it even closer to him, and Cedar felt herself sagging into him. He steadied her with one arm on her hip, and despite his loose, languid kisses, his claws clutched her tightly. When his tongue gently laved over the crease of her lips, she parted them, allowing him to slip through.

Still, he didn't invade, as he often had. Kargorr simply caressed the space, pulling her ever more deeply into him. If she wasn't careful, he would swallow her up—and yet she wanted it, in that place below her heart where all her rotten desires lay.

It was her tongue that reached out, hungry for his touch. Kargorr welcomed it, greeting the tip with his own, circling it and cupping it. Cedar's need grew as his teasing shed sparks upon her kindling, and soon the debris caught fire. She found her hand around his neck, pulling him in closer, insisting that he kiss her deeper. She was rewarded with a rumble in his chest, something between a chuckle and a groan.

At last, Kargorr gave in, slipping his tongue into her mouth and claiming it as his own. Cedar barely noticed when he dragged her toward him across the bed and the power of his kiss pushed her down into the furs. Still he held her hand, his thick, wide fingers twining with hers. He didn't let it go as his body settled over her, his thighs trapping her hips between them. She felt the wet tip of his cock skate over her belly, but he didn't move to use it. Instead, he drew himself back, releasing her mouth from his assault.

Now he rose high above her, his tusks catching the firelight, his broad chest heaving with his labored breaths. Those dark eyes traveled down her naked body, and she couldn't mistake the raw thirst in them. He crouched down over her and kissed along her cheek, down her neck to the hollow of her throat, earning an involuntary twitch in her hips. All while her heart beat frantically in her chest, her pussy already tingling, steadily warming for him.

With a painful slowness, he continued down, circling each breast with his lips but never touching her nipples. Cedar's back arched of its own accord, desperate for more, and at last he relented. He took one hardened point into his mouth, curling his tongue around it, then flicking back and forth, until she couldn't stop the gasps that fell from her lips. Still, he took his time, traveling from one to the other, torturing both of them with his easy touches. She sensed his hand slide down her hip to her belly, the softened tips of his fingers smoothing over it to the thatch of hair at the crux of her thighs.

And still, he only teased, only hinted at what he could give her, and Cedar was steadily tipping into the well of her desire. Soon, she would fall and crash to the bottom.

KARGORR

His Cedar needed delicacy. She needed courting, and tantalizing, and slow deliberation. But he would convince her, tugging on each of the strings of her unfulfilled cravings, until she finally unraveled.

She was his *yapira*, so he knew her body almost as well as he knew his own. He would find her wet when he at last reached her warm center, but he would wait as long as possible until she was starved for his touch. Only then would he offer her satisfaction. Now, he would build her want into a mountain and then climb it to the peak.

When at last her nipples were well-loved, Kargorr redirected his attentions to her soft belly, where he pictured their orcling curled up inside. He wondered what sort of orc it would be. A girl with bloodlust in her veins? A boy with a talent for metalworking? Perhaps someone else, someone just as fierce as their mother? It made his cock engorge even further, considering the future, this world where perhaps Cedar had forgiven him and he could care for them both as he meant to.

As his kisses swept south, so did Cedar's body rise off the bed against him, urging him onward. He only traced the inside of her thighs, which parted for him without any insistence, foreshadowing what he could do if he moved only a few inches up. His clawless fingers circled closer and closer, and when a quiet whimper fell from her lips, he couldn't resist any longer.

With a ferocious growl, he swept his fingers to the soft, warm place between her legs. Her hips bucked into his hand, driving him into her folds, where he was astonished to find exactly *how* wet she was for him. It filled her creases and dripped down from the bowl of her cunt, spilling to her ass. Kargorr's cock leapt, longing for nothing more than to feel that wetness around it, to give her empty body what it so clearly wanted from him—but he had more to do. He had much still to show her, to convince her hard shell to soften and crack for him.

He slid one finger between the swollen petals of her sex,

up and down, spreading that delicious moisture everywhere. His mouth watered at the memory of how she tasted, and at least that was one desire he didn't need to squash.

Swiftly, Kargorr kissed down her stomach, over her mound, to her pink, shiny cunt. He shoved down the painful ache growing in his groin and focused all his attention on her, on kissing over each of her lower lips, until she was wriggling and whining with her desperation.

At last, he brushed her small nub with his tongue, and the high, tortured sound that tumbled from her mouth was the prize for his patience. He treated it as he had her breasts, circling it slowly, refusing to touch the sensitive tip just yet. She shivered with each pass, and he was gratified by her hand finding its way into his hair, urging him on. Her taste was better than any cut of meat, any ripe fruit, sweet and salty and full of her desire. He couldn't help ducking down to lick up her juice, rolling it around in his mouth until he was satisfied and swallowed it. When he drew away, he found her small cunt opening and closing, narrowing into a small point as she swelled inside. How neatly his cock would fit there, how wonderfully she would squeeze him.

With the utmost gentleness, he lifted one finger to it and mapped out the edges, then slowly eased it inside her. This time her moan was big and full, the perfect music, and he rewarded her by brushing his tongue over the tender tip of her button.

"Please," Cedar murmured, her hand curling in his hair, pushing him closer. Kargorr could not deny his *yapira*, and so he gave in, latching onto her like an orcling to its mother, driving his finger deeper into that hot cunt. Her pelvis rose to greet him, and he sucked once again, burying his mouth in her.

What surprised him most was, as he pumped his hand and flicked his tongue, how easily she met her finish. She gasped and tightened around him, her heels digging into his back as he curled one finger inside her and dragged it along the textured ceiling of her cavern. He nursed her pleasure out of her, pushing her higher and higher, only to bring her back down to the ground again.

His meal wasn't over. He still had so much to give, so much to devour, and neither of them would sleep until they were both full and drowsy with their satisfaction.

Sitting back, Kargorr wiped his mouth and gazed down at her, this perfect human woman he had found.

31

CEDAR

What was it that gave him such power over her? How did he know precisely how to please her, where to touch her, in order to drive her off the edge of a cliff and into the vast nothingness down below?

It rattled her just how much searing bliss he could dole out. He worked her body like he was a master craftsman and she was little more than soft wood under his hands. How she wanted to be shaped, to be carved out and then filled with him, and the violent force of that need frightened her.

Lord Kargorr's dark green cock was enormous now, the head emerging from the skin. A thick vein pulsed along the shaft, and white fluid drizzled from the slotted tip. How he craved her, too, though he kept a tight rein on himself. At this moment, red glinted at the edges of his eyes, and she thought that taut rope of control was snapping one thread at a time.

"Little deer," he murmured, sliding his finger free with a slurping noise. He dragged it up through her folds, over her supremely tender clit, and she writhed under him. "Will you let me in?"

Cedar blinked up at him. He had never *asked*, simply taken. Those eyes were intense, brows sharp over them, as he stroked himself with his other hand. His great belly heaved as he awaited her answer, his knees keeping her legs spread wide and open for him.

Of course she wanted nothing more. She didn't just need him—she would, most certainly, perish if she couldn't have him inside her again. But the hurt was sharp and crystalline, shaped into a dagger that was still plunged deep into her heart.

Yet, she ached. She craved. Her body pleaded for reunion and for release.

What if it couldn't be fixed, but created new again? Perhaps she had to throw away this older version of herself and make a fresh one that could be with him. Otherwise, she might never have peace.

So Cedar nodded and spread her thighs further apart, her heart a skittering drum in her chest.

"Yes," she said. "Come in."

Kargorr snarled low in his throat, then fisted his cock even harder. Curling one hand under her, he drew her leg up over his hip to grant him access, and the ferocity in his eyes made her shudder. Never once did his gaze leave hers as he dragged his cock over her sensitive center, up to her shy bud and then down again, until that fat, wide, mushroom head was squeezing into her.

Cedar had forgotten how big he was, how his heavy, swollen cock had to force its way inside her. She was still tender from her climax and oh, how her body rioted in the most glorious way as he spread her wide for himself.

Then Kargorr paused and slowly pulled his fat cock back out. Cedar whimpered, because all she wanted, all she *needed*, was for him to finish what he'd begun. His lower lip curled as he pushed back in a second time, his thoroughly slick cockhead gliding through. Just that shadow of what he would feel like soon, buried in her, dragged a moan from her mouth.

"Is that what you like, little deer?" he asked, barely contained within her. He lowered himself on one elbow until she could feel his breath on her face. Her eyes traced the whitish skin of the scar that split his brow, cut jagged over the bridge of his nose, across his cheek to the groove in his tusk.

"Y-yes," she managed as he withdrew once more, leaving her empty, only to push her open again. "Yes, it... it..." As he moved faster, one short, shallow stroke after another, her words broke off. She whimpered and whined, her head thrown back, her legs winding around his hips. If he didn't take her soon, all of her, she might just burst into flames.

"More," she finally cried, raising blazing eyes to his. Cedar didn't miss the smirk that crossed his face as he obeyed, slipping in even deeper, demanding that she give to him. And give she did, welcoming him inside her, to the place where even she knew he belonged.

Still Kargorr toyed with her, venturing farther before retreating, then farther again. Each stroke he claimed more of her, somehow dousing her flames and nursing them even brighter at the same time. His hand crept up to her breast, taking on the weight of it as he thrust at a steady, rhythmic speed, still only teasing her with a fraction of what she knew he could offer. Despite the whirlwind that threatened to lift her off the ground and hurl her away, Cedar held Kargorr's steady gaze, daring him and begging him to give her everything. He plucked her nipple, then soothed it with his palm, and Cedar found her hips jerking, her voice coming out a pathetic whine as her body hungered to be filled.

"My *yapira*," he said, voice husky as his hand slid up her chest to her cheek. There he cupped it around her ear, holding her firm and soft underneath him. Leaning down, Kargorr paused with his lips only inches from hers. "Say that you are mine."

The words almost tumbled from her mouth before she could stop them, as desperate as she was to have it all. Once upon a time, he had asked this of her—demanded that she submit to him, and she never had, even as he drowned her in her ecstasy.

"No." She wanted the word to come out stronger, but she was steeped in the fullness he brought her, and the completeness he promised her. "No, I'm not."

Cedar thought certainly he would stop, that Kargorr would punish her for not giving him the answer he wanted by ending this. Instead, he groaned atop her and sank his cock even deeper on his next thrust. It tore an answering cry from her lips, because he still wasn't there, not quite there, where she so desperately needed him. Again he glared down at her, fire burning at the edges of his eyes.

"You won't say you're mine?" he demanded, withdrawing himself again, hovering on the edge of her. She canted her hips up, desperate to bring him back in, while nodding furiously. As long as he kept her a secret, she would never give in to this request.

"No," Cedar managed between gasping breaths.

Kargorr grit his teeth and finally, at long last, buried himself deep inside her. It sent a burst of heat racing across her body, to her hands and feet and throat. Once more he reeled his hips back, and once more he drove his cock in, demanding that she make room for him. Her cry was louder this time, and her hands gripped his shoulders tight, her legs locking around his hips. His hot breath fell across her cheeks as he plunged in again and again, filling her so full she thought she might splinter into pieces. Every stroke dragged the head of his cock along her channel, sending sparks from her belly up to her throat.

Then, she felt them: those two thick lumps at the base of him teased the edges of her, striking her tight opening with each thrust. Kargorr growled low in his chest.

"You will take my *sarga*," he grunted, seizing her hips so he could drag her up even higher, changing his angle to an even more searingly blissful degree. "My orcling will grow fat and strong inside you. And I will fuck you like this," he drove in hard, seeking out that tender place inside her and yanking a scream from her lips, "until you *know* you are mine."

Cedar had no words left as that bulge worked its way in, further and further with every snap of his hips, until nonsense was tumbling from her lips. Surely they would never fit inside her, not with how close she was, how tight he had wound her. But her pussy was soft for him, open for him, and when they at last slipped inside, she knew he was right.

But she wouldn't tell him, not until he could admit that he was hers, too.

KARGORR

Her obstinance was a drug, like those flower seeds he had heard about that could drive an orc to madness. She had so much will that he had been holding back his finish for too long, and his *sarga* begged to release inside her.

His Cedar was so lovely spread out under him, so ripe and full of life, that he bit his lip to keep from letting go too soon. No, he had work to do. His *sarga* made a lovely squelching with every pump of his cock, and her cries ratcheted louder and louder. Now she was squeezing him oh-so-tightly, her eyes closed and her head thrown back, her fingers digging into him like claws as she ascended. He'd never felt her so exquisitely tight, and as she finally reached her powerful finish, he struggled just to keep pumping.

"Yes, little deer," he growled as she wailed her pleasure, as her heels dug into his back. "Scream for me."

As his *sarga* swelled, he sunk into her one last time. She closed around him, sealing him inside her small body. All his muscles tensed with how glorious she felt, and with a roar, he unleashed. Cedar moaned again as he poured all of himself into her, as her perfect cunt held him fast. He managed not to fall on her, their panting breaths mingling in the air between them.

Finally, Cedar opened her brown eyes, which were soft and warm with her satisfaction, and gazed up at him. Kargorr leaned down and brushed his lips over hers, his tusk catching in her hair. With a breathless giggle, she reached up to untangle it. It was such a rare sound that he tried to memorize it, so he could keep it safe forever.

More than anything, he wanted to shout that she was his. That he had found his one, and the whole *parog* would recognize her.

But he couldn't. Not until he could secure their future.

Instead, he kissed her, savoring every inch of her lips. When the swelling in his *sarga* finally came down, he gently withdrew himself, and his seed spilled out onto the furs. Cedar moaned as he rolled over, then curled against him.

"Little deer," he murmured, wrapping his arms around her. "I must leave again."

She stiffened in his arms, then pulled her head away. A frown tilted her full lips.

"Why?"

"I am going to propose a coalition to another *parog*," he answered. "Work together to achieve my goals."

Cedar was quiet for a long time, and Kargorr thought perhaps she had fallen asleep.

Eventually, she spoke. "How long will you be away?" Her voice was small, uncertain. He pulled her in closer and pressed his lips to the crown of her head, inhaling her sweet scent.

"I do not know. It's two weeks' ride, if not longer, to reach them. It will take time to negotiate. I may have to work hard to convince Lord Gannag."

"And then as much time to come home," she said into his chest. Slowly, Kargorr nodded. He slid his hand down her side, then over the curve of her belly. It was still early, but he wondered if when he returned, his orcling might be larger, more prominent. The idea excited him, as much as he loathed leaving her alone for so long.

"You will have Rathka," he said, stroking her hair. "And Kiya."

Cedar huffed, and he was pleased to find her so reluctant to be separated. Perhaps while he was away, the wound would scab over and eventually heal.

"Rathka's a bitch," Cedar said, curling her hands into fists between them. "And Kiya... he's getting older. He should be with the others."

Kargorr sighed, wishing he didn't have to leave her so soon, when the fence between them was just mending.

"I will return as quickly as possible," he promised her, curling her leg around his. "To you and to our orcling."

She sighed against him—a resigned sound—and yet she wound her arms around his waist, pressing her face to his chest.

It was the first time Kargorr had slept so soundly in weeks, with his *yapira* finally at his side.

32

CEDAR

He was leaving again.

It was all she could think about that day as she walked Kiya around the camp, to the snowfields where he could play. Rathka was, surprisingly, rather talkative, and Cedar wondered if she and Kargorr weren't the only ones to make good use of their prior night together.

Everyone was busy preparing for Kargorr and Orgha's caravans to depart. Even Carn was fashioning leather sacks for the journey, so Cedar put herself to work helping him. It was easier than contemplating how slow the time would pass while Kargorr was away.

The thought made her pause. She was foolish for pining after him when he hadn't even left yet. He wouldn't feel the same longing for her when he was gone.

But the way he had been with her last night... Cedar shook her head. He told her all sorts of lovely things. He had moved so slowly, so intentionally, looking right into her eyes as their bodies worked in perfect tandem. And yet while he said them inside the privacy of their tent, out here, in the camp, she was merely a possession.

That night, when the work of loading the wagons was finished and both caravans were ready, Kargorr found her and dismissed Rathka.

"See to your *agsan*," he said under his breath, and Rathka gave him a startled look. Then she nodded and hurried away. Cedar could already hear the sounds of other orcs loudly finding their pleasure, and supposed they weren't the only ones saying goodbye tonight.

Again, Kargorr enjoyed her slowly, working her up with his tongue and his fingers and bestowing attention on every part of her body. Then he sat back on their bed, against the big bear pelt she'd made for him, and set her down in his lap astride him. His eyes roamed over her while he mapped her out with his fingers, as if memorizing her.

"So beautiful," she thought she heard him say. His hand slid up under her hair, pulling it away from her neck as he devoured her skin with his lips and teeth. He kissed every part of her as she rolled her hips.

"Take your pleasure."

So she did, angling herself so the head of his cock slid through her petals, dragging her wetness up as she ground her clit against the crown. Her damp center kissed his length when she trapped it between her thighs, and she used him like he had asked, seeking out what felt good and then digging ever deeper.

But soon Cedar couldn't bear it, and she needed too badly to be with him again, to swallow him up and be completed by him. His lip curled around his tusk as if he knew what she was thinking, and his big hands lent her strength as she sat up on her knees and, at her own speed, sank down on top of him. She brought him inside her body and cradled him there, and as she rocked, he stroked her breasts, hinting at the future with each pluck of her nipples.

Lord Kargorr let her stay that way, in control, guiding their speed and their motions, and she felt that tonight was different, that he was saying many unspoken things to her with his body, and weaving poetry as his black eyes bore into hers.

Cedar took as much as she could, knowing how long he might be gone, so that she could hold on to it and remember it. This new version of her would treasure it and use it to see her through until he returned.

She rode him until she had guided herself to her own finish; then Kargorr could no longer restrain himself, and he pushed her down into the bed, his eyes wild as he crouched over her. This time, he fucked her, plunging through her tight, wet heat while she was still swollen and sensitive. She soared again when those bulges at the base of his cock, his *sarga*, as he called them, squeezed inside her. Kargorr let out a grunt, almost painful sounding, as he shoved himself all the way in and at last, released.

He lay on top of her for a long time, their chests heaving in unison as they came back down to the ground. He lowered his face toward hers, his big hand now cupping the back of her head.

"Even when I am gone," Kargorr said with surprising earnestness, his dark eyes burrowing into hers, "I will be thinking of you. I will be remembering this with you, little deer." The swelling in his *sarga* had come down once more, and he gently eased himself out of her, turning her hips so he could lie next to her.

Cedar considered this, that he would be thinking of her, while surely she would be thinking of him. She couldn't deny it.

"And then I will return," he said with more certainty in his voice. "I will come back with great numbers and even greater strength. I will build up this *parog* into a force mighty and worthy."

As he always had dreamed—a dream that she was not a part of. As long as he fought for power, he wouldn't claim her.

So she took her hands away and curled them at her chest, because she didn't want to visit that place of resentment.

"With this *parog* at my back, and this fury and power at my behest," Lord Kargorr said, lowering his head closer to her ear, "then perhaps it will make your *agsan* worthy of you, too."

She tried not to give away how this affected her to hear. He wanted to be worthy of *her*? She was a human. A plaything.

Lord Kargorr drew her into his arms, crushing her against his chest. Cedar couldn't help touching him, her hands sampling the strong meat and thick skin, and his cock jumped against her thigh. His fingers returned to the place between her legs where she was dripping and sticky with his spend, and he pushed it back inside her, earning a low moan.

He took her again, slower, her back to his chest, her legs slung wide over his as he milked even more cries of pleasure from her lips.

Cedar wasn't sure how she fell asleep, but she did it surrounded by the scent of Kargorr.

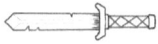

KARGORR

It was painful to walk away from the *parog*, from the way Cedar was tentatively blooming for him. But he had said his goodbyes and kissed her softly inside the protective walls of the tent, and ran his hand across her belly, feeling the soft swell of it. He did not relish leaving her while she grew his orcling inside of her, but this was what he had to do in order to build the life he wanted for them.

And once he had grown his force large enough to do what he wanted to do, and had advanced upon the larger human settlements and burned them to the ground, only then he would claim his *yapira* in front of everyone.

But within the first few days of their journey, he already hungered for her. Thirsted for her. Dreamed of her and pulsed with his need for her. They still had not had the opportunity to truly bond, to accept and fulfill the frenzy. It was an ache deep in his gut that worsened the farther away he traveled from her.

A few days from the *parog*, Lord Kargorr said goodbye to Orgha and the two groups split, one to court a new lord, and one to secure Lord Gannag's fealty and convince him to join Kargorr's cause.

Kargorr pushed his caravan hard, because the faster they reached their destination, the sooner he would convince Gannag and then return home.

A few of his warriors spoke of their own human concubines, some who had warmed up to their new masters, others who still resisted. There was an unspoken envy that Lord Kargorr's concubine now trained a cat of her own and walked around the village, helping where she could and behaving in such a trustworthy fashion. They worried about leaving their own concubines alone for so long, and Kargorr wondered what sort of hold humans held over the *grrosek* that they fretted this way.

It was a hard journey up into the snowy mountains, but their mammoths were sturdy and plodded one foot in front of another, dragging their sledges behind them. Kargorr had more gifts this time, valuable ones, but he believed he held the greatest gift on his tongue: the promise of obliteration.

Humans would once more bow before them if only the *grrosek* could work together.

At last, after two weeks of long, difficult climbing and crossing great tracts of tundra, they reached Lord Gannag's *parog*. It spread out across an immense clearing, surrounded on all sides by forest that had been cut away to make room and build walls.

Lord Kargorr was greeted by warriors, all bearing axes, even more standing a distance away on guard towers with arrows aimed and ready. He instructed his own band to lay down their weapons, and once they had been determined suitably helpless, Lord Gannag came out to greet them.

He was older, older than Kargorr, but age could be deceptive. He moved as if he were stiff, but Lord Kargorr would not make a mistake in believing him weak. No weak orc was in charge of his own *parog*, or another warrior would have ousted him already, someone younger and stronger.

"What brings you to our lands?" Lord Gannag asked as he approached, arms crossed behind his back. "One lord trespassing on another lord's territory..."

"I understand," Lord Kargorr said, letting his voice carry. "But I come bearing a proposal that I think might interest you immensely."

This caught Gannag's attention. He surveyed the gifts Kargorr had brought, and with a wry smile, he gestured into the camp.

"Fine, then," he said. "Come in, have a drink, and make your case."

It was a very good start indeed.

Still, unfortunately, it was a harder battle than Lord Kargorr had predicted. There was little love among the *grrosek* from one *parog* to another. Each of them had fought hard for their own territory and built their tents strong. What incentive did they have to leave it? And that's what he was asking: for them to leave their homeland behind and relocate south, into warmer human lands. It was a move that might put their orclings at risk.

Yet what Lord Kargorr offered was a powerful carrot at the end of a stick. Lord Gannag detested human scum and the way they had destroyed this land while the *grrosek* were trapped in the ice. Kargorr could detect the weakness in the other *kazek*'s armor, where he might be able to wedge a sword and peel him open.

Lord Gannag had no *yapira*, as many *kazek* didn't. Their only love should be for their *parog*, for victory, for pillage and death. And so behind the walls of their command tent, Lord Kargorr instructed his second Samrak, to bring up Kargorr's human concubine at the next opportunity.

"One of the delightful things about conquering," Samrak said over the fire that evening, "is the prisoners."

This piqued Lord Gannag's interest.

"I'm planning to take one of my own," the half-orc went on. "A human concubine. To sate my needs."

"They are very pliable," Lord Kargorr agreed. "Soft and small." He had to stop himself there, as his mind went back to Cedar, and it grated on him to even speak of her this way. But while the idea had sparked some gasps of indignation among Lord Gannag's leadership, the *kazek* himself considered it.

"You have one, then?" he asked Kargorr, picking under his nail with his knife thoughtfully.

"I do." All of his instincts wanted him to say the truth, that she was much more than that to him, but he knew better. "She has taken well to life in the *parog*. Humans are quite... adaptable."

This thought settled in with Lord Gannag, and Kargorr let

him sit with it for the following days. During this time, Lord Kargorr shared his plan, the size of the camp, the joined city he had planned should other lords choose to come to his cause. Gannag resisted mightily, hating the idea of living down in the warm lands and away from the tundra—but he could also see that Kargorr was right, and they would never be rid of the human pox unless they moved with a greater, more lethal force.

Though his campaign was going well, every night, Kargorr lay awake thinking of Cedar, of her belly getting fuller while he was away, how she was faring without him. Never had another consumed his thoughts like this before, and though it unnerved him to feel cold and hard without her presence there, he still answered the need. Every night, sometimes twice, he pulled out his cock and stroked it hard, his *sarga* swelling as they imagined being buried in Cedar's flawless cunt.

Then at last, after two weeks in which Kargorr wondered if the tension among his own band of warriors and their hosts might finally erupt in blows, Lord Gannag relented.

"We will pick up everything, as we have not done in many years"—the other lord gave Kargorr a significant look, as if he didn't know the pain himself—"and join you at your site. But if you've led me astray, know that I will gut you."

Lord Kargorr accepted this.

"The humans stand little chance," he said. He had already revealed how Orgha traveled now to yet another lord's *parog*, with the intention of recruiting even more *grrosek* to this cause and bring them together as they had never gathered before.

"Then lead us to victory," Lord Gannag said. "And we shall both hope that you are right."

33

CEDAR

The days were long and dreary, cold and dark. Bitter winds swept through the camp, and though Cedar could tell that her cat hungered to be outdoors more and more often, she kept him close by. It was selfish, she knew, but she needed his companionship. When the nights were coldest, she curled up with the bear pelt that still smelled somewhat of Kargorr, and stroked Kiya's soft fur. She always kept her dagger under her pillow.

Cedar hoped that spring would come soon, at least, and peel back the frigid air and endless nights that were suffocating her slowly.

Rathka was her usual ornery self, though she grew even more surly the faster the days that Orgha was gone became weeks. Cedar and Rathka snipped at one another from time to time, but had learned to co-exist in their loneliness. It was no secret now that Cedar cared for Lord Kargorr, that his absence affected her poorly, but Rathka was not cruel about it. If anything, she was sympathetic as they both waited for the caravans' return.

The other human concubines were known around the camp for their whimpering and whining, especially with so many of their orc keepers gone. Cedar had the opportunity to speak with them at the cook's tent, as they huddled in a group with a guard, but decided after listening to them gripe about their masters that she didn't have anything in common with them anymore.

One morning, Rathka remarked that Cedar's belly had grown, and Cedar reflexively covered it. Did she wish Kargorr was there to notice this, instead? So much was happening without him. Though she kept her memories of their last two nights together close, it was still stained with bitterness. He would never admit who she was to him as long as his mission remained at the forefront of his mind.

Would he still keep up this wall when her baby was born? Would she forever be seen by the rest of the orcs as a thing?

Sometimes Cedar touched herself at night, thinking of Kargorr, willing his body to return to hers. After three weeks had passed since the caravans' departure, Rathka insisted that it was time to visit the *shosek*.

Smoke filled the tent as they entered. Many pots full of odd ingredients covered the shelves, spilling over with leaves and herbs and dried bird legs.

The orc woman sitting on the other side of the fire was old, very old, with grooves on her dark green face that deepened when she frowned at them. She spoke none of the human tongue, only the Orcish one, and so Rathka translated. Little did she know that Cedar had been listening carefully, learning what she could just for moments like these. Cedar understood the ancient woman's discontent, that she resented the human who had taken their lord's affection so.

"The *shosek* is not pleased that Lord Kargorr chose you,"

LYONNE RILEY

Rathka said, in a matter-of-fact way. "But she will take stock of your orcling anyway. Be grateful."

Cedar pressed her lips into a thin line and turned back to face the healer, who was watching her intently. She ought to say something in Orcish, to put the old woman in her place as Lord Kargorr would, but Cedar didn't know what position this woman held in the camp if she was willing to speak so boldly, and she wasn't willing to give away yet that she could understand them. The less they thought she knew, the more unguardedly others would speak around her.

The *shosek* gestured for Cedar to come closer, so she obediently walked around the fire and sat. The old orc began to murmur something, words Cedar could barely hear, not to mention understand, as the smoke from the fire curled around them. While she spoke, the *shosek* reached for some pots off the nearby shelves and began tossing small objects into the flames. As they burned, the smoke reeked, and Cedar hastily covered her nose.

The old woman angrily objected.

"No," Rathka chided her. "The *shosek* says you must breathe it in."

Surely this couldn't be good for her baby, but Cedar was surrounded by orcs, and it would be another mark on her standing if she refused. So she inhaled the smoke and gagged, and the *shosek* watched her carefully. Then the old woman rose from her seat and went into the back, to return with a pot that smelled as bad as the fire. She scooped out some of the ointment and indicated for Cedar to raise her tunic.

With some hesitation, Cedar obeyed, revealing her rounded belly, and the *shosek* smeared the ointment all over her. Then the old orc woman bent her head and murmured again, keeping both of her hands on Cedar's stomach.

Cedar wished she could get up and run, because it all felt too strange, too intimate. Once again, Kargorr should be here with her, experiencing this with her, telling her what it all meant.

After some moments of silence, the *shosek* raised her head. She had a curious look in her eye that Cedar couldn't quite parse, but it made the hair on the back of her neck stand up.

Then the old woman spoke fast, too fast for Cedar to understand, but she picked up her disapproval. Rathka hesitated before translating.

"What did she say?" Cedar demanded.

Rathka's mouth pressed into a line, like she knew this would hurt and she wasn't eager to do it.

"This orcling grows outside the bonds of *yapira* and *agsan*," Rathka began. "So it will not be as strong as if it were cared for by a mated pair."

The *shosek* squinted at Cedar, the sheen of white cataracts over her black eyes giving her an eerie look. It was as if the ancient orc could see the truth underneath the lie—that Kargorr considered Cedar his *yapira* but refused to claim her.

Surely such a thing couldn't affect her baby. It was all superstition. But to fit in, Cedar would just have to bear it and pretend that the witch was right.

"Lord Kargorr should know this," Rathka said as the *shosek* bowed her head, then shifted back to her original seat. Cedar did not need to be told that they were finished, and she gave the old woman a cursory "thank you" in her tongue. The orc seemed surprised that she knew even that.

Then Cedar and Rathka departed the tent, Cedar's belly still slick.

"He'll know it when he returns," Cedar said firmly. "I want to visit the baths now, and not speak of it more."

Rathka did not argue.

As they settled into the hot water, though, Cedar hoped the old woman was wrong. This child would be strong, she knew. If just to spite the hag, Cedar would raise it to be so, with or without Lord Kargorr as her *agsan*.

She didn't need him in order to be a good mother.

KARGORR

After securing Lord Gannag's agreement to bind their forces together into one singular army, with a singular purpose, Lord Kargorr could at last return home.

It had been more than a month now, as Gannag's *parog* began packing up and Kargorr's own band of warriors loaded their sledges. It would be two more weeks before they reached their own *parog* down in the lowlands, and for a moment, Kargorr's head swam with the possibilities of what might have transpired while he was gone. If the humans had learned of the *parog*'s location...

He imagined his Cedar, at the center of a pile of bodies, and his stomach churned.

And so he pushed his warriors hard, probably harder than he should, asking much of their cats and their mammoths both. After many days of this, when the band was worn ragged, Samrak took the risk of advising him to let them rest or the animals would make their objections known.

Reluctantly, Kargorr allowed them to stop early for the night. But he was still full of his blood's need to be *home*, to see his hard woman and bury himself in her soft cunt, and to ensure his orcling was growing well. To fend it off and divert his mind, he snatched up a bow and left for a hunt with Liga, though she could have likely used the rest, too.

As they prowled through the woods, Kargorr tried to lose himself in the art of tracking, following footprints through the snow silently, while Liga sniffed the air to catch the scent of their prey. Spring was around the corner, and the animals would be careless as they began to mate and rut. Kargorr could use this to his advantage.

They moved silently through the snow toward the sound of males calling out to females. Then Liga leapt, and she was upon the stag before Lord Kargorr had even caught sight of him. Kargorr watched as his cat tore out the creature's throat, spewing blood across the white snow, wondering how far his mind had wandered that he hadn't seen it first.

Cedar. Thoughts of her were making him careless. His *sarga* had taken her, so why were they not now quiet?

Perhaps they would never be silent while she remained unclaimed.

But he had to wait. He would wait, until Orgha returned from his mission, hopefully bringing news that the eastern lord was open to Kargorr's plan. And then they would leave once more, to recruit another lord, and another lord still, until he had the force underneath him that he needed.

Only then, once he had secured the loyalty of all the *grrosek*, would he allow himself the weakness of fully taking his *yapira* in front of the entire *parog*.

He would learn to control himself until then. He would learn to keep his thoughts on the task at hand and break off the part of himself that craved her, all of her.

When Liga was finished feasting, Lord Kargorr tied the carcass to his saddle, and they dragged it back to camp.

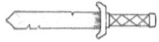

CEDAR

More than six weeks had passed when the call rang out across the camp: Lord Kargorr had returned.

For long moments, Cedar thought she was imagining it.

How many times had she hoped to hear that call? The drums beginning to beat, the cheers and whoops as other orcs left their tents and ran out to greet their returned friends and family?

Rathka surged to her feet and sprinted from the tent quicker than Cedar could track. But instead of running to Kargorr, Cedar felt frozen, remembering the last time he had returned.

How she had run. How he had chased her. How...

She took many deep breaths before steeling herself. She would not run this time. She had no reason to run, did she? He wouldn't replace her. He hadn't brought home the next iteration of her, a warm body to take her spot in their bed. He promised he wouldn't.

And though he was many other things, she did not know him to be an orc who lied.

Cedar squared her shoulders, intent on meeting Lord Kargorr at the gates. But before she could leave, the tent flap flew open—and in the entryway stood the biggest orc that had ever lived.

He had a great scar traveling from his temple, across his eyebrow, over his nose to his opposite tusk and then down, vanishing into his traveling clothes. His dark eyes were red around the edges, his lips peeled back in a vicious-looking snarl.

Lord Kargorr saw her, and that red in his black irises spread, nearly consuming them. He advanced toward her, and Kiya hissed from his place in the corner of the tent.

"Send him away," Kargorr commanded, his eyes never leaving hers.

"Kiya," Cedar said in a whisper, and gestured outside. "Go find your friends."

The cat understood this new word, *friends*, which meant

his siblings and the other cats in the snowfield, and he was happy to leave and join them to play.

Then Lord Kargorr took another step closer, and another, his sheer, feral intensity pouring off his skin in waves.

"Cedar," he rumbled, low in his throat, as if it were choking him. He seized her waist in one hand, while the other reached along her cheek to bury his fingers in her hair. Cedar gasped as he jerked her toward him, crushing her much smaller body against his huge, unyielding one.

He did not kiss her. He did not tear off her clothes. No, Lord Kargorr held her, enveloped her, clutching her as close as he could while he inhaled deeply at the base of her throat. She realized then that the arms he held her with were shivering, shaking, and so she wrapped her own arms as far around him as she could and squeezed him.

This was a different Kargorr than the one who had left her. This one was so desperate that he couldn't tuck it away inside, couldn't hide it behind hardness or cruelty.

Then, abruptly, Cedar was lying on her back on the furs, and he was on top of her, those red-rimmed eyes burrowing deep into hers, as if he could read her needs off the fabric of her soul. He crawled down her body and snatched the hem of her tunic in his teeth, using them to peel it back and reveal her belly.

"There," he murmured, sitting back so he could admire her. That's what he was doing, as a smile crawled across his unpracticed mouth. "My woman and my orcling."

He nodded, like he was agreeing with himself, like he was pleased at this outcome. Then he tugged on the laces of her pants, and Cedar helped him to kick them off.

She would not play coy. She would not hold herself back from taking what she wanted, what she'd been hungering for since he left. Perhaps she had not forgiven him, but she had allowed the flame to sprout anew in a different place. Here the tinder was even more ripe, more full of life-giving air, and when Kargorr braced himself between her thighs and spread them apart, she allowed the fire to consume her.

He reached down, dragging his finger from her protruding belly button to her mound, where he hovered for a moment before cursing to himself. He sat up and bit off the tip of his sharp claw, hastily filing it down on his tusk. He was muttering to himself in Orcish, something almost like a prayer as he got the tip dulled and returned to that warm, clenching place between her legs.

His finger skated over her lower lips, pausing to spread them, and Kargorr leaned down and breathed in deeply. Then came a low, throaty groan, as he dipped his finger into her, wetting it, before dragging it back up to her sensitive bead. He rubbed it in a way he never had before, just teasing it, circling it and flicking over the tip with small, precise movements.

Cedar had never felt anything like it. Her hips jerked involuntarily, and her cunt seized. With a hearty chuckle, Kargorr slid downward again, and tested the slit between her legs.

Then he dove down and devoured her.

Cedar cried out as that thick, black tongue of his lanced out, dragging up and over her clit, then across and down and every which way, while his finger worked its way inside her. She had touched herself while he was gone but had not taken an object, and now she felt small and tight around him.

As if he had just realized the same thing, Lord Kargorr snarled with barely contained desire. He began to pump his hand, fucking her hard with it while he ravaged her with his tongue, pausing occasionally to scrape his teeth over her swollen lower lips.

Soon, Cedar was high in the sky, above the tent, swaying and whirling with each lap he made, until she suddenly reached the sun and burst open. Her cry was high pitched as something unleashed inside her, and a rush of hot, wet liquid ran down onto the furs. She gasped and tried to wriggle away, but Lord Kargorr gripped her hips hard, pushing her back down to the bed as he thoroughly cleaned her.

She didn't realize her eyes had rolled back in her head as she shivered and shook with the force of whatever witchcraft he had visited upon her, until a shadow rose high above her, and something even warmer, even broader and softer than a finger swept through all that wetness. A moan escaped her as it pushed in, and she found Kargorr kneeling between her thighs, his great shape blotting out the dim lamplight. His eyes were intent on the place their bodies joined, his mouth open to reveal gritted teeth.

"Cedar," he ground out in a threatening voice. "I cannot promise I will not be rough with you." Even more of him slid into her, and though it shocked her body at first, it seemed to remember him and parted for him. More of that slick crown fit into her, and then came the shaft, all in one long stroke. Lord Kargorr groaned, toppling forward onto one arm so now his face was only inches from hers.

As he snapped his hips back, and then surged into her again, he attacked her mouth in a bruising kiss. He swallowed up her cry as he sunk deep, burying that thick, pulsing cock as far as he could, until those lumps at the base of him hinted at what would come. But she was still so tight, unpracticed at taking him after so much time apart.

But she could see in his eyes, could feel in the way his teeth ran over her lip, that would not last for long.

34

KARGORR

How slick she was, how perfect clenching around him this way, welcoming him in while squeezing and milking and suffocating him—it was almost beyond comprehending.

When he had arrived, Kargorr had barely managed to hand off Liga to one of the younger warriors before he stalked into the camp looking for Cedar. He would give her no reason to run from him. He would hold her and find solace again in her warm depths.

He had been gone too long, though, and her body had to stretch to accommodate him. But oh, how he would remind her of his size and shape, and she would remember.

Kargorr's body was determined to take his *yapira*, to invade her fully, to claim her and roar to the sky how she was his. But she wasn't, not yet. She would have to admit it first.

His blood howled in his veins as he pumped his hips faster, all his muscles tensing as he drove into her. Her belly had grown while he was gone, and now it was rounded with him, his orcling warm and small inside. His eyes rolled back in his head as he drowned himself in her again and again, his *sarga* seeking her with one gentle push after another. Cedar's perfect pink-brown lips parted as he began to wedge himself inside her, squeezing in one stroke at a time. She opened for him, and eagerly, without hesitation, Lord Kargorr fully sheathed himself in her small body.

A roar was pulled from his lips as Cedar's heels dug into his back, as her body seized, as her breasts bounced and at last, he found his way back to his place inside her.

But the last threads of his control were worn through, and he snapped apart. He plunged into her, then reeled his hips back to suck his *sarga* free from her, only to shove back in again roughly. She screamed a throaty scream, and so he plowed her spread, swollen cunt until she was writhing and her soft channel was fluttering. They danced on the edge of a sharp blade, almost teetering off the side.

Then she broke. He loved that he could make Cedar break this way, her chest arching and her fingers gripping his arms like claws. All her marvelous squeezing took him easily off the edge, dragging him down with her. His swollen *sarga* were trapped now, and Kargorr thrust once more before he finally followed her into oblivion.

They did not exchange words until morning, when sunlight crept in through the tent ceiling, and Lord Kargorr blinked bleary eyes. Rarely did he find himself in this state, sated like a cat that has just gorged on a fresh kill. He could move, he thought, and perhaps he ought to. But Cedar was curled up against him, her head resting on his arm, her breathing the only thing in the quiet.

But then he heard movement outside, and knew he had

matters to attend to, now that Lord Gannag's *parog* was on the way. Still, he watched her a few moments longer, and his free hand traveled down her body, exploring it, tracing the familiar edges of it and committing them to memory again. His blood warmed for her as he thought of all the ways he had rutted her last night, slinging her legs up over his shoulders, rolling her onto her front so he could lie on top of her, their legs and arms wrapped up together.

His cock was fully alert now, rubbing against Cedar's swelled belly, and she shifted in her sleep. With a soft moan, she rubbed back, and her hands drifted down until they were wrapped around his girth, and her eyes drifted open.

And then she smiled. It was an unguarded, pleased sort of smile, a smile he had never once seen on her face before. Lord Kargorr watched her, frozen, as she stroked up the length of him with her small hand.

There was certainly no chance of him leaving this tent now.

He fucked her while looking into her brown eyes, taking his time, working himself into her one slow inch by slow inch, languidly stoking her flames until she was burning, crying out, a twisting, panting, sweating mess underneath him. It gave him great pleasure to undo her.

"Tell me, little deer," he murmured to her, teasing her with his *sarga* but not yet giving them to her. "Tell me how you are mine."

"I'm not," she whined, jerking her hips up, trying to take more of him. "Please, I—"

And Kargorr swallowed her objections, scouring her mouth as his *sarga* filled her up, as he took pleasure in her and pleasured her all at once, until he had emptied his seed inside her twice more and she was utterly boneless underneath him.

But the time had come and he had delayed too long. Lord Kargorr sat up and rose off the bed, but a hand caught him.

"You aren't leaving again, are you?"

Cedar's question surprised and rejuvenated him, this not-so-hidden plea for his presence and company. Of course he would leave—he had to, in a few weeks' time. But for a moment, he considered lying, because her hesitance also meant that perhaps the bond between them was healing.

Lord Kargorr held her gaze. "Not immediately," he said, and she wilted. "First, Lord Gannag will join us here."

She blinked. "He agreed to come?" They had been too lost in their reunion for him to even convey this news.

"And his entire *parog*," Lord Kargorr said. "We will do as no *grrosek* have done before us and combine our forces. We will build an army." As he spoke, his vigor and his determination swelled. "And then I will bring more *kazek*, more *parog*, until we have the force to destroy all of humanity."

Cedar was not affronted, as he might have thought she would be, given he intended to extinguish her kind. Instead, she gave him a look that was almost... pitying.

"When will it be enough?" she asked. "How many lords?"

Lord Kargorr did not understand the question. He would walk to the ends of the earth to find his kin, bring them together, and lead the assault. In the ashes, he would rise as the unifier.

"Until we can walk over their bodies with our boots," Kargorr said, and began to dress.

Cedar didn't speak as he finished and headed for the tent door. There, he paused.

"I will remain here as long as possible," Lord Kargorr said at last. "And send Orgha in my place when I can. But this is what I must do, what I was called on to do."

Gazing upon her face, though, it was clear to him that Cedar knew this. She already knew how his mission superseded all else, including her. So Cedar simply nodded, then lay back down in the furs, resigned to it.

When he left the tent, Kargorr called on someone to find Rathka and bring her. Kiya slept on the ground, waiting for his mistress. Opening the tent flap, Kargorr sent the cat inside. Unlike Liga, who had grown up on the snowfields with the other cats, Kiya had an intuitiveness about him that surprised Kargorr. The cat understood many words and knew when Cedar needed him.

Lord Kargorr should be thinking about what came next, about the wave of *grrosek* descending upon them and everything their presence would demand: more tents, more land, more food, more everything. There was much to plan and many tasks to do, and yet even as he summoned Samrak and the two of them got to work, Kargorr thought of how his *yapira* had taken him so well last night, and how poorly he had left her this morning.

He could not give her what she wanted: true security, in his heart and in his *parog*. And he hated it.

CEDAR

The camp was bright with energy when she and Rathka emerged. A warm, spring sun was shining down, and it rather maddened Cedar that the world would only choose to warm up when Lord Kargorr returned. She was second-best, even in the sun's eyes.

Everyone was working, and when Cedar entered Carn's workshop, she found another young half-orc there, helping with some fresh kills. She was pretty, and had thick, braided hair that fell over her shoulder. She spoke Cedar's language, which was a welcome reprieve from most of the time, when no one except Carn and Rathka understood her.

But the orc woman did not meet Cedar's eyes. She spoke a

little of her mother, a human woman who had been taken decades ago and already passed away. It was comforting for Cedar to speak in her own language with someone who fully understood her.

Apparently, the hunters were out scouring the landscape for fresh kills, so the camp cooks could dry more meat for the coming orcs. Cedar wondered how many of these strangers there would be, and how the camp would accommodate all of them—more warriors, more families, even another lord.

Were he and Kargorr equals? Would Kargorr now be the one in charge? She felt a crawling sort of unease, wondering how power might shift.

That night, Lord Kargorr did not return to the tent until after Cedar had already eaten dinner. When the flap finally opened and he stepped inside, she was lying by the fire in a light doze with Kiya at her side.

Neither of them spoke as he took her to bed, as he licked her cunt and her sweat, as he held her on his lap and lifted her up, only to bring her down over his cock again.

When they were sated, and Kargorr weaved his fingers through her hair, Cedar asked him how the planning had gone, and he reported back that he had already tasked a team with clearing trees and flattening the earth for more tents.

"I sent an assistant," Kargorr said. "I thought she might be to your liking."

Cedar furrowed her brow. "The half-orc? You sent her?"

"To help Carn, and you, in preparing more tents. I'll be sending even more help as our hunters bring in fresh kills so that we might have plenty of leather ready to be sewn together into new homes for our guests."

"So Lord Gannag is your guest?" she asked. She wanted to know who he was, and what Lord Kargorr might expect of her.

His hand in her hair halted, his finger caught in a tangle.

"Yes," Kargorr said after a time. "He is a guest, but also an ally. A leader. If he feels that he's not being afforded the respect he is owed, then there may be trouble."

It was as Cedar had feared. There would be another pole of power introduced to the camp, and that could be unpredictable.

"I see." She thought for a moment, because such a transition portended conflict. "We ought to make a welcome gift, then."

Lord Kargorr sat up on the furs and arched a critical eyebrow.

"A welcome gift?" He snorted. "This is not the *grrosek* way. We have already afforded his *parog* many gifts in the courting stage."

"And once you court, do the gifts end?" She raised herself up on the bed, too, and pulled the bear pelt into her lap. "How does one maintain the relationship, then, and keep the other party pleased?"

She peered up at him, and Lord Kargorr's pitch-black eyes bored into her, searching her, digging inside her for the source and meaning of her question.

"An angle I had not considered," he admitted at last. "No *grrosek* has ever attempted what I am attempting. So perhaps you are right, little deer, and I should keep him fat and happy with gifts."

Once more Kargorr lay back down, and rather forcefully, pulled her to the furs with him. He pressed her back flush to his firm stomach, and his hands slid down her breasts, over her belly, where he spread his fingers.

"What sort of gifts should these be?" he asked, and there was almost a teasing note in his voice.

Cedar thought for a time over what the coming orcs might need, something they wouldn't think to bring for themselves but would show them better what the way of life looked like in Lord Kargorr's camp.

"Syrup-crusted pork," Cedar said, without hesitation. "Use some of my pigs. They have grown well and would be ideal for a roast."

Of course, Bread Pudding meant much to her—and her piglets were one of the last few reminders of her old life—but so did Cedar want to ensure that Lord Kargorr's gambit went peacefully. She feared what so many orcs might do in such close quarters when they harbored an easy willingness to resort to violence.

Lord Kargorr remained in a thoughtful silence for some time, then pulled her ass flush against his hips. He was already hard for her, wet and leaking.

"A clever woman I found," he muttered as she spread her legs, and he slipped through them. She was already covered in his seed, so his cock found its way easily inside her. "Such a good, sturdy woman."

It took six more days for the new orcs to finally arrive.

35

KARGORR

He would not just offer Lord Gannag's *parog* the syrup-crusted pork, though that would certainly sweeten the deal they had already accepted.

It wasn't enough to have an ally, just like it wasn't enough to have a *yapira*. One must care for them, too, and keep the pot appealing. Relationships had needs to be tended, and the better his bonds fared, the stronger they were.

He wouldn't just listen to his *yapira* because it was good and right advice, and he counted himself fortunate to have a companion who brought wisdom to his hearth. He would do it to please her, too, because the happier Cedar was, the better he felt, basking in her warmth instead of freezing in her cold.

So Lord Kargorr set about to creating an appealing campsite that the other *grrosek* could call home during the time they spent here, before they traveled south and conquered new lands. He considered their orclings and what they might need to be comfortable and find entertainment. He had the baths expanded and ordered new cooks to be trained to accommo-date the incoming force.

Orgha had not yet returned when Lord Gannag finally arrived. It unsettled Kargorr to not have his right hand at his side during such a momentous event, but he would have to trust himself to manage whatever might come.

Lord Gannag himself waited on his cat just outside the entrance to the *parog* for Kargorr to come out and greet him. They each thumped their chests and nodded.

"Welcome to our *parog*," Kargorr said. "As it is now yours."

He would make this lord feel like a valued guest, and then it would be easier to give him commands later, when it mattered most. That was when Kargorr would enforce who was truly in charge of this affair.

Settling in was no easy task. Lord Gannag had arrived with his own tents and poles, animals and gear, but his mammoths could not descend into the lowlands with their sledges. Lord Kargorr sent many of his own to assist, and it required days upon days of hard labor to transport all of Gannag's *parog* and their many belongings.

In the meantime, Kargorr was grateful he had commis-sioned additional tents, though his leatherworkers and tailors had labored themselves into exhaustion. He had to extract Cedar personally at night so she did not overwork herself and put the orcling at risk.

She had put up a surprising amount of fight about it. She wanted to be helpful, to put in the same hours of work the others were, but he would not allow his *yapira* to run herself into the ground.

Though the first wave of *grrosek* had only just settled into their new tents and others were still coming, it was a fine night, and Lord Kargorr was grateful for the clear sky and warm air that came in on a breeze as the bonfire was lit and the drums began.

His next gift: a marvelous celebration of Lord Gannag's arrival.

With her permission, two of Cedar's pigs were cooked alongside fresh venison, and even chickens that had persisted throughout the winter. Ale flowed, and though the revelers did not all have roofs over their heads that night—and many would have to share their homes with strangers—they were in high spirits, enraptured in the promise of their mission southward.

We will conquer the humans. We will take back what is ours. We will, we will, we will. Kargorr was glad to listen in on these conversations, and as Cedar sat on his lap at the raised table beside Lord Gannag's, a small smile played at her lips. She could hear it, too, and it pleased her.

He liked that it pleased her.

"Now that I've seen her with my own eyes," Lord Gannag said, drawing Lord Kargorr's attention, "I understand your attraction, Kargorr."

The other orc spoke in the *grrosek*'s own tongue, of course. Cedar turned her head and tilted it to show she didn't understand.

"He is complimenting you," Kargorr told her, possessively patting her rounded belly. "Indeed," he answered the other lord. "There is much to admire about her."

Lord Gannag laughed and lifted his mug of mead. "A good choice of concubine." Then he threw it back and drank.

The word *concubine* unsettled Lord Kargorr, and he couldn't help glancing at Cedar's face. She did not show she comprehended, though that perhaps irritated him more. She couldn't understand what Gannag said about her and telling her would only upset the balance between them.

"She will bear me a fine orcling," was all Kargorr said as he drank from his own vessel. It was dishonest, but necessary—perhaps a strategy more critical now than ever before.

This lord could not know how a human woman held Kargorr's heart in her tiny little hands, or how she could crush it into bloody flesh if she so chose.

CEDAR

She did not like the look of Lord Gannag, not at all.

It wasn't that he was ugly, or any uglier than any other orc. In fact, he might even be more handsome than Kargorr in a tedious sort of way. He had no great puckered scar, no blaze in his eyes, none of the same ferocity and hunger for action as her orc did.

And he was not nearly so tall.

Her orc. Cedar saw how many of the new warriors looked at him. They did not hide their interest in him, as many of Lord Kargorr's orcs did. Kargorr's own camp had seen what Cedar meant to their lord, but these newcomers were different. Orc men and women alike passed by their table with offerings to thank Lord Kargorr for welcoming them, but it clearly meant much more than that to some.

Many gifts were quite elaborate, valuable objects that made Cedar feel sick to her stomach. Those who left such gifts, she knew, were hoping for a measure of Lord Kargorr's attention in exchange. She did not like that, despite her presence, they felt so confident as to make their interest in him known.

But Cedar was a possession, much like these carved

animals and hunting knives and bone jewelry, and Lord Kargorr did not dissuade any of them from believing they might have a chance at him.

Cedar especially didn't like Lord Gannag's roaming eyes, how he stared at her when he thought Lord Kargorr was not looking. She could, though she pretended not to, understand what he said about her. His gaze combed her body, removing her layers of clothing, and Cedar resisted the urge to cover herself. Instead, she smiled prettily, though it unnerved her.

But Kargorr did not hide his ownership of her, frequently stroking her belly, and grinding her ass down against his groin as the night wore on and the alcohol worked on him. And as the orcs around the fire divided carefully into two groups, then began to mingle... the alcohol worked on them, too. Orcs from each side went out to greet the others, and many coupled off. This could be a great boon, Cedar thought as she watched them, as perhaps other orclings were being made between the two groups. It could unify them, help them work together better and serve Kargorr's cause.

She wondered when she had come to care so much about his success, about his mission, when it should haunt her.

Perhaps it was that she found life here much more suited to her. She ate well and slept in warm furs, and she had Kiya. It was more than she'd ever been given by humankind, so maybe it was best that they fell to the orcs. Orcs believed children should have childhoods and would not sell off their own young for a cow.

The moon was high in the sky when Lord Kargorr hooked his thumbs in her pants and pulled them down her thighs. His fingers ventured up under her tunic, and he growled in her ear as he eased himself inside her. Cedar watched the other orcs, many buried up to the hilt in each other, as Kargorr fucked her in his lap, and she would have met her finish much sooner had Lord Gannag not been avidly watching the entire time.

Kargorr carefully did not use those lumps at the base of his cock on her, his *sarga*, which felt significant. That was only for them, in private, she understood now.

His seed was still dripping from her thighs when she heard Gannag speak.

"Perhaps when you are done," he said dryly in Orcish, "I could whet her on my own cock."

Lord Kargorr sat up abruptly, still lodged in her. "I must not have heard you correctly," he said in a warning tone. "Surely you are not asking for my concubine's cunt?"

This time, Cedar could not hide that she understood. Her eyes went wide and she gaped at Lord Gannag, as Kargorr's hands tightened around her.

"Ah," Gannag said, smiling ruefully. "She knows more of our language than you think, Kargorr. Still, she is but your toy, is she not?"

Was that how he spoke of her when she wasn't around? Of course it was. They all knew her as his concubine, and concubine only.

"She is bearing my orcling," Lord Kargorr said at last, his cock sliding out of her.

"Then she'll bear mine next," said Gannag. "Once she has shown she can produce such strong offspring as you predict, perhaps your next gift to me can be this lovely wet basket of yours."

A ripple of pure rage spread down Cedar's spine. Surely he wasn't asking this.

That's when she heard a growl behind her, low and rumbling, as threatening as one of the cats when they fought over a scrap of leftover meat. Lord Gannag quirked a brow as Kargorr clutched her closer, tighter.

"She is not for sale," Lord Kargorr said gruffly. It was clear that he was reining in his baser impulses, because his body was nearly vibrating underneath hers.

"But you have given me so many lovely gifts tonight, perhaps you can grant me this one more?" Lord Gannag stumbled closer. "No pretty orc woman from your *parog* has propositioned me tonight. That is rather unfair, isn't it, when your own cock fares much better?"

The big orc leaned forward, so his face was in Cedar's. Lord Kargorr surged to his feet behind her, immense, scarred, his eyes like the night.

"I think it fair that I have a hole in which to spend myself," Lord Gannag said with an eerie smile.

Cedar answered. She answered quickly, her hand moving before she had a moment to think twice about what her actions might mean, what consequences they might have. The slap of flesh echoed, carrying in the night air.

She withdrew her hand, holding it close to her chest as if protecting an offending animal that didn't know better. Lord Gannag's head was turned to one side, the skin across his cheek dark green from where she'd struck him. Her fingers reflexively fell to her dagger, tucked into the belt around her waist.

It was only then Cedar realized the whole gathering had gone quiet, and every orc nearby was watching. Others approached, now that it had been noticed the two lords were already in conflict.

This was everything she had been trying to avoid, and now she was right at the center of it.

36

KARGORR

His marvelous woman.

Lord Kargorr's rage quieted just for this moment as he gazed upon her, at her shaking shoulders and proud, angry face. Cedar had understood precisely what Lord Gannag said about her, and she had acted. She was beautiful and strong, and would make a fine mother to his orclings. Her ferocity represented everything he sought to create, the shape of the world he wished to carve from stone and flesh.

It would all look like her, right now, having spoken against a great, powerful, terrifying lord.

"A concubine?" asked Lord Gannag, slowly turning his head back to face them. He glared down his nose at Cedar and raised his own hand. "A concubine would *hit* me?" He was rippling with his fury, and when his fist swung in retaliation...

Lord Kargorr caught it. He seized the other *kazek*'s wrist, and slowly, with a far superior strength, lowered Gannag's arm.

"Perhaps you have not heard me," Lord Kargorr snarled. "This woman is *mine*, bearing *my* orclings, forever until the end of time. You will not put your cock in her. *Ever*." His own rage burned bright as he brought Cedar to his side, and his hand fell to the long knife he kept at his waist for eating.

"She is a plaything." Lord Gannag spit on the ground. "A body for our pleasure, and I've had to watch you have all the fun." His beady eyes hung on Cedar, who now remained at Kargorr's side. "She is human, Kargorr. She is nothing. And now, she will die for what she's done."

"You will not *touch* my *yapira*!"

Lord Kargorr's bellow rang out over the silent camp. As soon as the words were spoken aloud, though, an audible objection rose up from the assembled orcs.

But many on Kargorr's side of the fire were silent. He saw them nodding, as if this had come to be understood already by many.

He had said it. He had said it aloud, for everyone to hear.

"Your *yapira*?" Gannag asked, aghast. "This human?"

"Yes." Kargorr couldn't un-say what he'd said. It was the truth, after all. "I bonded to her many moons ago."

It felt as if a great weight had fallen from his shoulders. Though he faced judgment out around the fire, for the first time since finding Cedar, he felt as if he was truly himself.

"And you have used your *sarga*? On a *human*?" Lord Gannag shook his head. "And this is the orc I've chosen to align myself with."

"You will not question my character," snapped Lord Kargorr, and he pulled the knife free. "I can cut you down for your insults, or you can sit back down, and drink your mead, and perhaps find a ripe woman tonight."

Quiet fell as Lord Gannag shook with his fury. He sized up Kargorr, and it could be a bloodbath between them—but that would sow chaos and death among their *parog*.

"We share a purpose, a mission," said Lord Kargorr, running his hand down Cedar's side. "Do not throw that away because I have chosen a mighty *yapira*, whom you have deeply insulted."

Lord Gannag growled, but did not advance. Kargorr was prepared, his muscles taut and ready. He would do whatever he needed to defend Cedar and his *parog*.

With a great sigh, the other *kazek* picked up his mug. Then he slung back his mead.

"Then give me a woman," Gannag said with a growl. "I want one of these humans, who has so fine of a cunt that she can call an orc lord her *agsan*."

Kargorr's shoulders loosened, and he took a heavy breath before he slapped Lord Gannag on the back.

"Of course," Kargorr said amiably, as if none of this had ever happened. "That's the wonderful thing about conquest. There are many more humans to be found. Perhaps you will find your own *yapira*."

Lord Gannag scoffed. "I will not succumb to that weakness," he said gruffly. He glanced at Cedar, who now stood stricken. "Though some fine, half-orc offspring..."

He went on about the virtues of half-orcs, their superior sight and fine craftsmanship, but Kargorr could not forget his own words.

He had, at last, announced to the world who Cedar was to him. It was now done and could not be undone.

And he was grateful for that.

CEDAR

She had fully expected to die. Or at least be lashed until she bled and begged.

The revelry went wild after the lords settled their conflict. When at last Kargorr rose to his feet and announced he and his *yapira* were off to bed, it was met with hoots and hollers and cheers.

Kargorr took Cedar's hand and brought his lips to her forehead before whisking her away to their tent. As they passed through the crowd, Cedar caught sight of Rathka, who had her arms crossed with a touch of amusement playing on her lips.

Once inside the tent, Lord Kargorr did not even let them reach the bed first. He whirled her around in his arms and slid up her tunic to expose her growing breasts.

"My fierce woman," he said, pausing to lick her nipples, panting as he sucked on them. Cedar's chest arched into him, and he curled his arm around her waist to hold her fast. "Willing to strike a *grrosek* lord for his insults." He hungrily took her whole breast in his palm and feasted on it while she moaned and tangled her hands in his hair.

"I... I would not be a *hole*," Cedar said, interrupting herself with gasps.

"Indeed," Kargorr murmured, finally releasing her. "You may be human, but you have the ferocity of an orc."

That felt like a compliment. She wanted to be ferocious, to be feared, as Kargorr was.

"Now," Kargorr said, kneeling to pull her pants down, which were still wet with his seed, "will you say it?" He dragged his lips from her calves to her thighs, then to the crux of her legs. He continued upward, rising to his feet, until he stood high above her, one hand on her cheek.

Cedar pressed her lips together. Was she his now? It begged another question: Was he hers?

"Will you ever take another?" Cedar asked instead, and Kargorr furrowed his brow.

"Another?" His mouth tilted up at the corner. "No. I do

not have the time or energy for another one of you. You are enough for a single orc to manage."

It was, perhaps, the first time he had made a joke in Cedar's presence, and a startled laugh came out of her.

"And you will make me your partner, and not your concubine?" she asked, and his roaming hand stilled at her side.

Kargorr let out a great sigh and bowed his head.

"You already are this," he said, surprisingly quiet. "You have given me great wisdom and tempered me. And I have shown you very little care or thanks in return."

Cedar merely stared up at him, for she didn't recognize this behemoth of an orc, with the scar across his face and the hard, downward curve to his tusked mouth. What were these words of his?

"Then," Cedar said, reaching to stroke his chin up to his tusk, "I suppose I can be what you want."

His eyes went wide, then they narrowed in a plain, feral hunger. He snatched her up off the ground and carried her to the bed, where he set her down and quickly disposed of his own clothes. Then he sat before her, his legs spread, his huge cock jutting up toward the sky, and held his hands open, palms up.

"Come to me, then," he said in a low voice. "Make use of me and show me your orcish fire."

KARGORR

She did.

How gloriously Cedar sank down on his cock, sitting astride him on her knees. When she raised herself up and then took him in again, her belly bounced, and her round breasts teased his eyes as they responded to every movement. She would feed his orcling quite well, and he would never fear for its safety as long as it was with her.

When her thighs grew tired and she had already sought her finish twice, Lord Kargorr flipped her onto her back and fucked her deeper, harder, nursing cries and screams from her plush lips.

"Tell me," he growled, sinking further into her, his *sarga* insisting that she open for him.

"I'm yours," she sobbed in return. And then, he was fully encased in her wet warmth, fully with her, inside her, reveling in her.

They lay quietly for some time afterwards, his swollen cock still firmly rooted inside Cedar's perfect cunt. His hand wandered her body, pausing at her belly.

"The old witch," Cedar said suddenly. "She told me the baby would be weaker if... if you weren't my *agsan*. Does this change anything?"

He scoffed. "She is wrong." Kargorr let his hair fall over both of them like a curtain. "But perhaps you have been my *yapira* since the beginning, and that is why the leaves turned red as blood. Our orcling will be mighty, fearsome, powerful. I know this already." And he did. This offspring would take the helm for him someday, and once the world was theirs, he would quietly recede with Cedar at his side, for the rest of eternity.

"I hope they are wise, too," said Cedar carefully. "Not just strong, but quick. There is as much strength in cleverness as in brute force."

Kargorr arched an eyebrow at her. "That is what you will bring, then. Teaching our orcling to use their head, as much as their fists."

That night, for the first time, perhaps in his life, Lord Kargorr slept knowing that it all was as it should be. Though there was far more to do, for now, this was the right place, the right time, with the right woman at his side.

The camp was slow to wake the following day as the *grrosek* shook off the fog of drink and the haze of copulating. Lord Kargorr wondered in the silence, as Cedar still slept, how many orclings were made while the sun was down.

What roused him from his bed was the sound of a beating drum and a few scattered cheers.

While Cedar yawned, he quickly dressed and left the tent.

"*Kazek*!" He would know that voice anywhere. It was Orgha, at last returned.

And he was not alone.

Behind him was the caravan he had departed with, and behind them, a horde of *grrosek*, that went on as far as Kargorr could see. He slapped his right hand hard on his back, and Orgha coughed.

"You have brought me a gift," Kargorr said, his face slack.

"Indeed. Lord Rukhan heard my missive and responded well." Orgha turned as another orc appeared, a behemoth of a creature with a wide, mighty face. He was even bigger than Kargorr, truly a beast, and he rode the biggest cat to ever live.

"Your presence is greatly welcomed," Lord Kargorr said as Lord Rukhan dismounted. Rukhan thumped his chest, as did Kargorr in return, and then the other orc's stern lips broke out into a mad, wicked smile.

"I am only here because Orgha promised me many human heads would roll," Lord Rukhan said with a feral look in his eye. "I will join any effort to this end, as strange as it might be to find so many of our kind squirreled away in one place." He eyed the massive *parog* that had doubled in size already. "I hope that there is still room for us."

"We will make room." Kargorr's voice carried over the sound of drumbeats. "And we will then move southward, to take what is ours."

He knew Cedar was approaching before he even saw her, and turned to bring her under his arm. Orgha quirked a brow, but did not speak.

"Make yourself at home," Lord Kargorr said, "though please, do not insult my *yapira* or she may strike you the way she struck Lord Gannag last night."

A huge, booming laugh streamed out of Lord Rukhan.

"A human, no less," he said, eyeing Cedar's belly. "I thought we were here to kill them, not breed them."

She tensed at Kargorr's side, but he stroked her arm.

"I do not know if all of them are as bullheaded as mine," said Kargorr, "but she is as fierce as any orc and will raise fine warriors. Many of them."

Lord Rukhan seemed to consider this as they began welcoming in the new arrivals. It would be madness for some time, Lord Kargorr knew, trying to get them all settled. But he handed out commands, and Orgha spread the word, even as he reunited with his own *yapira*.

They would have time later, but for now, the construction of Kargorr's mighty city would begin.

37

CEDAR

The clan grew and grew, until the camp had become more of a city. Carn kept Cedar busy curing new hides to be sewn into tents, to help accommodate the massive influx of orcs that had taken over the camp. More trees had been felled and carved into posts, then piled high for future bonfires.

Though there were more mouths to feed, there were also more hunters and more livestock that had come with the travelers. And every night, more orcs crossed the lines, and Cedar foresaw dozens of ceremonies in the future between those who had been here, and those who had recently arrived, their unions tying all the groups together.

A distinct change came over Lord Kargorr in the days and weeks following. In the evenings, he told her everything that he had done that day in the new, larger *parog* as he rubbed *kuja* over the pink lines forming on her swollen belly. He had conflicts with the other lords over how to proceed, and the role of peacemaker did not come naturally to him. He would tell her what they argued about, and to her surprise, asked Cedar what she thought.

She gave him as wise counsel as she could, advising him how to play the other lords against each other to get what he wanted, how he could weasel them into agreeing to his proposals by doling out fodder for their egos.

And Kargorr listened raptly to her, then reported back how well it went.

"Orgha thinks I have lost my mind," he said one evening as they sat on the floor in front of the fire, blankets and furs piled around them in a nest. "Allowing them to 'walk all over me,' as he put it."

"You are the puppet master." Cedar leaned back into his hard body, and he reached around her belly to cup it in his hands. "The puppet master's moves should be invisible."

He chuckled into her hair. "My clever *yapira*." He kissed her there, his lips traveling down to the nape of her neck, his hand trailing up to her breasts, which grew larger with each passing day. They were also more sensitive now, and so Kargorr was gentle with her nipples as he teased them. "Is this how you mastered me? With your tiny strings?"

She chuckled as she kissed the palm of his hand. "Like gentling a cat."

When he took her, he was more careful with her, and Cedar had to ask for him to fuck her harder.

Kiya was old enough that he could no longer sleep in their tent, as big and clawed as he had become, and so he moved out to sleep among the other cats. There were many new arrivals, and Kargorr appreciated it would improve the diversity of the group and prevent inbreeding.

Though Cedar missed Kiya at times, she went and saw him often, and whenever she called his name, he came running. He would snuffle at her hand, purring as she scratched behind his ears, and she always fell to her knees to hug him before she left again.

He was happier there, she knew, and the pang of loneliness she expected to feel never came. Day by day, Cedar grew more anxious to meet their orcling. Carrying it was no easy task, either. She grew quickly and often visited the healer to see that all was well. The old *shosek* still sneered down her nose at Cedar, but she didn't dare speak out against her lord's *yapira*. She applied salves to keep away stretch marks and tested the orcling's position in Cedar's belly with her hands.

"It is healthy," she would say in Orcish. "Healthy and... strong." She hesitated on the last word, as if she didn't want to admit it, but it was too true to ignore.

And their orcling was growing strong, Cedar could feel it with every passing day.

"You are full to bursting with me," Lord Kargorr would say, cupping her belly as if to take off some of the weight and carry it for her. Then he would kiss her throat, and palm one of her swollen breasts, even in the middle of the *parog*. Other orcs gave him appreciative nods, showing their respect for him and his *yapira*.

Kargorr had a knowing look in his eye one day as they went to visit Kiya out in the snowfields. Even though she was big and awkward, he told her it was as good of a time to learn to ride as any.

"What if I fall?" Cedar asked, wrapping an arm around her middle.

Her *agsan* merely smiled, and it was a rare expression. "The orcling will be fine. It's mine, and it will be resilient."

Cedar called to Kiya, and he happily jogged over to them, searching for treats. Cedar had practiced climbing onto Liga on her own, and Liga was much bigger, so Kiya shouldn't present a problem.

She grabbed his scruff and slung her body up and over his

back. But Cedar missed the first time, because her weight was strangely distributed. Kiya shuffled to one side, giving her an odd look.

"Hold still," she said, and gave it one more try.

Then she was up on Kiya's back, and he grunted underneath her.

"Sorry," Cedar said, stroking his neck. "Do you want to go for a ride?"

So she leaned forward, as Kargorr had taught her, and ushered him into a run.

Kiya flew. Cedar's body remembered how to move in time with the snap of his spine, to rise and fall with each stroke of his long legs. They ran and ran, making circles around the enormous camp, until both of them were exhausted.

When they returned, Lord Kargorr was waiting for her, a smug smirk on his face.

That night, he took her slowly, telling her how good and strong and beautiful she was atop her cat, and how he looked forward to riding side by side to their new homeland.

Kargorr was planning something, but would not share what it was.

After finishing at the leatherworker's, Cedar hustled to the baths because she knew he detested the scent. He had worked many long hours today, as he did every day, preparing the camp and his warriors for their next mission.

She did not like that he would be leaving again soon, when the baby was so close to being born, but he promised it would be a short campaign to clear out villages that lay between the camp and the larger human city to the south.

"We will relocate then," he had said, stroking her hair. "To bring all of you closer to the front line. It will be more dangerous, but with such a force amassed, I believe it will be more than safe for you and the orcling."

Cedar was even rounder now, and Kargorr was the one to notice when the indent in her belly popped out. He was elated to discover it, that she was that much closer to giving birth to their first child. Sometimes he showed her off, leading her around the camp with him as he did checks and was called to oversee preparations.

Tonight, she was dressing herself for such rounds when Lord Kargorr returned to their tent. He was wearing unusual clothing, with necklaces of bone and teeth around his neck, and an elaborate jerkin with a swooping collar, so that his big chest was bare. His loincloth matched, and underneath it, his cock hung in a sling that hid very little.

"Cedar," he said, leaning down to capture her lips. "Wear this?" He produced a long dress, sewn in a way she had never seen before, with elaborate hems and bones along the seams. Curious, she stripped down and changed into it, and his gaze traversed her with a pleased nod.

"Come." He held out his arm, and curiously, Cedar obeyed, linking them together. He led her out of the tent, toward the pit in the middle of the camp.

The fire was already lit, but no one was dancing or drinking or singing. Many had gathered, but they were all silent as Lord Kargorr led her through the masses, toward the fire.

There, he stopped and turned to face Cedar.

"It has taken me far too long to do this, little deer," he said, his dark eyes capturing hers and holding them there, riveted. "But now I will amend that." He pushed her hair back from her face and tucked it behind her ear, and then he swallowed in a way that was, she thought, almost apprehensive.

"My *yapira*," he said quietly, as if just for her ears. "You are mine. You have always been, and you always will be."

Cedar nodded slowly, a subject they had covered before. But then, Lord Kargorr reached into his mouth, behind his right tusk. Her eyes widened as he yanked hard, and with a gush of red blood, he pulled one of his teeth free.

KARGORR

No woman radiated light the way his *yapira* did. Cedar was even keener than he'd thought, with a quick mind. Her heart could be as hard as it was soft, depending on who she showed it to.

Now that his orcling was nearly here, there was something he had neglected. A path of showing her what she meant to him—how he now lived in service of her pleasure. He had chosen the correct partner for his vision of the future. Now it was time to claim her, to give her the *grrosek*'s truest symbol of devotion, a piece of himself to prove that she would always have his heart, as all his ancestors had done.

"Kargorr!" Cedar cried, reaching up toward him as he removed the tooth from his mouth, but he wrapped his fingers around hers and clasped them tight to show her it was all right. Orgha approached, carrying a pick and a hammer, and took the tooth away with him. A hole was made, and Cedar watched with horrified eyes as the bloody bone was slipped onto a string and returned to Kargorr.

"Your mouth," Cedar said quietly, wiping away some of the blood that trickled down his face, but he shook his head and licked it up. Kargorr had suffered far worse, and this suffering was special—blood shed for his affection, for his one and only.

He brought the necklace to her throat, where he wound it around her neck and tied it at the back. That perfect throat, long and slender, that always held up her head so proudly. He let the necklace fall to her chest before sliding his hand up to her cheek.

Cedar was beautiful this way, cast in the light of the fire, her eyes huge and round as she took in what he had given to her. Her dress cradled her broad belly, and he knew his orcling was getting closer, so much closer, to life.

"You are mine," Kargorr repeated, leaning down toward her. He kissed her forehead, and then her nose, taking in the scent of her that always awakened his cock. It was already growing thick in its sling, imagining how they might celebrate later.

"And I," he continued, pausing with his lips only inches from hers. "I am yours."

When he kissed her, he gave her everything in that kiss. Lord Kargorr told his *yapira* that he belonged to her, and to their children, and to their children's children. The world he intended to create would exist in her honor, as his gift to her and the orclings she bore him. And when the time came that he and Cedar withered like trees in winter, they would lie together in their graves, their hearts rising up to the stars as one—a single flame vanishing into the everlasting night.

THANK YOU FOR READING!

I hope that you were swept away by Cedar and Kargorr's love story. If you enjoyed the book, please consider leaving a review! Reviews help indie authors like me find new readers.

JOIN MY NEWSLETTER!

For all the latest regarding books, and to get a FREE Trollkin Lovers novella, join my newsletter!

www.LyonneRiley.com

ABOUT THE AUTHOR

Lyonne Riley published her first book at age five, which was written on tiny sheets of notebook paper, and she insisted on giving a copy to everyone she knew. She's been writing ever since, from fan fiction in her teen years to original fiction as an adult. After a stint in traditional publishing, she discovered what she truly wanted to write: very smutty stories about monsters and the little humans they worship.

Now she lives in the middle of nowhere with her dogs and spouse, writing sexy fairy tales.

ACKNOWLEDGMENTS

I would like to thank everyone involved in helping me through the process of putting out this book. I can't say enough how much I appreciate the help and encouragement of the people around me—especially Amber, who told me I could do this in the first place.

Huge thank you to all of my friends for encouraging me to write this book, especially Jenifer Wood, who cheered me on from the beginning with this difficult novel, and Ash Raven, who inspired me to write it. To my critique partners, who gave me phenomenal editorial feedback: You all make this possible. And of course, my amazing spouse, who has always supported my dreams—and given me lots of inspiration for my characters' sexy adventures.

I couldn't have done this without the expertise of my fellow self-published romance authors. Thank you for inviting me into your circles and helping me through this process.

And thank you to my readers, who gave this book a shot.